U Up?

Catie Disabato

MELVILLE HOUSE
BROOKLYN • LONDON

U Up?
Copyright © Catie Disabato, 2021
All rights reserved
First Melville House Printing: February 2021

Melville House Publishing
46 John Street
Brooklyn, NY 11201
and
Melville House UK
Suite 2000
16/18 Woodford Road
London E7 0HA

mhpbooks.com
@melvillehouse

ISBN: 978-1-61219-891-0
ISBN: 978-1-61219-892-7 (eBook)

Library of Congress Control Number: 2020948930

Designed by Betty Lew

Printed in the United States of America
10 9 8 7 6 5 4 3 2 1

A catalog record for this book is available from the Library of Congress

For Mike and Anne

The intense desire—
and the fulfillment of that desire—
experienced through looking.

—SCOPOPHILIA, AS DEFINED
BY THE ARTIST NAN GOLDIN

In the land of gods and monsters
I was an angel
Lookin' to get fucked hard.

—LANA DEL REY

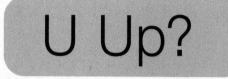

Friday, 12:03 a.m.

u up?

My phone blared with the incoming text, a noisy alert I was as relieved to hear as an almost–murder victim is by the wail of police sirens. For hours my phone had laid inert, as useless as a lone brick, while I watched endless Netflix lying on my back and poked at my barely concave belly button.

How glorious it was to hear my phone, to see it light up again, at a late enough hour that it was a true surprise to hear it wake.

u up?

Oh yes, sweet phone and glorious late-night texter, yes I'm up.

EzralsTexting

Thursday 6:55 PM

u wanna go to that new tiki bar?

can't tonight, i'm knocking off work
tomorrow to go to the desert with noz

like for the day???

she got us a room at two bunch palms
for the weekend

Friday 12:03 AM

u up?

The text was from Ezra Levinson, my best friend. We've known each other forever because we went to the same Jewish summer camps in high school, then to the same college and latched onto each other during orientation, panicked about moving away from our families, hungry for a familiar face. We got really close, we've continued to be really close, and over the years we've become a part of each other, what I imagine having a sibling must feel like—or even a twin. Our hair grows exactly the same, so over the past five years or so we've semi-accidentally maintained the same haircut.

I was surprised to see Ezra's name on my screen, I hadn't expected to hear from him. He was supposed to be on his way to Desert Hot Springs, sitting in his girlfriend's, Nozlee's, passenger seat, Noz steering her ancient Jeep Wrangler with one hand on the wheel and one on the gear shift, one of Ezra's big hands wrapped almost halfway around her thigh, the desert spread in front of them like a landscape painting, cacti growing in dirt along the freeway. I'd expected to spend the weekend watching their Instagram stories from Two Bunch Palms, the chic hot springs hotel, and liking their rusty, desert-brown pictures, then meeting them in Palm Springs on Sunday night, like we'd been planning for weeks. I'd been so ticked off at both of them when Ezra told me they were going away this weekend, before our night in Palm Springs, and even though Nozlee was supposed to be one of my closest friends, she hadn't seemed dedicated enough to apologizing to me about it. On the other hand, Ezra had apologized profusely and promised me they'd be on time.

EzraIsTexting

she got us a room at two bunch palms
for the weekend

Friday 12:03 AM

u up?

im UP

u wanna come out for a last one at la
cuev?

La Cuevita was one of our regular bars, recently renamed from the English (Little Cave) to the Spanish, potentially to make it seem more authentically Mexican. It wasn't authentically anything, really, but it was cave-like to be sure; the ceilings were low and the rooms were dark and what lighting there was was red. I liked red bars. I looked good in pictures in red light.

I jabbed at my keyboard erratically, so Ezra would see that enigmatic ellipsis, *dot dot dot,* appear in our message chain. Then I deleted the random letters I'd typed and closed the app, so the ellipsis would disappear, so he'd know I'd seen it and thought about responding but then didn't, just to give him a little scare. Even though he'd apologized, I couldn't get over being a little miffed with him. It was a bad weekend for both of us, and I had expected to spend every hour in his company, at bright brunch tables or in dark movie theaters, sharing plates of french fries and sitting in companionable silence when we ran out of things to say to each other. I had imagined the moment he would start telling me some story of our shared past, "Do you remember when we drove out to the Rose Bowl and it was suddenly raining . . . ?" trailing off as we both remembered the moment, and who had been with us at the time. Our other best friend, Miguel. One year ago, on this same weekend, he'd hanged himself in a hotel room in Palm Springs. That day at the Rose Bowl, Miguel had pulled us both out of the car and into the rain, expecting a movie-like moment, but all LA rain is actually drizzle and the only thing that happened was that our hair got really frizzy, and that story is actually a story of nothing, and it's only worth telling because I will never see Miggy's hair get frizzy again. On this weekend, of all weekends, Ezra was supposed to spend time with me, and instead he'd agreed to go to the desert with somebody else.

And yes, Nozlee was our other best friend and, yes, she had suffered/was suffering the loss of Miggy alongside us, but she wasn't a twin. Maybe it was racist for me to think that, because she was Iranian and Ezra and I were white (Ezra's grandfather, who had survived a concentration camp with a name I can't pronounce, not Auschwitz, would say that Ezra was "Jewish, not white" but we knew that wasn't true because we had always been considered white). But I wasn't talking about appearance. I was talking about the emotional experience of being linked together. And even though I'd known Nozlee forever and loved her, and even though Ezra had dated Nozlee forever and loved her, she was not linked into us in that nearly biological way.

I put off answering Ezra's text again and opened my text chain with Miguel:

Miggy

Yesterday

i know it's harder for him than it is for me

but that doesn't mean i'm not hurt that he ran off to the desert

You have to let him deal with his grief in his own way

i don't want ot

i want him to deal with his grief in LA with me

Today 12:07 AM

if u were me, and u were mad at ur only living best friend for abandoning u, and u were very snug in your nice bed, would u get up just to keep ezra company?

I hit send and glanced back at the television screen. In the show, a lady detective who had a very dykey way of dressing was kissing a doctor guy who was so bland in his handsomeness that I'd never recognize the actor in a coffee shop, even though I'd seen every episode of his show. Seen and *loved* every episode of his show. I love the way formulaic cop dramas allow me to blank out, the way people must feel when they're really good at meditating. I know a few people who stopped watching all cop shows around the time Black Lives Matter was really picking up steam, because they don't want to watch anything that casts cops as heroes or glorifies the justice system, and I get that. And it does seem kind of weird and rude to defend the pleasure I take in the inherent emptiness of these shows, which for me separates them so solidly from the real world, so I don't even try.

Because she apparently wasn't hanging out in the desert, I texted Nozlee a semi-joking text about stealing the leather jacket the dyke-dressing lady detective wears during night-time scenes. I thought we could have a cute little back-and-forth about it, and then she'd have a perfect opportunity to segue into an apology to me for going out of town.

The text was only half a joke because I knew Nozlee actually had access to the jacket in question, one of those strange things about living in Los Angeles, the way that movies and TV shows could accidentally break the fourth wall because I knew so many people who worked in """"The Industry."""" Nozlee worked as an assistant art director on the lady detective show and once set me up with the costume designer; so, the detective dressed like a lesbian because the costume designer on the show is a lesbian. The costume designer and I had eaten brunch on the gardeny back patio at Bowery Bungalow and I'd ordered a pitcher of sangria before she told me she didn't like to drink in the mornings, and I'd resented her and started to hate our date. But then she didn't make me feel bad about drinking the entire pitcher myself and fed me a bite of her shakshuka, somehow managing to make a spoon thrust across a table both sexy and not-messy, and I'd started to like our date. After, we'd gone shopping in Silver Lake and based on her guidance that day, I now had clothes that would allow me to cosplay as the lady detective. Our banter wasn't enough to overcome the obvious difference in our lifestyles (who doesn't drink at brunch?) and when she texted me, it was both sweet and way too normie, and I couldn't think of anything to say back right away and then got distracted by something and then it was two days later and I hadn't texted her back at all and Nozlee was hearing about it on set. She'd had to prod me to apologize. Suffice it to say, we didn't go on a second date. Even though maybe we could've if I'd wanted to and had composed a more emotionally expressive apology text and had allowed her to verbally process my ghosting.

My phone lit up, I looked away from the hetero kissing.

Miggy

Today 12:07 AM

if u were me, and u were mad at ur only living best friend for abandoning u, and u were very snug in your nice bed, would u get up just to keep ezra company?

You should go

If you're going to be upset with him bc he's leaving, you should at least tell him you're upset.

In death as in life, Miggy was always annoyingly certain he had the right answer for everything; once he had an idea in his head, it was impossible to dissuade him from it. One of the ideas that he'd had for years was: "Eve expresses her anger incorrectly," which was a hugely reductive take on my emotional state. I texted back with two thumbs.

Miggy

Today 12:07 AM

if u were me, and u were mad at ur only living best friend for abandoning u, and u were very snug in your nice bed, would u get up just to keep ezra company?

You should go

If you're going to be upset with him bc he's leaving, you should at least tell him you're upset.

maybe getting laid in the desert is his way of grieving

It would certainly be an effective way to honor my life.

Most of the time when people die, they leave the rest of us behind forever, but occasionally an impression of them remains: a ghost, obviously. Some people, like me, can see and communicate with ghosts. Nozlee, too. From the ghosts we understand that the afterlife is like you're napping most of the time, and when you're awake you're driven by unchecked desires; hungers and thirsts so intense they are all-consuming. In every werewolf movie, they have a scene of the body mid-transformation: a hunched and contorted back sprouting hair, claws growing where fingernails should be, eyes glowing yellow, teeth elongating and sharpening. Ghosts are creatures constantly in that mid-transformation state, their non-corporal bodies sometimes half-formed mist, sometimes a fully defined body, sometimes that body is contorted and growling and almost fully a beast.

Most of my friends know that I "see ghosts" but almost all of them, even Ezra, think I'm being, like, hyperbolic. I've always been into the now-trendy pseudo-witchiness, into candles and moon ceremonies and crystals. They know I grew up in Los Angeles, and they remember New Age-y Topanga from *Boy Meets World*, and they remember when "being Wiccan" was a thing in junior high school, and they also watched *The Craft* on cable in high school and, after, bought a necklace with a Pentagram on it from Hot Topic. When I say, "I see ghosts," they think I mean that sometimes in the corner of my eye, I see a flicker of a shadow that I've decided is a ghost. It's easier to not correct them. It's easier not to insist, *I experience an actual materialization of the dead.* Life is too exhausting not to make the easiest choice when it comes to the kind of thing that used to get my kind burned at the stake.

When Miggy died, he didn't return to me as a physical presence, but as a contact in my phone. We text a lot. Though he had little to report from life after death, it was a pleasure to still get a sense of his voice in my ear. Miggy didn't have a voice anymore, not a throat, not the capacity to suck air into a throat to produce sounds, but I could remember what his voice sounded like. As a ghost, his driving thirst was conversation. He was like that when he was alive, too; when we die, we just become extreme versions of ourselves, our traits and preoccupations amped up so high that it's monstrous. When he was alive, Miggy loved detailed descriptions of my days, gossip (even about people he didn't personally know), and deep conversations about divisive topics like the efficacy of meditation and the future of the Democratic Party and if there is such a thing as a truly selfless act. Miggy still loved all those things after he died. As a ghost, he's devoted himself to texts with me, with Nozlee, and with any other mediums I knew, or who were friends of friends and willing to provide their phone numbers and text with a ghost on those long, lonely, spooky nights.

I keep the texts secret so none of our other friends get jealous, so I don't have to explain to them that I can see ghosts and re-traumatize myself when they don't believe me or have me committed, and also so that if they did believe me, I didn't have to be the conduit when everyone else wanted to say hi to Miggy. Getting to talk to Miggy is my prize for all my early-in-life suffering as the result of seeing ghosts—visits to childhood psychiatrists who asked leading questions trying to determine if I was seeing hallucinations or just had an active fantasy life, social isolation from the other kids who thought I was a "weird

Wiccan bitch," waking up in the middle of the night to hear my mother crying softly to my father that it was her fault that I was "different" because her mom was manic depressive and her aunt had depression and it was actually so selfish of her to have passed on those genes, and I was lying awake knowing it was because of my strangeness that my parents choose not to have any more children.

The only person I can talk about it with is Nozlee. We met in this sort of witch-skills apprentice program in Brooklyn, back when she tweezed her eyebrows too much and claimed to be a bisexual. We studied under a more experienced witch to hone our otherworld communication and exorcism skills; unfortunately Witch Colleen didn't offer much in career training, so it was about as useless as our BAs in Comparative Literature in helping us pay our rents. Some of Witch Colleen's students tried to make witchcraft into a career, but it was harder to make a living than even if we'd been freelance journalists. At Colleen's suggestion, Noz and I both moved to LA because it was easier here to use our skills to make money on the side. Sometimes, I did exorcisms for rich people. Before her set work picked up, Noz made good money reading tarot cards, which is completely unaffected by her ability to see ghosts. Colleen herself had vanished from New York a little while after we graduated from her program, and was rumored to have moved out to the desert to find work as an exorcist or shaman; Nozlee insists that Colleen reaches out to her sometimes, but since Colleen had never reached out to me, I was sure she was exaggerating, conflating a like on Instagram with an actual reach-out.

I glanced again at my screen, at my thread with Miggy.

Miggy

> if u were me, and u were mad at ur only living best friend for abandoning u, and u were very snug in your nice bed, would u get up just to keep ezra company?

You should go

If you're going to be upset with him bc he's leaving, you should at least tell him you're upset.

> maybe getting laid in the desert is his way of grieving

It would certainly be an effective way to honor my life.

You should go

You should respond to him

And then go

Though I was pissed at Ezra's decision to semi-abandon me, I appreciated that he'd thought of spending these last few hours before his desert trip with me at a bar we loved. I would try to take Miggy's advice and be direct with Ezra, but it would be better if I could just erase the feelings of being hurt and have fun with him during the small window of time between now and last call. I could spend the car ride doing a kind of cleansing breathing exercise (in for four, hold for four, out for four) to eject my feelings of abandonment which were probably misplaced aggression and definitely a product of my anxious attachment style (I was sure Therapist Lauren would say as much in our next session, whenever I got around to scheduling it). I could clear all the passive-aggressive bullshit out of my veins and lungs and just be present for Ezra. If I went as is—hair scraggly, bangs damp with night sweat, eyes bloodshot from staring at the computer and internet's endless scroll—I could get there an hour and a half before closing. And if I was being totally honest with myself, there was little I wouldn't do for Ezra if he asked.

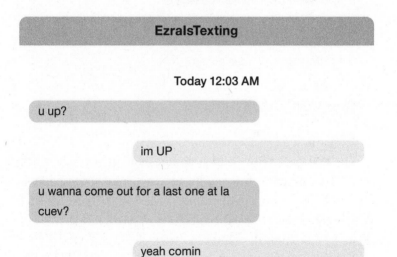

EzraIsTexting

Today 12:03 AM

u up?

im UP

u wanna come out for a last one at la cuev?

yeah comin

After hours lying on my back on the left side of my bed, I left it warm and rumpled when I got up. The right side was cold; it had been empty all night. And for a few weeks previous.

The wood floor in my bungalow creaked when I walked, haunted-sounding. The bathtub faucet perpetually dripped and the drain in the kitchen sink occasionally made a glugging noise like it was a throat looking for something to swallow. I could hear all of it in the quiet dark. My phone lit up again; maybe Ezra was calling it a night after all. I thumbed the message open.

EzraIsTexting

u wanna come out for a last one at la cuev?

yeah comin

Noz broke up with me this p.m.

The text gave me a sudden anxious energy, my grievance with Ezra immediately insignificant. I scurried around, found my black jeans, and then dropped them in disgust when I remembered that they used to belong to Noz and she'd given them to me when she was done with them. She was giving away Ezra now, as easily as the jeans, without even consulting me or warning me. With Miggy gone, our group had been reduced to three, and everything was fine as long as Nozlee and Ezra stayed happy together, and I loved Nozlee and she loved me and she loved Ezra and I loved Ezra and he loved both of us in different ways. But maybe Nozlee didn't love Ezra anymore and so I couldn't let Ezra see me in her jeans.

I put on my Levi's and the muscle tee with the blue stripes that I'd stolen from Ezra, and the jean jacket that matched the wash of my Levi's; I put my glasses on. I blew out the blue comfort and protection candles that I'd been burning while I lingered bed-bound, and dug through the crates I kept under my bed and pulled out three candles: one black, one white, one red. I put all three jarred candles into my bathtub and used an eyeliner to write three names on three squares of toilet paper: Nozlee, Ezra, Eve. I thought hard about a general anti-negativity vibe and lit one black candle and burned my name. I thought hard about Ezra's heart healing and imagined him smiling, not caring and lit the white candle and burned his name. I thought about Nozlee's heart pumping hot blood and her mind growing amorous, relit with revived love for Ezra. I left the candles burning in the tub, laced up my Gazelles, and finally ran down the stairs.

EzraIsTexting

Noz broke up with me this p.m.

oh babe oh fuck im sorry IM COMING

Ezra and Noz weren't what you'd call a solid couple. They were both bad communicators to some degree, and stubborn, and both had demonstrated some capacity to kamikaze the best parts of their lives. It was something I could relate to. Therapist Lauren called it my "death instinct," which didn't necessarily mean I was suicidal, just meant that I had the drive in me to self-destruct, but gradually, muting my suffering with "ritualized comfort-seeking behaviors," like drinking or making enemies or paying to soak at the Korean spa with the only money I had left to buy groceries. My death instinct came up often in therapy, even though Therapist Lauren doesn't know I see actual dead people. She thinks I'm holding onto my death instinct out of some kind of fear, but I'm not scared of anything.

In my car, I tossed a bag of Haribo Golden Bears onto the pile of sweaters and empty water bottles that lived on the passenger seat. The gummy bears were another instinct or reflex, born in me by Ezra. Ezra was the kind of friend who would reach his fork into your salad bowl or pick up a taco off your tray to try a bite—but he didn't have a sweet tooth. My gummy bears were mine, and mine alone. I dug my fingers in the small hole I'd ripped into the corner of the bag, I scissored my fingers until the bag split at its seams, I took a handful.

Chewing, finishing a bear, popping another in my mouth, I began the agonizing process of easing my car out of its tight parking spot, accompanied by a vision of spending the rest of my life executing endless, agonizing three-point turns. It was a likely future for me; I planned to live in LA until I died, and then probably for a while longer. As I twisted to make sure I wasn't going to smash my taillight into the corner of the building, the Levi's dug into that part of my side in between my ribs and hips, unprotected by bones and vulnerable. I untwisted, and the Levi's dug into the small swell of my stomach.

I actually introduced Ezra and Noz years ago, when she was in LA to visit me. Noz wears her desire on her face, and I could tell from the moment she saw him that she wanted to suck his fingers into her mouth. Before they made it official, Ezra and Noz were on and off again for more than two years. Noz was an assistant art director and mostly working on indie movies at the time, always traveling to whatever state was giving the best tax incentives and coming back with some story about how Anna Kendrick's eyes crossed when she took shots of tequila or how Walton Goggins remembered everyone's names, even the production assistants and grips. Last fall, she got a job on the pilot of my lady detective show, and it obviously got picked up to series. That meant Noz had been in LA for more than ten months and she and Ezra had been exclusive for most of that time. For years they'd always been texting someone else, or fucking someone else, but given long months in the same city together, they couldn't commit to anything but whatever it was they had; the smell of each other's bodies, the familiar fights. Devotion like that turns a fucked-up thing into a real romantic love affair.

One more boring micro-adjustment in my car's trajectory, one eye on the rearview mirror and one hand on the wheel, I was finally able to drive out of my parking lot and turn onto Sunset Boulevard, heading east. My phone connected to my car's Bluetooth and the car started playing what I'd been listening to before, "leaves" by Miguel—the singer, not my dead friend—an LA song. *"The leaves they don't change here / You know I'm from here, I never saw it coming / Where did the summer go, when you loved me?"* I sang along as I drove, the streets uncommonly empty, my voice mixing with Miguel's in the closed environment of my car; I could trick myself into thinking that I sang well.

Sunset took me almost all the way into Chinatown before I swung north, onto the 110. This stretch of the 110 was like a country road converted to a freeway, twisting and hazardous to speed on, but everyone did it anyway. The mountains bloomed on either side of me, a state park bracketed the freeway. What should've been an uneasy claiming of territory, the roads taking over where mountains were supposed to go, was actually a natural-seeming partnership. The roads looked like they grew out of the earth the same as the mountains, both black at night, both dotted with degrading color, yellow for lane lines, green for the tree plants that clung goat-like to the sloped sides of the mountainous ridges.

I took a sharp right onto the Avenue 60 exit, stopped at an excruciatingly long red light, slid into a parking space in front of La Cuev, nodded at the familiar door guy, went through a gaping doorway that barely kept a boundary between street and building, and was inside.

The bar inside La Cuev is horseshoe-shaped and massive, with rickety uncomfortable chairs that no one sat on except during happy hour when the rest of the place was full. So close to closing, I knew I wouldn't find Ezra there. Nevertheless, it had to be my first stop. The sole bartender left on duty was a woman named Meghan who I know as well as you can know a bartender, from slices of conversations while she mixed margaritas or cut limes. She has a band, she doesn't have a boyfriend anymore. She'd gone home with my friend Georgie, once, but I didn't know Meghan to date girls regularly; Georgie is pretty masc. of center.

Meghan put down her phone when she sensed someone come up to the bar and smiled when she saw me. I tip well.

I ordered: "A beer, whatever is on special please, and a shot of tequila, Well is fine." Meghan heard me but took the bottle of Patrón off the shelf; it was late enough, I was enough of a regular, or maybe it was a flirt. I took the shot then ate the sour meat out of the lime, leaving behind a ravaged peel.

"Did you see Ezra?" I asked.

Besides the bar, La Cuev had two areas: a shadowy, red indoors to the right and a narrow outdoor smoking zone to the left.

"He's outside," Meghan said, taking my card.

"Will he need another by now?" I asked.

"Probably, he doesn't look so good," she said. "He also had a boilermaker."

"Add it on, and another shot of tequila for me."

She swiped my card and got to work preparing my order. I glanced into the corners, looking for apparitions. Seeing none—only the normal shadows and cracked stone walls—I closed my eyes to feel for unseen spirits. I'd felt a presence in La Cuev before—most bars are haunted, and I used to spend a little time with this one ghost man, a Mexican dude who'd died sometime in the 1990s, who had never given me his name, spoke only Spanish. I'd been trying to use a translation app on my phone to communicate with him, but after I brought my then-girlfriend in, and he saw us kissing at a dark table, he refused to acknowledge my presence. Now when I come into the bar, he floats on the ceiling, or disappears entirely. I could feel him lurking somewhere, but he wasn't showing himself.

I somehow picked up the two tallboys and two shots, and made my way outside, past all the rickety tables and chairs, looking for Ezra. I looked for his familiar body; his heap of curly hair, his slender six feet and three inches, the slice of his cheekbones. I almost didn't see him, because of what he'd done to himself. He'd cut off his hair, down to the root. It saved me that he was sitting with his back to the door, so that he couldn't see the horror on my face at this mutilation; I took a moment to collect myself.

I'd last seen Ezra in person yesterday morning at Thursday Trash Tennis, wearing white linen pants and a white tank, greeting the day with a tennis racquet in one hand and a Tecate in the other. His curly hair had been intact then, bobbing as he smacked a ball almost to my baseline. (Ezra and I had been a doubles team for years, before things got serious with Noz; last Thursday I'd partnered with Dorothy, who had a good serve but much less charisma on the court.) It looked like he'd buzzed it without being able to see the back of his head, awkward tufts everywhere he couldn't reach. Ezra had a good enough face to basically always look good, but he might've finally found the outer limit of his appeal.

I could tell by the rattle and the angle his neck curved back when he sipped that he was at the bottom of his previous tall-boy. I slid the full one onto the table in front of him.

"Hi honey," he said. I put the rest of the drinks on the table and he got up and wrapped me in a big hug. His eyes were red-rimmed, but pupils were small, his focus sharp; he wasn't drunk yet, or on downers. The skin on his arms prickled in the cold night air, and I had no stretchy sweater to offer him; it was unfair that he was the sad one and I was warm and fine in my jacket. I watched his limbs for the restlessness of coke or Adderall or the Ritalin we got last time we were in Mexico.

"Hi honey," I said. I sat down, put my phone on the table next to his, and rubbed my fingers on his scalp. "It's all gone."

"Yeah, I don't know," he ran his hand over it. "Some Britney Spears shit."

His face was just so there now, without the hair, so unhidden; cheekbones, a forehead, eyebrows arched and expressive and rough like men's eyebrows are. His lips, too.

"It looks good," I lied. "It makes your face look good."

He smiled big. Ezra has one of the world's most beautiful smiles, a magnetic sun-like smile. The single drawback: his eyes squinted into slits when he grinned and I preferred his eyes to his mouth.

We clinked shot glasses, then tapped the bottoms on the table, then took our shots. Drinking with Ezra is always an act of physical nostalgia, a version of "going through the motions" without the negative connotations. Though the emotional circumstances of our lives are as temporary as fast fashion trends and so the conditions of our drinking together are always changing, that shot was an echo of every single shot we've ever taken together, an amassing of our long friendship, an expression of our love for each other. Love, like alcohol, is something the body consumes. Ezra reached across the table to squeeze my upper arm, reminding himself that I was there; then he lit a cigarette.

"So what happened?" I asked on his exhale.

He shrugged like he didn't know, but that was a lie. Ezra had a PhD in Nozlee, the preeminent scholar in all her various forms of glory and bullshit. I sipped on my beer and waited. If he didn't want to tell me, he wouldn't have texted.

"I went over to her house after I finished my work, and she was in the shower," he said, a storyteller setting the scene. Ezra ghostwrites "autobiographies" of aging male celebrities, and young adult novels "written by" young female celebrities, and an upcoming series of novels not unlike *Gossip Girl* about a warring group of Jewish high school students attending pri-

vate school in Los Angeles. He's comfortable telling dramatic
stories about emotional melodrama.

"We'd been fighting on text for about like, the previous
three hours," he continued, ashing his cigarette on the ground
even though there was a perfectly good ashtray on the table in
front of him, unnecessary and a little gross, like the way sometimes men insist on peeing outside. "I expected we'd squash
the fight sometime during the drive to Joshua Tree, and get
In-N-Out, and have our weekend. She came out with her hair
up in a towel, and she was really calm and said, 'Let's not fight,'
but I'm a fucking idiot, and I still wanted to yell at her about
whatever the fuck, about her *mean tone* all the time.

"I mean, goddamn it. What do I care about her tone? If
I hadn't said anything we'd be on our way to the desert right
now."

"It's not your fault," I said, and instantly regretted it. I knew
it wasn't about fault, it was about cause and effect: Ezra had
pushed for a fight and it didn't matter whether or not he knew
that it would be relationship-ending. He was in desperate disbelief, understanding the reality of his situation, sure, but fixed
on his last moment of control, his last action. He was circling
some kind of drain.

"What did she say?" I asked.

"She was very direct. She said, 'I'm breaking up with you.'

"She said we fight all the time and it was getting too toxic
for her and she might get an offer to be an assistant to the art
director on a Marvel film and leave LA anyway, so we might
as well call this a good try and cut off the cycle of abuse right
now. She said she deserves to feel good. She said we needed to
start the process of getting over each other."

"That doesn't sound very generous," I said, "it's not like she's some angel."

"But whatever, I like a girl who's mean to me."

Ezra was drawn to the dynamism of a negative dynamic. Or actually, a dynamic that quickly flips from positive to negative and back again. "What does she want you to do to fix it?" I asked.

"Nothing," he said, stubbing out his cigarette. "Go choke."

"She should go choke," I said, reflexively on his side in that moment, even with one close friend vs. another. "But like," and I needed to be delicate about the next bit, so Ezra wouldn't think I was accusing him of melodrama. "Are you sure this is real?"

"I'm sure," he said. He looked really pitiful, defeated and tattered, the lines of his body a poor container for all that was going on inside.

"Because," I said, still being careful, "This isn't the first time."

"This isn't anything like the other times she broke up with me," he said. "She wasn't screaming at me or freaking out, she was very quiet."

I could see how that would be a bad sign.

"The other times," he continued, "she was deciding emotionally in that exact second to break up with me. This was like she'd thought it through and had already made her decision and was just, like, informing me of the new situation."

I reached over and grabbed his hand, and he squeezed me hard, tight around my lowest knuckles, to anchor my body to his. I tried to squeeze back but there was nothing for me to do in the grip but take it.

"Well fuck her then," I said.

"Fuck me, I guess," he said, almost making a joke again.

I remembered a screenshot he'd sent me, it was of sexts he'd sent Noz right after they got back together after one of their screaming breakups; she'd asked him if he would fuck her from behind, and he'd responded in detail exactly how he'd do just that. Reading the exchange had sent a tremor of arousal through my whole torso; I've learned that other people's sexts are the best porn. This was a particular guilty and twisted moment of lust, considering the circumstances.

He backed off, let me go, had a sip of beer. The bar was closing down, emptying out. We were slowly being left alone. Behind the bar, Meghan cleaned glasses with routine disinterest.

"I've gotta go to the bathroom," Ezra said, thumbing his nose. So he did have coke.

I nodded. "I'll go after you."

He stood up, and from below his hair looked even more dramatically ruined. I thumbed open Instagram, looking for a few specific old posts. Ezra and I had a series of Instagram pictures from our urban hikes in the hills of Silver Lake and Echo Park and Highland Park. We'd have a stranger, or a third person with us, take a picture of our backs, our boyish brown curly hair, us looking out over a vista, some neighborhood of LA spread out below us. On our hikes, in our pictures, we had been twins, but we wouldn't be anymore; I'd still have my hair and he'd have some shaved head thing (shaved heads had always been too Nazi-ish to me). We wouldn't look the same anymore. We looked nothing alike from the front, from the back was our only opportunity to match. Now we were separate, in some new and unsettling way.

When Ezra came back from the bathroom, he passed me the little baggie and a pen cap under the table. From her bar perch, eyes locked to her phone, Meghan shouted last call with all the enthusiasm of someone contractually obligated. I took what remained of my tallboy in a single gulp and Ezra rattled his can, checking its level of fullness. We could both do with another.

"Another round? Close me out?" I asked.

Ezra nodded, and I went to *el baño* while he went to the bar. The *Mujeres* room was cramped, two stalls and a cracked porcelain sink, no graffiti. Someone was in the back stall. I heard her tearing plastic, one last tampon before bedtime. In my stall, I pulled down my jeans and peed a little, gently, while I got a big bump ready on the scooped stem of the pen cap. I flushed to cover the sound of my sharp inhale.

U up?

The door banged, I was alone in the bathroom. I looked at my phone.

I had three new texts. Nozlee had texted me back "lol" and then "hey can we talk?" and I thumbed her away, not ready to hear her side quite yet. Second, some incoherent nonsense from Lydia, who was with a group of our friends at a whiskey bar downtown. Then also a complaint about Lydia from Georgie; they were in some kind of cold war. I scrolled, I opened my text thread with my ex, Bea. I closed my messaging app. I opened Instagram, I closed Instagram, I opened my text thread with Bea. I wanted to, I shouldn't, I did.

DONT TEXT BEA

Wednesday 5:37 PM

i didn't do it to hurt your feelings, i just
wasn't thinking about it!

you not ever thinking about me is
basically the whole problem

Today 12:59 AM

u up?

We'd only broken up two weeks ago, so I wasn't yet used to all the absent moments in my day and brain that came from the lack of her. In moments like this, my guard down and my mind alight, the gaps where she used to be seemed so unnatural, something that desperately needed filling. Not by just anyone, but by her specifically. Not knowing precisely what she was doing, thinking, and feeling at this exact second made me feel crazy. I wanted the certainty of her love, of her body in my bed, and instead I was stuck with the uncertainty of whether or not she'd text me back, and when she'd do it, and what she'd have to say when she did. When someone breaks up with you, what they're saying is "you don't get to know my thoughts anymore." I really, really, really wanted to know her thoughts.

I had to put my phone down fast before I further succumbed to temptation; luckily I had other temptations to distract me. I took another bump, into my left nostril this time.

I'm not a saint of restraint, so I picked my phone back up again immediately. I summoned all my strength, used it to avoid Bea, and opened my text chain with Miguel.

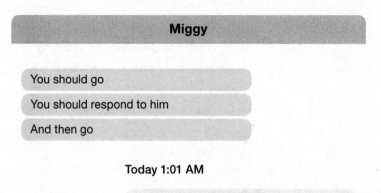

Miggy

You should go

You should respond to him

And then go

Today 1:01 AM

are you reading this shit?

The response ellipsis indicator popped up immediately. Apparently there's not much to do when you're dead except text back, but it still took a few seconds to actually generate the text; what I didn't know about the afterlife could fill the entire universe—apparently Miggy was, in death as in life, still typing out texts with his thumbs.

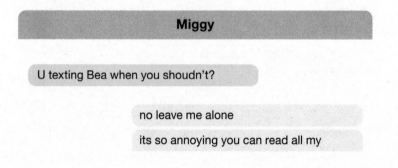

Miggy

U texting Bea when you shoudn't?

no leave me alone

its so annoying you can read all my

texts, im supposed to be allowed to have privacy

what am I supposed to say to georgie and lydia? i see both sides

lydia should be allowed to have a life outside her friendship with georgie, and georgie should be pissed that lydia is lowkey abandoning her

bea texts me more than i text her, it doesn't matter if i occasionally text her when i shouldn't

She's not forcing you to text her back

And you're texting her at night

Fix your own side of it or stop complaining, imo

Miggy always thought he knew better than me what to do about my life.

Miggy

Fix your own side of it or stop complaining, imo

i've gotta put my phone away or i'm gonna hit her up again

I left the bathroom stall. In the dark mirror, I checked my nose for white residue and, finding none, scrutinized all the other facets of my appearance, to remind myself what my face looked like. I fussed at my hair (my hair, alone, un-twinned); I licked my left index finger and rubbed it roughly under each eye, as if I could wipe away the dark circles. My fingers jerked against the vulnerable skin beneath each eye. I left the bathroom.

Ezra was still at the bar, flirting with Meghan over the end of his tallboy. She looked semi-interested; her shoulders were sloped towards him. Her phone, tucked into the back pocket of her jeans, was the only thing giving her ass any definition. I stuck my hand in Ezra's pocket, passing him back the baggie. He wrapped his arm around my shoulders and gave me a little squeeze. His side was warm and he smelled like the end of the night, when all the deodorant has worn off and bodies smelled human again. I felt a warm crackle in the part of my brain that was right behind my eyes and also in the tips of my fingers. I felt happy, realized it was the cocaine, still felt happy. I hoped Ezra felt happy, but he just looked exhausted. We paid, we left together.

Outside, Ezra looked both ways on a mostly empty street, a few neon signs crackling, late nighters like us leaving the cluster of fancier cocktail bars a couple of blocks down the street, giggling as they got in their cars, revving their engines.

"You wanna kick it at mine for a bit?" Ezra asked.

"For sure," I said. "I have my car, do you have yours?"

Ezra has a high tolerance for alcohol but even so, I was glad to hear he'd taken a Lyft to the bar, so there wouldn't be a moment of uncertainty when I tried to figure out if he was sober enough to drive.

We slid into the Fit. Ezra clicked his seatbelt on, then I lurched out of the parking spot and onto the mostly empty street, lit up all night long by streetlamps. Ezra put on Lana Del Rey, "Ride," something for us to sing along to. He rolled down the window and smoked out of it.

"I'm sorry if I'm holding you hostage," he said.

"You're not."

"I'm not going to fall apart if you don't want to hang out and just want to go to bed."

"I feel good, I want to stay up."

The coke had me feeling good, like the little blue Adderalls my best friend used to give me in college, like hiking the hard path of Runyon Canyon and all your effort rewarded by the stunning vista, like the moment in a horror movie when the haunted teenager finally destroys the ghost that killed all of her friends. I chase all the little euphorias that life offers, chemical or physical or recreational. No single joy is more valid, more objectively good, than any other. They are all available for us, and meant for us to feast on.

At each glowing red stoplight between La Cuev and Ezra's, I checked my phone to see if I'd gotten any more texts from Bea (nope) and then watched Ezra while he watched after-midnight LA. In theory, I wanted to hear Nozlee's side of the story and give her perspective equal weight as Ezra's, but he looked so piqued and furrowed and plucked, like the life had been wrung out of him. All the pain on his face was as a result of Nozlee's actions, Nozlee's selfish choices; and when Ezra felt bad, I felt bad. I started to simmer a bit with anger towards her; even though the breakup had been with Ezra, it was a blow to me as well.

The night breeze rumpled my hair and didn't rumple his

because he didn't have any anymore. I touched the back of his head again, at least the stubble felt nice, and he leaned into it like a happy cat.

"I'm really grateful you came out tonight, you're such a good friend," he said, low like it was a secret. But of course I was a great friend; I was always there for Ezra. I took the last few turns and curbed my car in front of his apartment.

The building was gateless, a mansion divided into seven apartments sometime in the early seventies, and much more recently completely refurbished—new pipes and deep sinks, garbage disposals, gas stoves that looked vintage but worked like new (with big, reliable flames), central heating and AC, hardwood floors, and the holy grail of apartment living: in-unit washers and dryers. Above a recessed garage, the new landlord had painted a new name for the building: the Monte Vista. Twin palm trees decorated the front yard and at night, the dimmed floodlights made the fronds into claw-like nightmare shadows on the walls, like monster hands that were dragging the whole building back to hell for the crime of obnoxious gentrification. Ezra's building had been featured in several articles in the *LA Times* and *LA Weekly* as an example of the changing nature of the neighborhood; the online-only hyper-local newspaper *The Eastsider LA* dedicated a slew of posts to it, just after the building was repurchased, during renovations, and at the unveiling of its new pink grotesqueness.

Ezra had been living there for five years, the building had gentrified around him. But the landlords hadn't tried any tricky tactics to get him to leave, even paying for him to stay in a hotel the week they re-piped and re-painted his unit and letting him stay on at his old below-market rent price, because Ezra looked like the kind of person they wanted in the building. After he'd moved back in to his new and approved apartment, he'd felt vaguely embarrassed to bring girls home. The younger, newer ones hadn't seen anything wrong, but some girls—a bartender who'd been working in La Cuev since it was Little Cave, a Latinx community organizer who advised everyone on which city council members to vote for, a Cal Arts graduate who'd made us come to her readings of incomprehensible experimental prose poems—they all had paused on the sidewalk and said, "Oh my god, you live at the Monte Vista!?" Not that it stopped them from going inside.

One girl had even posted about it on Medium and had gone viral, "10 Things That Happened When I F*cked a Guy Who Lived at the Monte Vista." It was actually a pretty good piece, more an astute musing on living in a changing neighborhood than a review of Ezra's length, girth, or prowess. But still, the headline made it seem like early Gawker shit. Ezra immediately decided not to be offended and to LOL it off, posting it to his Twitter feed, but he didn't go home with another girl for a few months; even when he spotted someone he'd normally go for, he stayed with Miggy and me instead of going over to her.

Although I often cringed at my own role in gentrification, the slow eroding of communities and neighborhoods, I secretly didn't mind the Monte Vista upgrades. I liked that the building no longer smelled like an ashtray. I liked the way the new paint job looked in Instagram pictures. I liked that it wasn't pretending not to be pretentious; that is another form of authenticity, somehow. Monte Vista means "mountain view" and even that wasn't a lie, the apartment sits on the rounded peak of a small hill street and there is in fact a small view out of Ezra's living room windows, a swath of the city that gets all lit up at sunset; I liked to look out of it and watch the sky grow darker.

Inside, Ezra turned on all the lights, including the strand of white Christmas lights taped to the inside of the massive IKEA shelf that covered one entire wall and was stuffed with records, books, and a few crystals that Noz had brought in to cleanse the space. Ezra's orange outdoor cat, Lotus, sat on the open windowsill licking her wrist delicately. She was petal-like in her composure, but our presence must've displeased her because after a few more deliberate licks, she decided to leap gracefully from the window ledge into the foliage below, away on her next hunt. Ezra would wake up with her wound around his neck like a furry noose. She, like all those girls he brought home to the Monte Vista, must've loved the smell of his pheromones, because she always cuddled closest to the place where his smell was the strongest, in the delicate spots on either side of his neck.

Out of my purse, I pulled a little baggie of my homemade Cascarilla and poured a little hill of powder into the corner of either side of the window, where Lotus had trampled through and scattered the Cascarilla I'd left there before. Cascarilla is just finely powdered eggshell; I make my own in a coffee grinder, to get it soft and fine. It protects spaces and cuts off communication with spirits, and I use it to keep bad or needy ghosts away when I'm trying to have a fun time. Ezra's house contained a very annoying and obsessive spirit that I constantly had to tamp down by spreading Cascarilla all over the place.

The thing about Cascarilla is that it looks like very finely chopped coke. More than once, I've done a line only to find that I was inhaling eggshell. Cascarilla doesn't make me high of course, but for a few hours after that kind of mistake, I couldn't see a ghost if I wanted to. I know a few mediums who wish they weren't; they snort the stuff regularly. Sometimes they start doing it when they get married or when they have children, when suddenly the presence of a ghost while going about the normal day-to-day stuff is something to be scared of, instead of just a ripple in the natural ecosystem of the world. It's a bullshitty impulse, hiding from themselves like that; Witch Colleen had always warned us against associating with witches who didn't want to be witches.

Ezra, at the fridge, ignored my ritual protecting of his space; he was used to my witchy gestures by now, allowed them to fold into his life. Ezra cracked us two beers and I, with the baggie of coke, started cutting out some lines on the surface of a nonfunctional iPad mini that lived in the catch-all tray in the middle of his small kitchen table for this exact purpose. I'm good at details, fine motor skills: rolling joints, painting molding, chopping onions, decorating protest signs, shaving (my own legs and bikini line, other people's), and slicing homemade pizza into eight slices of the same size. My lines always come out exactly even. In my purse, I carry a 2.5-inch black glass straw that I commissioned from a glass-blower hobbyist with an Etsy shop. 2.5 inches is the exact length of a dollar bill rolled up. The glass was fresh and cool as it dipped into the shallows of my nostril, and with a sharp inhale, I took in a narrow track of cocaine. It woke me up like orange juice. I passed the straw to Ezra, who snorted two lines in short order.

"So why did she just suddenly make this decision to be done?" I asked. "It can't have been just the one fight."

"I think I know what did it, ultimately," he said.

I thought of a party last weekend where Noz would leave

the room every time Ezra entered it. At happy hour last Monday, she didn't ask him what he wanted when she went up to the bar.

"She wasn't being nice to you," I said. At Trash Tennis, she'd screamed at him over a pivotal missed shot. It was supposed to be a noncompetitive sport.

As the cocaine nasal drip wormed its bitter way down the back of my throat, I reached for the beer; it was a cobalt blue commemorative can of Budweiser, released when the Rams football team returned to LA in 2016. Ezra, Noz, and I had found the old, full case of beer in the back of Ezra's closet the previous weekend, and made some good jokes about a time capsule. We had decided beer didn't go bad and put it all in the fridge.

"There are some real problems with our relationship, right? The way she always wants to tip exactly 15 percent at restaurants, like, down to the penny, that dives me insane. Or how she sometimes zones out when I talk to her, or how she always complains about my friends—"

That one was new to me. I drummed my fingernails against the can of Bud, wondering what friends he meant.

"—But the essential problem, the thing that really made us be shitty to each other, was the fact that she never really apologized for sleeping with Andrew and I never really forgave her or let myself forget about it. Like, those nightmares."

Ezra had very literal anxiety dreams, mostly of watching Noz have sex with Andrew, his now ex–best friend. In some dreams, Noz would be naked, giving Andrew a sweet, deep blow job; in some, she was on the bed in bastardization of the yogic child's pose, her ass angled as high as possible, so Andrew could thrust into it. In one dream, Andrew assumed the same position, and Noz lapped delicately at his asshole. Ezra didn't know what sex acts Noz and Andrew had performed so his mind filled in the details with versions of their own sex life, literally recasting his role with Andrew, down to the shirt Andrew flung into a corner during his and Noz's passionate pre-sex make-out.

Because Ezra and Noz had been technically nonexclusive at the time and hadn't even texted for the whole week and a half before she actually fucked Andrew, he'd been able to forgive her. Though I guess not thoroughly, not actually. Andrew, of course, was ostracized completely.

"You never had a real conversation about it, right?" I said.

"Exactly, it was like, I always suspected she was fucking someone else, right now I'm honestly convinced she's fucking someone else. Like, tonight. I'm convinced of it. I know it sounds paranoid but some of the things she said made it sound like she was breaking up with me for someone else."

"What did you guys say about the Andrew thing?" I asked. "Did you talk about it when you guys got serious about each other?" Ezra hadn't been forthcoming at the time, just gave me the news that Noz was staying in LA and they were staying together and that nothing else was important, so like him I'd brushed the whole Andrew situation under the rug and acted like I'd never heard of any such thing.

"She said that if we hashed it out we'd end up in this big fight right when we were trying to start over, and that was no way to begin a real relationship, so we decided not to talk about it. She said she'd never do that to me again and I said I forgave her, which I guess was a fucking lie, even though I didn't mean to lie at the time. I should've asked her why she did it, a real emotional reason, so that I didn't have to wonder and resent her and act like a jealous dick."

I could guess at Noz's reason to not talk about Andrew, to get some control over Ezra, whose affection often felt like an untethered kite. I also think she liked being mean to him. I didn't say so. I had never said so.

"I think it was a rotten hidden core," I said. "From the second you decided not to have that conversation, you were doomed."

"I'm an idiot," Ezra said.

"It was her decision as much as yours."

"I wanted to talk, I let her convince me not to."

"Then she didn't want to make it work in the first place," I said. "You're an amazing guy who is going to find a person who deserves all the good you can bring into their life. You're going to make someone's world perfect. You don't deserve someone who won't even have the conversation."

Ezra squeezed my wrist. His hands were dry and his grip strong. I let him keep me there, roped to him. I thought of the only time I'd actually seen him and Noz kiss—as opposed to the times when he'd described it to me. Noz, Ezra, Miggy, and I were all hanging out at this big house with a pool in the Hollywood Hills; Miggy was housesitting. Under the sinking sun, my arms were getting cold, and I'd gone into Ezra's bedroom to get something, a sweater; Ezra was sitting in a tan leather chair, and Nozlee was on his lap, facing him, her knees on either side of his hips, legs spread so wide it was straining those dumb raw denim jeans she had been breaking in at the time (I'd seen the welts at her hips, she'd been so happy to show them off, completely ignoring that this chosen form of suffering was wholly unnecessary). One of Ezra's hands was on the back of her neck, one was on her hip; both of her hands were in his hair. When I walked into the room they stopped, I flushed hot like I was under the noon sun again, Noz turned her head to see who it was, and seeing that it was me, laughed. It had been unearthly tender.

Ezra let go of me to wipe his nose. Bodies drip. The fluids of a stranger are so gross; we gag on a hair in our restaurant food, we lose our appetite. But when we love someone, their bodily fluids are de-gross-ified, and not just the obvious, the spit and cum exchanged during sex. I've popped Ezra's pimples, peeled itchy sunburned skin off his back, watched him vomit and piss in the street. I'm long past the point of being icked by any of it. I'd lick the snot off his upper lip without blinking.

"Can we talk about something else now?" Ezra asked. "If we keep talking about this I'm going to totally lose it."

"Sure, of course," I said. "Do you wanna play the game?"

The game is a game of choices, an either-or. We alternate picking a similar pair of things—sushi or Italian food, *Chinatown* or *Citizen Kane*, going to the ocean or going to the pool, *The Vampire Diaries* or *True Blood*—and then we guess which one the other person would choose as their own favorite. We type our answers on the Notes app on our phone and simultaneously reveal them, reveal what we think the other person would prefer. We are rarely wrong about each other now, after so many years playing the game together. Often it's easier for us to guess what the other person's response will be than our own answer; Ezra knows what I like before I know what I like, which is a form of precognition. When we get going with the game, we can play for incredibly long stretches of time, until our brains can't think of any more movies or places or activities or objects; until we are empty of thoughts or ideas, a raw nothing.

Ezra tapped his foot and reached up to tug at the ends of his hair but he no longer had hair. "Blind or deaf?" he asked. Ezra would prefer to be deaf, I would prefer to be blind.

"You're a fucking fool," he said, smiling big at me.

"Why??"

"Because the worst thing in the world is to not be able to see what's right in front of you."

Then he put a hand over my eyes and walked me around the apartment, gently bumping me into the fridge and the doorframes and the couch until I was giggling so hard I couldn't suck in a breath.

With the little pile of cocaine on the table, and the Cascarilla on the window sill, we were able to keep our brains full until 3:45 a.m., at which point Lotus returned to nuzzle at Ezra's feet, and we both decided it was time to finally end what had ultimately been a good night, because even though Noz was a bitch and Ezra was brokenhearted, as deep night settled in over the palms in the yard of the Monte Vista, we still had each other.

Friday, 10:37 a.m.

When I parted my curtains in the full flush of the morning, it was like creating my own sunrise. The light came in as incrementally as if the sun was chugging up over the horizon, because the curtains are so heavy and hard to move out of place, thick blue velour I bought on sale at some home goods store in West Hollywood, waiting for a margarita buzz from El Coyote—the last restaurant Sharon Tate ate at before she died; what did she order? Taco Salad?—to fade off enough for me to drive home. As I pulled them open, squinting in the sudden slivers of light, I waited to feel a headache, but somehow one didn't come; my window-unit air conditioner churned, trying its hardest and failing in equal measure to keep my apartment cool. It only just keeps the summer at bay, that's the best it can do.

All the plants—my cactus points, the spider plant that keeps producing cute little baby leaf clusters, the on-the-edge-of-death jade plant on my kitchen table that makes me feel like a King Kong giant looking down at a tree—strain towards the sudden burst of light. When illuminated, my apartment, its plant life, and the crystals and Cascarilla on my windowsills, all glitter.

I made some coffee and ate straight out of my big container of Fage 2%; I always eat alone in the soft morning light and can dip my spoon in anything I please. I checked my phone. There were a few emails, a work assignment for the day from my boss James Danielson, a marketing email from Thinx, and a nice note from my mother about one of her friend's daughters getting married to her *girlfriend,* because now my kind can marry; I responded with practiced fake enthusiasm and vagueness. A few Twitter notifications, new pictures on Instagram to scroll through.

On Instagram, I watched a video Ezra had taken of me last night, right before I left his apartment. Lotus was in my lap and, through the window, the glowing palm fronds ringed my head like a halo. In the short video I laughed and snorted; I can't remember what Ezra had said to make me laugh, but I remember the joy, some joke stacked on top of another joke, riling me up so that I was laughing so hard I almost squished Lotus when I doubled over. Watching myself laugh, I didn't laugh, but I felt a pleasant echo of having had laughed. My life Xeroxed, and doubled back.

The only new text I had contained a set of pictures of my friend Leslie and me in a Jacuzzi from this time last year; she liked to send little friend memories. I sent back a series of red hearts. Then I sent a few messages to see who was up out there.

EzraIsTexting

Yesterday

Noz broke up with me this p.m.

Today 10:52 AM

👋

how's the morning treating you?

DONT TEXT BEA

Today 12:59 AM

u up?

Today 3:57 AM

I'm up

Today 10:52 AM

i guess we missed each other

Georgie

Not tral

Out

I' didn't meant to yell at u, I love you the most!

Today 10:53 AM

woman, you were ful of a smoky scotch whiskey and spouting inanities, are you feeling filthy & disgusting this a.m.?

Lydia

Yesterday

their old fashioned is such garbage

it smells like gasoline and tastes like a jolly rancher

ugh fuck Georgie is sloppy wasted and annoying the shit out of me she's crying abt our friendship, i just can't

our friendship is fine she's the one with the problem

sorry i just have to vent to someone

now she's yelling at me, i'm going home

Today 10:53AM

sorry hun I was fully asleep

sounds like a shitty night, do you need decompress and vent this morning?

DOT DOT DOT

morning beautiful woman

i'm okay actually

georgie and I had a little fight then hugged and made up, i don't even really know what it's about, we're both on our periods and it's the day after a full moon so we were probably filled with big female energy and spewed it out at each other, i'm feeling good tho

Their fight wasn't about periods, it was about how Lydia finally got Hannah, a good girlfriend, nice to her and friendly with our group and tall and hot, and stopped drinking so much, started going to the gym more often, so her codependent friendship with Georgie was shifting. It was happening slowly, like erosion on the cliffs in Malibu, which made it rougher than if Lydia had ended the friendship with a Band-Aid rip. Lydia, self-help books written by formerly single women hidden under her mattress like 1980s teenage porn, didn't know that she was slowly murdering her best friend; she didn't know she couldn't have both Georgie as a nonsexual mostly girlfriend and a Hannah. I was watching them writhe in my text message window like dolphins caught in a tuna net.

I showered to de-sweat and de-tangle my hair, put on my bike shorts and my running shoes, found my glasses case and switched out my regular glasses for sunglasses, grabbed my keys, and left. I opened the work email I'd seen in my inbox earlier; James Danielson, with his usual Hemingwayesque lack of greeting or explanation, began with: "Start at the intersection of Effie Street and Silver Lake Boulevard."

I work as a researcher/copywriter for a company that had published an app called LA by Foot, which they advertised as a series of "definitive walking guides to the secret history, hidden paths, pedestrian staircases, and beautiful architecture of Los Angeles." I didn't write that copy. My bosses did, two men named Jason who left LA for San Francisco when their app that helped demystify train schedules for English-speaking tourists in Japan made a literal billion dollars. They keep LA by Foot going as an easy-to-manage side project, with one part handled by an engineer who, based on the boringness of his emails, I never, ever want to meet in person. James Danielson, a Los Angeles historian who teaches at UCLA, comes up with ideas for locations that should be highlighted on the walks, then I write the copy.

James Danielson is old, and fat, and all the cartilage is gone from his knees, so he needs me to actually do the walking. I could do it all myself, research the history of Los Angeles by reading any or all of the many books James Danielson has published, but he has something I don't have: the social power that comes from having a masculine name that starts with a J.

James Danielson, in control of me, was sending me to Silver Lake.

I couldn't bear to leave Echo Park just yet, with its welcoming familiarity on a fresh sunny morning, so I created the unnecessary errand of getting another cup of coffee and walked down to Stories Books & Café on Sunset Boulevard. The sun made the whole world glimmery, even the grubby Little Caesars and uneven gray sidewalk had a shimmer.

Most of the dives and Mexican restaurants where I'd slurped margaritas and ate enchiladas for years had recently been replaced by fresh businesses, designed to appeal to white people with money. The owners of The Gold Room had attempted to transform the old ratty narrow dive bar into a cocktail bar, but they wound up with a Frankenstein, the new aesthetic stapled over the old like poorly done plastic surgery, too-inflated lips, too-narrow nose, too-sharp cheekbones. On the back of the empty parking lot across the street, flowering bougainvillea vines grow through the concrete, pink and green and white.

Some mornings, I can't walk down Sunset without remembering that the empty building across the street used to be a perfect Mexican restaurant with five-dollar margaritas on Wednesdays, where old Mexican men posted up at the bar and would buy me a drink in exchange for a few lines of conversation; without remembering that the Gold Room used to sell me a shot and a beer for five dollars; without remembering that the 99 Cent store, lumbering to its death like an aging Brontosaurus, used to be one of two competing and always bustling hyper-discount enterprises on neighboring blocks; without remembering that it was me and my kind that had done this to the neighborhood.

It should've been a bummer morning, with the coke leaving behind an internal twitch of anxiety, and with the depressing thoughts of Ezra feeling crushed and maybe still sleeping. I tried to feel down, but all I felt was the warmth of summer sun, the way walking through Echo Park made me feel like I was flying, and the strange sensation that everything ahead of me was going to be better than everything behind.

As I walked, I let this feeling crest, unaware for a few blissful moments that it and I were Icarus-like, as I walked into Stories and made my way past the bookstore in the front to the coffee bar in the back, and saw her: hip-cocked, slouchy jeans, striped shirt, waiting in line, no chance of mistaking her, obviously Nozlee.

Noz gets her brown skin from her Iranian-Jewish father and her round breasts from her Russian-Jewish mother. Her hair was dyed platinum blonde, the same color as Kim Kardashian's when she first bleached her hair, and she wore it like a boy or a lesbian: a choppy bob, styled like she'd run her hand from her forehead to the back of her head. She is a Virgo sun, Scorpio rising, Cancer moon, and her teeth are faintly yellow. She has a major paranoia about the dentist, she can't even drive herself to an appointment because she'd have a panic attack in the car. One time when she and Ezra were on the outs, she'd asked me to take her. When she got in my car her face was blotchy and blanched like she was about to throw up; when she'd cried, I'd pulled over and hugged her around her shoulders.

When we were studying under Mother Witch Colleen, we'd bonded because among the eight other witches in our apprentice group, Noz and I were the obvious stars and haughty about it in a way Colleen neither encouraged nor tried to suppress. She taught us a witch needs confidence, but must always understand that compared to the four elements from which we draw our power, we are less than nothing, a blip in geographic time and as easy to tear apart as a piece of paper. Back in New York, we'd been the person each other texted first every morning, that kind of friendship. But it always had an undercurrent of uncertainty that came out when we hung out in person, because she always had a look on her face like she was asking me a question that she couldn't say out loud. Noz was more sensitive than me, more of a true medium, ghosts developed attachments to her and would do her bidding; whenever I tried to bond with them, they tried to eat me.

Noz and I had left New York at the same time. I'd learned all I could from that kind of city and I wanted to know what it felt like to live in the sun. Noz's mother in Chicago had gotten sick so Noz went there to help her. We'd tried to stay in touch, but drifted. When her mom went into remission, Noz wanted to ditch the Midwest. She'd decided on LA independently of me, for the same reason so many witches do, because our kind belongs here. She hit me up when she moved here, with Twitter DM like, "can I have some you friends please?" I introduced her to everyone I knew; besides people she worked with on set, she had me to thank for all of her friends in Los Angeles. Including Ezra, of course.

We'd tried to recapture some of that best friendship, she read my tarot and we went on ghost hunts in Griffith Park and even got wine like normal women. But something of the magic (lol) was gone, and I had these weird instincts that she was looking at me differently, like before she looked at me and now she was *looking at me,* which is not something that made actual sense so I couldn't talk about it with anybody else. Our friendship shifted, adjusted, and suddenly our best times were in a group with Ezra and Miggy. We gelled into a dependable little foursome, and I was never bothered that at the end of our nights together, when we were strung out from coke or tipsy or high, when we'd said everything we could say and our brains were empty and ready for the vacancy of sleep, I'd go home by myself and Ezra and Noz would go home together. It would've been nice to have sex with someone on those nights, but there was always a girl I could catch up with the next day, and the sex they were having couldn't have been the best part. It was the hours we spent with each other that mattered; that was the way we gave each other our lives.

Seeing her waiting in line for coffee the morning after she'd decided to leave him, all I could see was the end of everything.

I looked at my phone.

DONT TEXT BEA

Today 3:57 AM

I'm up

Today 10:52 AM

i guess we missed each other

Today 11:32 AM

how's your hangover?

"Eve."

I looked up, Noz had me in her sights.

"Hi," I said. "How's the bright, sober light of day treating your emotional wounds?"

"So I guess you heard," she said.

"Well, yeah," I said. "Ezra and I met up last night, we talked about it for a while."

Noz winced, Noz sighed. "I wish I'd gotten a chance to talk to you before, but at least—can we talk now?"

I pretended to check my watch. "As long as you don't make me late for my one o'clock."

Noz was startled by a gentle throat clearing from the barista behind her, a bearded, pretty man who was, in terms of his exterior, Noz's type. I watched her closely to see if she extended small flirts to the guy while she ordered an iced coffee for here. The barista filled a mason jar with cold brew. Drink delivered, she lingered, sipping her coffee, while I ordered my espresso. She followed me to the pick-up counter while we waited for the other barista with a beard to prepare my espresso. This one was less pretty.

At the same time, we felt a shiver. There was a presence in the coffee shop, something mild and likely benign, not the kind of spirit either one of us would spend time trying to exorcise or communicate with; not the kind of spirit that would take a form, much less a human form; not the kind of spirit that would be visible. As invisible as a smell, something that only the two of us could sense. Flimsy, Colleen would've called the spirit.

"Flimsy," Noz said.

I didn't even nod, as much as I wanted to. Again, like a teenager, Noz sighed. The barista delivered my espresso, which I normally drank quickly, standing, but instead I got us a table near the front, where the light came in through the glass.

"So what'd he say?" she asked.

"Everything he told me, he told me in confidence. I don't want to get in between you guys."

"I'm not trying to get the gossip, I just don't want to waste your time repeating."

Actually, she wanted to know how to spin it. I love Nozlee, but one of her great talents is making her own perspective as real as the truth. I sipped espresso.

"We mostly talked about, you know, feelings," I said. "Rather than practical matters. He's really upset. He hasn't even texted me this morning."

Noz had the decency to look ashamed, and as the warm morning light struck her I could see her normally pristine hair was snarled in places and she hadn't bothered to apply her usual makeup, so the bags under her eyes showed—but so did the scattered row of freckles across her cheekbones and nose. She usually kept them hidden so it felt like a misplaced intimacy in this public place. But I loved those freckles and how beautiful they made her face look.

"It's not easy for me, Eve," Noz said. "It wasn't a relief to let him go."

"I would hope not!"

"When I was thinking about breaking up with him—"

"Thinking about it, and not telling me you were thinking about it, you meant to say," I said.

"Come *on* babe, you absolutely would've told him," Noz snapped back.

"You're my friend too, I can keep a secret."

"You would've felt obligated to tell him."

"I wouldn't have," I said.

"Can you just hear me out and try not to argue with me?"

"Yes, sorry, yes." I finished my espresso, already cold and too bitter, and put my hand on top of hers. She squeezed my hand and lingered with it a little and then let me go.

"I'm having a hard time right now, trying to figure out what I want from life. Did you know that when I was a kid, I knew my stuffed animals were inanimate and didn't have thoughts but I still rotated which one I slept with every night because I didn't want them to know I had a favorite? But I did have a favorite and it was my penguin. I wished I could sleep with the penguin every night. And somewhere in the back of my mind I knew that I could do whatever I wanted but in the front of my mind, an anxiety would overtake me, and it wouldn't allow me to sleep with the penguin every night. And on top of that, when my brother asked me to give him the penguin, I did it! I pretended that the penguin wasn't my favorite and I just gave it to him."

It was cute to think of little Nozlee and her stuffed penguin and her babyhood anxiety, but I wasn't sure what the metaphor was supposed to mean.

"Is Ezra the penguin?" I asked.

"My point is that I act against my interests. That I refuse to acknowledge what I want. My therapist makes me talk about the penguin a lot but it's not actually important, it didn't even have a name. It's just a good framework."

"What is important then?" I asked. I wanted to be generous

to her, but I was also deeply desperate for her to get to the point and tell me what I needed to hear, that things weren't going to change, that uncertainty would never reach me. Miguel had decided to die and Bea had decided to leave and maybe it was unfair but I couldn't abide Nozlee choosing to disintegrate my last safe, comfortable unit.

"Sometimes I feel so anxious and sometimes I feel so empty, and I can't tell if either of those feelings are real. I started to take out my uncertainty on him, and it didn't feel good."

"Like how?" I asked.

"Like, I used to beg him to come pick me up at the airport, but now I would just prefer to get home by myself, but instead of being able to tell him calmly I snap at him like, 'Oh suddenly you are so happy to pick me up at the airport? Where was this when I actually wanted it?' But then when he actually did it, I felt so much love for him I thought maybe it would break me in half. And then two hours later, I'd be so annoyed with him and looking for that love and I would just feel empty.

"When I was thinking about breaking up with him, I was also thinking about how I could stay with him forever and get married, all of it."

"Well then why didn't you propose instead?" I asked.

Noz laughed, and it was sort of a joke, but it sort of wasn't, and she realized that a second too late. She was so pretty when she was upset.

It wasn't like I'd never thought about it, with Nozlee—that's how she always showed up in my brain, a tangle of double negatives, the vagueness of "it." A few hot nights in Brooklyn, pressed close together at Union Pool or some other straight-people shithole, I reveled in the scent of her slightly sweaty body and the gleam of her big eyes made a little glassy by whiskey and admired the ladder of her spine revealed by a backless top. I reveled in any expression of physical or emotional intimacy. But I didn't like the idea of longing, pining for someone who wouldn't reciprocate, who might make a gesture of sexual experimentation and openness but ultimately "settle down" with a guy. I don't like gay pain stories, and it's not like I never chased after a straight girl, I just never got so deep into it to actually give myself to them. In that regard, Nozlee presented a danger.

And so it was a relief to me when she and Ezra got all twitterpated when they first met, and they wrapped around each other like the pair of rattlesnakes I once saw fucking on a hike in Elysian Park. It gave me an opportunity to braid myself in with them without opening myself up to the possibility of my heart getting curb-stomped. When they got serious, I thought that braid had turned to steel. I actually had allowed myself to imagine officiating their wedding, getting seminude FaceTime calls from them during their honeymoon. I'd given them, in my mind, a straight person's dream life with space for myself inside it.

Nozlee breaking up with Ezra reminded me the braid wasn't made of steel, it was made of hair, and if you took the hairband off, the braid would come apart. Nozlee saying she just as easily could've married him was like saying she'd undone the braid for no reason at all.

"That's kind of sick, actually," I said.

Noz scrunched her face up, confused.

"It's twisted and a little gross to be thinking, 'I could either marry this guy or break up with him. What should I do? I guess I'll break his heart!'"

"That's not what I'm saying. I'm saying I've been complacent—I haven't been allowing myself to live my fullest life, and part of that was him."

"So you're blaming him for holding you back? No wonder he felt so shitty after talking to you."

"Eve, that's not what I'm saying. I am trying to take responsibility for the fact that I want something else and that maybe it was a bad idea from the beginning, him and I," she said. "Maybe it never should've started."

"That's a nice thought, but now he's fucking in love with you and you've gotta take some responsibility for that."

"That's what I'm trying to do."

"By giving him half of a real shot, then deciding to fuck off?"

"That's not what happened. I'm trying to tell you, the relationship was always a placeholder."

So maybe she *was* fucking someone else, maybe even Andrew again. I'd have to scour his social media for any evidence of her. He wouldn't do something as obvious as post a pic, but maybe he'd tweeted something that contained a particularly Nozlee-esque turn of phrase, evidence of proximity.

"That's a pretty rude and ruthless thing to say about your boyfriend of two years," I said.

"God you piss me off so much sometimes," Noz said, frustrating and whispering harshly like if she didn't keep her voice down she'd just scream at me. "I'm one of your best friends, my feelings are important, I'm trying to communicate them to you. Please just try to understand me, I need you to understand me."

I felt the edge of the chair dig into the back of my thighs. The flimsy presence took notice of two witches, both heated, sitting in a corner. It turned into mist, it started to congeal into the shape of its body. I saw its teeth, I saw its hungry throat, I saw its dripping tongue. The door opened as some new patron walked in and I felt it beckoning me out, out of there.

"Fuck this," I said, as Noz tried to start talking again.

"If we stop feeding it, it will go away," Noz said, glancing over her shoulder at the ghost.

I hopped off my chair.

"Eve, wait," Noz said, trying to quickly stand up as well, but the barstool-style chair was too high for her to descend from elegantly, and she half tripped, stabilizing herself on the table, which shook like a little earthquake. "I have more to say to you," she said amidst her own bodily chaos.

"Save it," I said. "I have work, I can't sit around all day listening to you justify."

I left as fast as I could, squinting, fumbling to exchange my glasses for my sunglasses.

No texts yet from Ezra.

DONT TEXT BEA

Today 11:32 AM

how's your hangover?

Today 11:59 AM

I'm not hungover. I know how to hydrate.

I had nothing at all on my phone that justified a response.

Friday, 12:15 p.m.

The new walk I was working on was in the tony hills of the Silver Lake neighborhood; in Los Angeles, the higher and more precarious, the twistier and more narrow the roads, the greater the threat of mudslide and earthquake damage, the less available street parking, the higher the average income. The new walk was part of a series about residences and public buildings across Los Angeles that used glass bricks in their construction.

Every email from James Danielson consisted entirely of a series of commands that read like the barebones instructions in a treasure-hunting game. I parked on Silver Lake Boulevard and went to the corner of Effie, like James Danielson had instructed me to do. I pulled my phone out of the black leather fanny pack I liked to wear while I walked, to read through Danielson's message. Strangely, still nothing from Ezra.

James Danielson: "Start at the intersection of Effie Street and Silver Lake Boulevard. Don't continue on Effie Street, take W Silver Lake Dr. north. Explore the streets to the north/west of Silver Lake Boulevard. Note any houses with glass bricks easily visible from the street. Keep a list of their addresses. Take clear, well-lit photographs. Framing and artistry is not necessary in these photographs, as they will just be used for my reference and for further architectural/historical research."

I also ran the Instagram account for LA by Foot, as well as all the other apps and properties owned by the parent company, so framing and artistry, were, in fact, necessary. James Danielson didn't think the Instagram was a worthwhile endeavor, but I knew 67 percent of new downloads of the LA by Foot app came from our targeted Instagram sponsorship campaign. The guys that owned the app liked to tell James Danielson he was in charge, and it felt insane sometimes, to know my job was more important but that none of the men I worked for would acknowledge it to my face. I took the scouting pictures so they'd look like the posts my friends made during their hikes in Griffith Park: expansive views of Eastside neighborhoods from above, houses nestled between patches of green; bent palm trees against bright blue skies; spindly cactus gardens, artfully manicured; ombré sunsets over Dodger Stadium.

This email was exactly the kind I liked to find in my inbox on any given morning. I liked to walk on hilly streets with good views, where I could be alone, with and inside the city. I was always so in love with Los Angeles. I turned on to W. Silver Lake Drive, and headed north, north, up into the hills.

I've spent hours climbing the residential hills of the Eastside of Los Angeles by foot, but still my quads burn when I ascend, and my breath gets hard and fast. My work walks usually give me the opportunity to get out of my head, to focus on the burn in my calves and thighs as I trudge up steep streets, or to go into the blank space in my mind in between what I see and how I'm feeling about it—there is a gap there I can inhabit, where nothing bad can reach me. I worked on dismissing invasive thoughts of Noz's quivery face and the way she rushed after me when I left the coffee shop. She was reaching out for me, I was reaching away from her, and I didn't want to think about it, and I didn't have to. I sucked in a hot breath hard through my mouth and tried hard to forget about her. The sun was bright and my steps were heavy and I almost, almost succeeded.

I wound up a few of the lower streets, houses still small, or poorly maintained, or cracked at the foundation, or divided into apartment units, their sidewalk gates adorned with misshapen metal mailboxes.

When I hit a flat expanse of street, I stopped to catch my breath and stepped into a shadowed patch of the street. Under a fresh-flowered lavender jacaranda tree, I looked at my phone, to see if anything had happened on there.

12:27 PM	DONT TEXT BEA

how's your hangover?

Today 11:59 AM

I'm not hungover. I know how to hydrate.

Today 12:16 PM

You aren't making this breakup easy.

Bea and I had split a few weeks ago, an inevitable parting; we'd begun dating right after Miggy's funeral, in a heady rush, a very lesbionic nesting. The hot early times lasted really super long, almost the full year, before devolving quickly and dramatically into a series of huge fights, during which she dissociated from what was happening and I stormed out dramatically, pulling my car precariously out of the narrow driveway and halfway into downtown Echo Park before I had any idea where I was going. That is to say, when things got tough we ran away from each other. We were still running away from each other, further and further away with each late-night *u up?*, with each ill-advised post-breakup after-midnight hookup. Bea was probably the hottest person I'd ever dated and it was hard for me to reconcile the ugliness I wanted to pile onto her with the beauty of her body, so round and strong. And so, I fought with her and I fucked her and didn't stay away from her even when it hurt.

I sent Bea a screenshot of a few texts she sent last week that claimed, even with my pettiness and quick temper with her, she'd rise above and be compassionate and generous.

DONT TEXT BEA

Today 12:29 PM

It's like you're not even trying.

what do you want me to do?

Be less mean

Stop hitting me up in the middle of the night.

you hit me up in the middle of the day all the time

you ask me my opinions on, fucking, like, movies! casual shit! like we're still friends!! and, what, ur surprised that i think its okay to hit you up??

You don't have to make it a national crisis every time I'm not perfect

Reaching out to you to keep things friendly and civil, when we have so many friends in common, is not the same thing as texting me whenever you're drunk and full of cocaine

Emotional situations that other people experience as a drizzle, I experience as a thunderstorm; a thunderstorm, as a hurricane. Therapist Lauren wants me to do breathing exercises and visit a psychologist who can prescribe something that will calm the tornado-like spikes of anxiety that ravage me, that turn a dashed off late-night text, which others could easily ignore, into the kind of crisis that makes me lash out. Bea should know better than to fuck with me, but eight out of the last ten post-midnight texts I've sent, she's answered by inviting me back to her apartment, and asking me to fuck her the exact way she wants it, and slipping out at 4:00 a.m. Bea doesn't want more of me or none of me at all, she wants both of those things at the same time.

I made a sharp left onto Westerly Terrace and encountered a bungalow, partially hidden behind a huge bird of paradise plant, with a row of glass bricks instead of a front window. I made a note for JD and flipped my camera so I could take a selfie for my Insta story, with the banana leaves behind my head and the light diffusing through my curls. I made sure to get the glass bricks in the pic and typed a quick "#glass-bricks" in white glowing script, hidden in the bottom corner of the post. I turned off my phone before posting. I turned on my phone again. I turned it off. I looked hot enough to attract thirst-follows, maybe, from some freshly minted baby dykes who went around with their undercuts, following everyone whose faces they recognized from the last Gay Asstrology dance party or Cruise, the dyke night at the city's oldest (I think) leather bar, the Eagle. I wanted everyone to look at me and think I was hot, but I didn't want them to know I wanted them looking, not so soon after a breakup. I wanted them to look at my face and thirst for it, I didn't want them to think about what was inside. I retook the photo with a new framing, so that my pretty little face was a bonus feature but the glass bricks were the most prominent subject of the pic.

Glass bricks are having a moment. Looking at something, looking for something, can make it into a trend. My friends started Instagramming pictures of glass bricks; then a new bicycle store in Echo Park made sure to say in the announce-ment to lease their building that they would ensure that the glass bricks would remain; then a new bar opened in the build-ing with an Elliott Smith mural and took down part of the mural to install a wall of glass bricks, and we were all so mad at them for doing it, but that's capitalism, that's gentrification. The deconstructed pieces of the once-public mural were now hung on the walls of the bar, where you had to spend money to look at them.

Glass bricks are a trick. They are neither translucent, like a window, nor reflective, like a mirror. Glass bricks obscure, they provide nothing to the observer, but to the person inside, they let in light. Despite their opaque properties, which shrug off inspection, we bring our gaze to them, we spot them in the wild, our urban safari, phones up like binoculars, snapping pics.

I approached the base of three consecutive pedestrian staircases, steep and long, made of concrete and painted bright turquoise greens and sunset oranges and marigold yellows. I sprinted up all three of them as fast as I could. Halfway through I couldn't think anymore; on the last staircase I couldn't breathe, my thighs burned, I neared collapse. I landed, heaving, into the highs of the Silver Lake hills, where the real houses stood.

I walk so often among the houses of wealthy Angelenos that their exteriors feel like something I own, the way I feel ownership of public spaces in the city: the area of Echo Park Lake where I always sit with friends, the winding trails of Elysian Park, the good places for Instagram pics near the abandoned zoo. The interiors of the houses, though, I need an invitation to see, like everyone else, the way we are all vampiric. But I've seen inside dozens and dozens of them over my years in Los Angeles, of course, like everyone. Sometimes friends would housesit and throw a party. Also, a small subset of young married Silver Lake and Los Feliz couples pass around my contact information to new people in their neighborhood, so I have a steady supply of clients who want their spaces cleansed from the bad energies of previous owners. Every now and then, a neighborhood house suffers a real haunting and I do a quick exorcism. Ghosts, like pests, aren't welcome in the houses of the wealthy.

DONT TEXT BEA

You don't have to make it a national crisis every time I'm not perfect

Reaching out to you to keep things friendly and civil, when we have so many friends in common, is not the same thing as texting me whenever you're drunk and full of cocaine

Today 12:39 PM

maybe we just shouldn't ever text, like a full texting fast

so that every time we see each other, its awkward? That's what you want?

maybe it's my job to actually enforce the breakup

I walked along San Jacinto Street, where house after house features glass brick accoutrements. At 1823: a drab-gray concrete block enhanced by art deco-style cutouts in the doorway and windows shaped like cubes, glass bricks three by three. I would live in a house made of them, and feel safe enclosed in my opaqueness that didn't reflect back at me a single speck of my body or mind.

12:44 PM	DONT TEXT BEA

maybe it's my job to actually enforce the breakup

That's ridiculous

You're the one texting me in the middle of the night!

u were up

u just decided not to text me back for hours

maybe I should just block your number

At 1706, near the middle of the downward slope on the street, another concrete house with cube windows, this time painted purple and glass bricks four by four. The numbers escalating.

DONT TEXT BEA

maybe I should just block your number

Do people customarily tell you before blocking?

You're not going to do it.

> If you were going to, you would have already.

At 1672, more concrete architecture, and this time glass bricks walled in rooftop sun garden. I spotted a woman of indeterminate age sunbathing; when she turned away, I snapped a picture of the building and the back of her head. She looked like she was modeling the wide-brimmed sunhat she wore for protection. I couldn't tell if I thought she was hot, because she didn't look anything like Bea.

DONT TEXT BEA

> If you were going to, you would have already.

> i'm just so like, fucking tired of your shit.

> Is this how you're going to be acting to me at the memorial party thing on Sunday?

Down the street, something that looked like villa, Moorish architectural style, with curly wrought-iron gates and much more decorative glass brick windows in diamond shapes, lined with blue painted tiles. I wish I knew the owner, and they would invite me inside.

DONT TEXT BEA

12:54 PM

If you were going to, you would have already.

i'm just so like, fucking tired of your shit.

Is this how you're going to be acting to me at the memorial party thing on Sunday?

maybe you shoudlnt come.

I suffer from volcanic thoughts. As I stood in front of a house that wasn't mine, the stillness in my body seemed to force violent words and mean ideas out of the heavy, black parts of my brain and into the world. Words, now, that I couldn't take back. An attempt to banish her from a celebration of our mutual friend's life, a reckoning with his death. I don't know much about volcanoes except that the lava that comes out of them hurts people.

DONT TEXT BEA

I'm not going to sit at home crying

Watching everyone's fucking instagrams

Just thinking about Miggy alone

> I know that, like, I really hurt you when
> we broke up but that doesn't mean
> you're allowed to just be shitty to me

But wasn't a volcano an imperfect metaphor? I wasn't spewing lava all over Bea out of some, like, sadistic impulse. I didn't want her to suffer. I wasn't some geologic thing, some rock formation; I was a can of pop and if you shook me up, I was just going to explode.

DONT TEXT BEA

> I know that, like, I really hurt you when
> we broke up but that doesn't mean
> you're allowed to just be shitty to me

> we don't have to talk then

> Maybe you could say sorry to me.

The blue patterned tiles gleamed and nearby vegetation rustled, ASMR, and I did a calming exercise I'd made up for myself where I imagined that I lived in the Italian villa from the movie *Call Me By Your Name* and I could hear piano music playing faintly from a faraway room and everything was warm, and suddenly I could imagine being nice to Bea.

DONT TEXT BEA

i can do that.

i'll tell you I'm sorry in person.

i don't want you to be left out.

i want you to come to the party.

I know.

I'm going to come

I already paid for the hotel room anyway

I turned onto North Dillon Street, which curved sharply to the left. Midway through the curve, I felt an uncanny, apocalyptic vibe: a motorized hedge cutter left unattended and the clippings strewn around, carnage on an otherwise neat street. Where had the gardener gone? As I continued down the slope, I saw around the trimmed hedge to what was alongside it: a pile, taller than me, of still-leafy tree branches, recently cut, sawn off the tree they used to be a part of, stacked like dismembered bodies. They had been let alone, left behind. Something moved into my periphery.

I stumbled as I turned, startled. I thought I saw Miguel. But there was nothing.

Then there was a woman. And yes, she was a ghost woman, but her body was so distinct that I could tell the shade of brown her skin had been when she was alive, which usually meant that she was freshly dead, but she was dressed like a dandy from the forties or fifties (and not like someone from 2018 who was trying to look like a dandy from the forties or fifties). Maybe she'd died in costume. I hadn't seen a ghost with a body this steady in a long time, which was unsettling enough to encourage me to take a few steps backwards.

"Hey Eve," the ghost said, very what-the-fuck, because I was absolutely certain I'd never met this particular ghost before. I would've remembered her solid body, and her gorgeous round face.

"How the fuck do you know me, ghostie?" I taunted, sort of shakily.

"We have a lot of friends in common," she said, enigmatic as fuck. Then, within the space of a half second, her mouth got really big and bloody, like she was ready to make me a meal.

A shock of sound, as the motor of the hedge cutter started up again. I turned my head fast, saw a Hispanic man in a fluorescent vest was back to work trimming the hedge. When I turned back, the freaky ghost was gone. I walked away as fast as I could, outrunning the odd feeling of something unreal happening just outside what I could sense, which shouldn't happen to me or any ghost-seer. It took me a few minutes to get my breath back.

DONT TEXT BEA

1:04 PM

I'm going to come

I already paid for the hotel room anyway

> We'll both have fun and be nice to each other.

> i'm always nice.

I kept moving. I climbed as fast as I could, one foot after another, up a steep street called Hill, the cars parked precariously along one side, wheels turned in and parking brakes on to prevent slippage. I knew the ghost was gone, I couldn't feel her anywhere, but I wanted to get far away from the place I'd seen her as fast as I could. My breath came out stuttered, but the more my quads burned, the safer I felt.

At the crest of Hill Street, on a brief asphalt plateau before the street again sloped downwards, I saw a dilapidated Spanish-style residence with impressive sparkling glass bricks bordering the doorway. The yard was empty and brown, but I could imagine how chic the house would've looked with a manicured garden of orange trees or palms, or even the rose bushes favored by some houses a few blocks over. It was summer, everything would've been in bloom. I took reference pics on my phone.

At one corner of the yard, a poster for the real estate agent representing the property was stuck in the ground. I took a few pictures before I realized I knew the woman in the picture on the sign, Paris Montgomery, a name like a TV character. She had light brown skin, long wavy black hair that was probably a weave, a blue blazer, and sparkling white teeth; she looked nothing like the boho-chic Coachella girl I'd known a few years ago when she was fucking Ezra. I wasn't surprised to see that after she'd gotten tired of taking shrooms, she'd ended up getting a real estate license. She'd always had a normie vibe, unseemly corporate. But who was I to judge? I, a trashy piece of Silicon Valley runoff? Not dedicated enough to my job to be a real User Experience Specialist, not dedicated enough to my witchcraft to be a real Medium, not dedicated enough to other people to be a real girlfriend to anybody? On the poster was Paris Montgomery's work number, a 310 area code.

I saw, to the left of the poster, a sparkle; it turned out to be sun reflecting off the metal of a crumpled beer can; blue shine. I was surprised to see the can was a Budweiser Los Angeles Rams commemorative can, just like the ones Ezra and I had been sipping from the night before. I didn't think there were any left besides the ones in Ezra's fridge. I zoomed in and took a few pictures, tapping my screen to adjust the focus. I snapped an artistically shadowy picture, with a rainbow-y spark of reflected light bouncing off the top of the metal.

I immediately texted the pic to Ezra.

EzraIsTexting

🖐

How's the morning treating you?

I found a clue

I waited for the *dot dot dot* symbol of Ezra texting me back, but my screen was as still as the photograph. Ezra is always tethered to the phone, and even after a bad night he should've been up by now, conscious enough to send me at least a thumbs-up emoji.

Neither Ezra nor I have any family in the city, and neither one of us goes to work in an office; with no one else keeping track of where we are and if we're okay, we've become accountable to each other. Because of Ezra, I know my absence will be noticed, I can't just disappear into my apartment, or onto the narrow unpopular back-trails in Elysian Park, or into the anonymity of a dark, crowded bar. We keep the lights on for each other.

EzraIsTexting

i found a clue

are you awake and not answering?

jus tell me if you're alive out there bc i have a bad feeling

I rewatched the Instagram story Ezra took of me last night; I watched myself: I laughed, I snorted. This time, I was listening closely enough to hear Ezra's faint chuckle, see the shake of the camera as he laughed too. Maybe I wasn't laughing at something Ezra said, maybe I'd said something to crack us both up, and we were laughing together.

I walked for twenty more minutes, noted the houses with glass bricks, stood at the apex of Redesdale Avenue, towering above the glistening Silver Lake Reservoir, made a quick two-picture Instagram post of an old photo of the reservoir that I took at the same spot years ago, when the reservoir was dry and empty. I took a selfie under a large swath of purple bougainvillea, draped over a clay-colored wall like a folded heavy blanket. Ezra didn't text me back.

EzraIsTexting

if u don't answer imma come over to
your place

At the intersection of Redesdale and Fall Avenue, I walked uphill on Fall, relying on the strength of my now-quavering thighs to take me up. I was wet with sweat; sweating is a kind of purge, like vomiting, because it takes something that should be inside the body and pushes it outside to fix some perceived bodily problem. Vomiting saves us from poisoning, sweating from catching on fire. Fall curved and turned into Webster Avenue, and I found myself at the top of the three brightly painted staircases I'd walked up earlier. I walked back down to Silver Lake Boulevard and at the crosswalk, red light, I stopped and looked at my phone.

1:17 PM   **Lydia**

Georgie and I had a little fight then
hugged and made up, i don't even really
know what it's about, we're both on
our periods and it's the day after a full
moon so we were probably filled with big
female energy and spewed it out at each
other, i'm feeling good tho

Today 1:15 PM

whatcha upto bb

DONT TEXT BEA

I already paid for the hotel room anyway

We'll both have fun and be nice to each other.

i'm always nice.

You don't have to say sorry to me in person. I know you're sorry. I am still very effected by your moods and I'm working on that.

Nothing at all from Ezra. I typed his name into the Instagram search bar, and nothing came up. In the past five minutes, he'd deleted his Insta. He was up. He was somewhere. He just wasn't answering. I checked Twitter, I even checked his Facebook. He was deactivated everywhere, he was gone.

Friday, 1:22 p.m.

Back in my Honda Fit, I merged onto the 2, roaring up to Highland Park under a clear blue sky with nearly empty lanes ahead of me. I kept looking at my phone while I was driving, looking at the blank spots where Ezra's content was supposed to be, and looking back and forth between the gray highway concrete and the white empty screen made me feel like I couldn't actually see anything, which is a terrifying feeling to have when you're driving. I wanted to put my phone away, but my anxiety was boiling over like a pot of pasta and I needed to do something with it. One hand on the wheel, I put in my headphones and called Lydia.

"Sup babe," she answered.

"Hi hi hi," I said, "Have you heard from Ezra today?"

Lydia and Ezra had slept together once, drunk but in daylight, trying to be quiet in the back bedroom of a Palm Springs Airbnb, during my twenty-fifth birthday weekend.

"Why?" Lydia said.

"I haven't heard from him all day."

"I haven't heard from him either." I heard the delicate, wispy change in audio as Lydia switched me to speakerphone. "And he didn't answer my text from this morning. Rude."

Ezra, twenty-five in Palm Springs, chewing a piece of his hair but smiling too big to be sheepish as he loaded the sheets from the bed we had planned to share into the washing machine to make sure the bedding was clean for me, so that after a full night of reveling, when I finally knocked out mere minutes before the arc of a new sun crested the enclosed back-yard, the bed didn't smell like his cum.

"It's not that late in the day, babe. I'm sure he'll text soon."

"I have a bad feeling. Noz broke up with him last night."

Lydia was silent for a second, then said, "Shit."

"He deactivated all of his accounts."

"Shit."

"He texted me at midnight-thirty and I met him at La Cuev," I said. "He was really broken up about it."

"What did he say happened?"

I relayed the highlights of my convo with Ezra.

"Sounds brutal," Lydia said.

"He was wrecked," I said. "That's why I'm so worried."

"You guys do coke?"

"Yes, but who cares?" I said.

"You could have second-day anxiety."

"Yes, I absolutely do, but there are tangible things here to be anxious about!"

"A lack of texting," Lydia said, gently but skeptically.

"A lack of texting, plus he deactivated his accounts, plus we didn't even go to bed all that late, plus an extra-bad thing happened."

"But like . . . Ezra sometimes drops out. He's deactivated accounts before when he's needed breathing room from the internet and everyone."

"He does that with other people but never with me," I said,

following the Verdugo Road exit off the highway, into the numbered surface streets of Highland Park.

"Never?"

"Not ever."

"His thing with Nozlee is a shitshow, yes, but it's theirs," Lydia said. "No one but them can really know what it's like between them, and that's okay, that's good even. To have private things. To go dark a little bit, when things get rough between them."

I could never live inside Ezra's mind and he could never live in mine, no matter how often we extended the invitation to each other; conversation is the only tool I have to give Ezra a sense of my inner life, and language is so stumbling and imperfect. True understanding is an exercise in futility, and yet, with Ezra, I try; with me, he tries. Endlessly, endlessly, we talk, across brunch tables, sipping champagne flutes filled and refilled and refilled and refilled with bottomless mimosas; curled up on scratchy outdoor blankets in the public parks and manicured lakeshores of the greater Los Angeles area; hiking Runyon Canyon in lululemons, looking for reality TV stars walking their pit bull rescues; in leather booths in the corner of dark bars: faux-tarnished cocktail bars with faux-clever drink names like "Beast of Bourbon," narrow wine bars with rickety stools and daily specials artfully chalked onto the slate menus that decorate the walls, and all the old-school tiki bars, with their saccharine cocktails served in plastic coconuts and specials on rum punch, that have seen all the fluctuations of Los Angeles and Hollywood, all the rises and falls, and kept all the inhabitants delicately inebriated under the constant beating of a sun so hot and bright that nothing stays hidden.

While Lydia was right that I couldn't know what it was really like for him with Noz, and while Ezra had sometimes gone inward, he'd never completely gone dark with me. If he'd sent even a single emoji I could've taken Lydia more seriously. If Ezra was asking for space, I would've given it to him, but he wasn't asking for anything. He'd have to be present to ask, and he wasn't. He was suddenly and completely not there.

"Plus," Lydia said. "It's Miggy's weekend. He might need some time alone to process that."

"Then why would he plan to go away with Nozlee?"

"Well maybe he didn't know he'd want alone time," she said.

"All these hypotheticals you're offering up aren't helping," I said.

"I don't mean this meanly, I know you've gone through a lot this year and I don't want to add anything to your plate, so I really don't mean this in a shitty way: but your ideas of what Ezra is thinking are just as hypothetical as mine, you just aren't phrasing them as such."

"I'm about to drive through a dead zone," I said. "Can I call you back in a bit?"

"Yeah okay babe," Lydia said, "But don't just say that though. Actually call me back. Promise."

"I promise," I said, and clicked out of the call. I pulled up in front of the Monte Vista, it was pink in the sun.

1:40 PM	Lydia

Promise me!

> i promise Mom.

> Do as mother says.

> yes mami

Because I was answering Lydia, I remembered that I'd been texting with Bea and feeling tenderly towards her before the shock of Ezra vanishing from the internet.

DONT TEXT BEA

> You don't have to say sorry to me in person. I know you're sorry. I am still very effected by your moods and I'm working on that.

> im sorry i texted u on coke

> im sorry i got bitchy.

> i won't be passive aggressive at the party.

> or aggressive-aggressive.

> i will hug you like everything is fine

Comfortingly, Ezra's red, nineties-era Volvo was in his parking spot, where it should've been. It was a brownish red, the color of dried blood, which Ezra had picked with annoying/pretentious poetic intention; he called the money he used to buy the car "blood money" because it came from ghostwrit-

ing the memoir of an aging former A-lister who was both a Sci-
entologist and a closet case; the book was a tool to spread the
word of his cult as well as reaffirm the illusion of his heterosex-
uality. I'd read it because I read every book Ezra ghostwrote
and had him sign the title page. I was the only person who
knew the name of every single book he wrote, which thrilled
me because it was tangible evidence of how important I was to
him; if I ever doubted Ezra's affection for me or the deepness
of our friendship, I could go to my bookcase and hold a book
and know I was the only person in the world who both wasn't
responsible for the production of this book and also knew the
name of the person who actually wrote it. From the books, I
knew he loved me, so I read even this horrible straight Scien-
tology nightmare, and noted that Ezra filled in the star's pretend romantic relationships and sexual encounters with details
from his own sex life. In my copy, I filled the margins with
names of women I recognized from Ezra's descriptions. Lydia
was in there, but most of my notes were the same: Nozlee,
Nozlee, Nozlee.

At Ezra's door, closed and locked and painted the same
pinky red as his building, I knocked. I realized I was tapping
my foot like Sonic the Hedgehog and stopped tapping it. I
waited, as still as I could possibly be.

DONT TEXT BEA

1:42 PM

i won't be passive aggressive at the
party.

or aggressive-aggressive.

i will hug you like everything is fine

Maybe everything IS fine.

I knocked. I waited. I looked at my phone and skipped through several Instagram stories from last night, of a few of my friends doing karaoke—I never, ever watch karaoke stories because they are universally shrill and terrible—and watched a video of Lydia wiggling her toes and then one of her drinking a glass of rosé and then a second one of her toes. I like videos that capture quiet moments in my friends' lives, a cinema verité via inverted camera, where the subjects invite their audience into their gentle mundane.

Hands in my big purse, I swapped my phone for my keys. Ezra's spare was sandwiched between my Ralph's rewards card and my YMCA key card. I unlocked his door and peeked inside, shouting his name in case he was home. Maybe someone had stolen his phone and deactivated all his apps, not just the social media ones, as part of the theft. Ezra's living room was empty, so I went in, turning the deadbolt closed behind me and crouching to pet Lotus. She was affectionate, pushing her head into my palm over and over again while I quietly waited to hear sounds of Ezra stirring in the kitchen or bedroom. His apartment was silent except for the scratch of Lotus's eager claws against the wood floors. Very characteristically a cat, Lotus suddenly lost interest in my petting and darted away, leapt onto her window, and eyed me, asking *what are you doing here.*

"Just checking on your dad," I whispered.

Lotus turned away to lick at her hip.

The kitchen had been cleaned, last night's beer cans in the recycling bin. Ezra's bedroom door was partway opened, but I couldn't see the bed through the crack. I pushed on the door gently, hoping it would open silently just in case Ezra was still sleeping off yesterday, or masturbating with headphones on. The door, unfortunately, creaked, but it didn't matter. Ezra's bed was empty, and made. From my vantage point I could see into his bathroom, also empty. The fuzzy light that came through the venetian blinds hit the bed in LA-noirish stripes. I called out for Ezra in case he was . . . What? Hiding behind the shower curtain? Under the bed? No response, of course. Nothing on my phone.

Ezra's slender silver laptop was sitting open on his desk, magnetically drawing me in. I fit easily into the grooves of his desk chair, flakes of his skin and stray eyebrow hairs clung to his unclean keyboard; I, of course, know all of Ezra's passwords.

Online, I checked his Gmail first. His inbox was clogged with an annoying wave of pointless emails: newsletters from a dozen or so companies that Ezra had once purchased something from online; urgent calls for donations from the Democratic Socialists of America, from one of our senators' reelection campaigns, from a political action group that was doing something good either in Mexico or at the Mexican border; a notice from Bank of America that his monthly statement was available. I was tempted to delete them all to save him the chore; once he turned up he might not even notice anyone had done that for him, do we even recognize the absence of our usual digital trash? I decided not to answer that particular question now. No new emails of substance.

I opened a search tab and typed "Find My iPhone" into Google. I typed in his Apple ID and the alternate password he used to protect his Apple account. Once I logged in, I clicked on the "All Devices" dropdown menu at the top of the page and saw the iPhone image that represented Ezra's own phone; in little gray letters it was designated "offline." I clicked on the icon anyway, and the website bloomed under my gentle clicking fingers a list of powerful options: Remove from Account, Erase iPhone, Lost Mode, Play Sound. I clicked "Play Sound" and waited. No sound.

Like I was creating an insert shot in a high-octane internet thriller, I moved the arrow icon so it hovered over the "Lost Mode" icon. I didn't click. I waited. I did click.

The "Are you sure?" window opened up and, okay, yes, okay, I was sure. There was a small field where I could enter my custom message to whomever turned the iPhone on. I typed:

"Ezra, it's Eve. If you get this, turn the lock mode off and call me the fuck back."

I felt Lotus rub against my ankle before I heard her claws on the wood. "I'm going to find your dad," I told her, closing his laptop and reaching down to rub between her ears. She wouldn't tolerate the touch, she sprinted away, over her windowsill and out into the garden. It was then I noticed the windowsill was wiped clean of Cascarilla, and I felt a spirit gathering, the kind of spirit that liked to cut me off from the outside world. Fucking Bonnie.

I found her hovering in the kitchen, with her ghoulish smile and nasty bloodied fingernails, trying to hold onto a human form.

"Sup Bonnie," I said.

Bonnie was the ghost of a teenage girl who lived in the

house the Monte Vista once was, in the 1910s. She hated me, would've haunted me constantly if she had the power to do so, and she was deeply, passionately in love with Ezra, who of course couldn't return her love for many reasons, including the fact that he couldn't see ghosts but also because ghostlife had turned her insane. Bonnie had once tried to be cool with me, but had turned against me when I refused to be the conduit between her and Ezra so she could try to start something up with him. Once when she got violent and shitty, when she managed to log on to Ezra's phone and text Noz a death threat from his number, we tried unsuccessfully to exorcise her. Bonnie's hold on the building was as strong as its foundation, and she'd stayed with the building for decades while the neighborhood shifted: home to Hasidic Jewish families in the twenties and thirties when the whole neighborhood walked every Saturday morning to Temple Beth Israel; home to Hispanic families in the sixties and seventies; home to members of the Avenues gang in the nineties.

Now Bonnie hovered, mostly incorporeal, the Cascarilla keeping her at bay whenever I was around; she learned internet memes over Ezra's unsuspecting shoulder, she listened to true-crime podcasts with him, she scanned the fashion blogs Ezra used for research for his girl novels, she tried to stir up drama. If the rest of the world could hear the voices of the unliving, I'd try to land Bonnie her own reality show.

"Sup you mangy dyke bitch," Bonnie whisper-howled, her ghost-voice like a whistling wind through clacking tree branches at midnight. She'd gotten extra haughty and shitty since my failed exorcism, a real check on my ego.

Lotus, back on her sill, watched Bonnie obtain form. Cats can see ghosts. With the way Lotus was always knocking my protection powder astray, it's also possible cats can communicate with them, that Bonnie and Lotus were in cahoots. Bonnie floated away from me, to Ezra's bedroom. I followed her. She dawdled by the closet. Her almost-there body whisked around Ezra's long-sleeved button-downs, just like any one of his ex-girlfriends.

"Bonnie honey," I said, "were you watching us last night?"

"This isn't your house," Bonnie said, as usual. "This isn't your house, get out!" All the windows rattled in their panes, a show of force that I ignored.

"I'll let you hang around today if you tell me when Ezra left."

"You're stupid," she said, flickering. "You're as bad as that other bitch. She thinks if she can't feel me I'm not here. She thinks I don't see how he hates eating her nasty fishy pussy."

Bonnie hated Noz even more than she hated me.

"They broke up," I said. "Isn't that nice?"

Bonnie's whole body nodded. She was thirsty for news like that.

"If you tell me when Ezra left, I'll give you something you want," I said. It was medium self-protection 101 to never make a deal with a spirit, but I was wigged out enough by Ezra's prolonged silence to slide into slightly dangerous territory. Bonnie's eyes sparkled with the prospect of a present. Ghost facial expressions are exaggerated, easy to read.

"Tell Ezra about me," Bonnie said.

"Not a chance," I said.

"Fine then, you can go fuck yourself."

"There has to be something else you want," I said. Ghosts are beings made primarily of desire, their wanting is their only drive, which is why their actions and movements take on a sexual tinge even without an alive-person's sex drive.

"I'm a singularly focused person," Bonnie said.

"There must be something," I said.

"Only one thing," Bonnie said, slipping her ghostly bod into one of Ezra's shirts and hovering there like last night's conquest. "Stop putting down that white stuff, so I can't be here."

"For a month," I said.

"For a year," she said.

"No deal," I said.

Bonnie shrugged, her lower body turned to mist and her face faded.

"Wait!" I said. "Wait, wait. Six months?"

Bonnie snapped back into focus. "Deal," she said.

It was a bad deal. Bonnie liked to eavesdrop when Ezra had girls home. When he fucked them in bed, she liked to hover above their bodies like an uninvited and unseen third party in the sexual encounter, then tell me or Nozlee that she'd done it. With Ezra's recent breakup, there would be plenty of new encounters for her revel in; unlike her feelings towards Noz and me, Bonnie liked Ezra's one-and-done girls, their absence after that one night made space for Bonnie's fantasy relationship. It was creepy, and I felt a little sick that I knew it was happening and had never been able to tell Ezra about it—a medium problem I never envisioned while studying with Witch Colleen. I'd just bargained away Ezra's privacy for a long time. Every time we were out to a bar and he left with someone new, I'd have to silently know that a thirsty spirit pervert was salivating over another hot conquest.

"He texted for a little while after you left, he looked upset," Bonnie said. Probably clashing again with Noz, worse than before, from exhaustion and intoxication. "He didn't sleep, and at around six in the morning, he got up and left."

"Then what?"

Bonnie dropped out of Ezra's shirt, she looked see-through. She'd been semicorporeal for longer than ten minutes and after years of being weakened by constant exposure to Cascarilla, she didn't have the strength to stay present for much longer. I wondered how strong she'd be after six months without it.

"Then what?" I asked again.

"Haven't seen him since," she said. "Can't wait until he comes home." She floated higher and her body started to disappear.

"If that's all you've got, the deal is off!" I shouted, and she smiled a big toothy smile and shook her head 'no.' Witch Colleen had warned us against going back on any deal we made with a ghost, which is why we weren't supposed to make any deals with ghosts. But it couldn't count this time, considering how little she'd given me.

"Fuck you," I said, as she disappeared. I'd give her maybe a month before putting down the Cascarilla again; that was all she deserved.

I assessed the information she'd provided; it wasn't much of a puzzle, really. After a late, coke-y night, manic and heartbroken, there's only one place Ezra would go before 9:00 a.m. A dark dive bar: the Drawing Room.

It might've been easier for me to slip out of Ezra's apartment and get on with my search if some element of Bonnie's presence had remained, a ghostly hand against the wall, an uneasy stillness, anything; because I knew even though I couldn't feel her, she could still feel and hear me and terrify me by choosing to appear at any moment she wanted, and I'd just given her the power to do that unfettered for a while. Witch Colleen had told me too many stories about witches going back on their word to ghosts and suffering great consequences, up to and including their own death, so while I could fudge the agreement at the edges, I couldn't consider fully going back on it. I felt the familiar unscratchable itch of rising anxiety, a twitching panic; I spotted a small pile of Cascarilla on the windowsill above Ezra's bed.

Without thinking about it, I plopped down on Ezra's IKEA bed and pulled open one of the storage drawers in the base of the bed, the place where he kept notes on his ongoing books. There was also a bong we never used anymore, his old medical marijuana card (a piece of history), small cardboard boxes full of Ritalin and Klonopin we bought on a trip to Mexico, small baggies of cocaine dregs, and the broken iPad we do it off of. The iPad had been cleaned after last night's use and put away in this drawer, but there were no little baggies or other signs of the cocaine we had left over; curious, but no problem, I wasn't after uppers. I pulled out the iPad and an expired credit card he'd left lying at the bottom of the drawer; I held the iPad beneath the windowsill and swiped the Cascarilla off the ledge and onto its gleaming surface. Though Witch Colleen had preached over and over again about a witch's responsibility to remain aware of the spiritual world around them, I've been lately creeping towards a forbidden road of avoidance and disassociation. I've been snorting Cascarilla every now and then, and though I don't like to admit it, with increasing frequency. The whispers of the spirit world are getting too sharp, the presence of the ghosts too haunting, I don't want to know the secrets they always want to whisper in my ears; only Miggy knows about my bad habit, and he only knows because sometimes it's as long as ten hours before I answer a text from him, something that would only happen if I couldn't see it.

I slung my purse from the floor nearby to the bed beside me, dug around for my phone, and pulled it out alongside my little pouch, which held my glass straw. I opened the phone first:

Miggy

Today 2:02 PM

i've gotta put my phone away or i'm gonna hit her up again

i have to take a lil hit off the ol' cascarilla

but im only going to do it when i have to hide from bonnie, from now on

and I'm gonna tell you each time

I felt bad lying to Miggy, but I wanted to give him a real and serious reason why I had to do it, not some intangible uneasiness that I didn't know how to explain. I wanted to do something that would make him mad, but have him not be mad at me.

Miggy

why can't you just lay down the powder like you've been doing?

i had to make a deal with her

> to get her to help me figure out ezra's whereabouts

You made a deal with BONNIE?? She's unSAFE what did you promise her?

I'm like very anxious over here because I know you did this to, like, "find Ezra" but like, girl.

He'll text you back when he's ready

I bent over the iPad and snorted a line of eggshell white in two consecutive deep inhales. I glanced at my phone screen, and I couldn't see Miggy's text chain anymore, which meant the ghost blocker was working. I tapped out another line and inhaled it. Unlike cocaine, which has a sick smell, Cascarilla is scentless as you inhale it, so I could smell something underneath it, something familiar, something coming from the sheets: a sweat smell I recognized, a body I was familiar with, the smell of Nozlee still clinging to Ezra's bed.

From the car, back on the 2, going south, I called Georgie.

"Baby, are you home?" I said.

"Sure am."

Georgie had a smoky voice, and she was a softie, not a mean bone in her body. She never had enemies, even though she had plenty of opportunities to make them. When she had been femme presenting, guys used to come up to her in bars and uselessly try to talk her up, with an incredibly actually insulting opener, along the lines of, "So, where do your par-

ents come from? You look like you're from [name of South
American or Middle Eastern country]." Now that she has a
dykier presentation, she mostly gets those questions from
women, during a hazy post-coital downward spiral. She
leaves girls' beds a lot.

"I was going to dip into the Drawing Room for a second," I
said. "You wanna meet me for a quick one?"

"Sure thing," Georgie said, amicable as ever.

"I'll be there in like fifteen," I said. "Have you heard from
Ezra today?"

"Nope. We texted a little yesterday, he said he was going to
the desert with Noz."

I didn't know whether or not to tell her about the breakup;
Ezra wasn't super close with Georgie, and I didn't know how
close to the vest Ezra wanted to play the split. It veered uncomfortably towards spreading a rumor. I decided to see how I felt
inside the bar.

The day was starting to get very hot and I spent the rest of
the drive moving my thighs from side to side so that the gathering pools of sweat between my skin and the car seat wouldn't
condense into a smelly glue. I was unsuccessful. Pulled into
the parking lot and my car turned off, I still had to painfully
peel my legs away from the seat.

The Drawing Room was the only bar on the east side of
Los Angeles that opened at 6:00 a.m., a dive bar that trafficked
in real drunks. It had no windows, it was dark and cold. It was
where Ezra would've gone.

Inside, Georgie was already at the bar, drinking from
a pint, thumbing through something on her phone. Instagram, maybe, from the style of her scroll, an upward push
interrupted by tapping twice on the screen. She waved when

she saw me, put down her phone. She stood up to hug me, gave me a good squeeze. She was wearing a dashing beige linen dykey coverall "flight suit" thing that I'd advised her to buy at what we thought was going to be a lowkey summer collection release party for a brand we liked called Everybody, but that turned into a very high stakes see-and-be-seen event for a group of the chicest eastside lesbians and a parade of all of our ex-girlfriends. The flight suit was devastatingly flattering on her, though, but had made me look like I was drowning inside clothes, and I was jealous because truly all the coolest dykes are out there have been wearing flight suits lately; they're either femming it up with heels or keeping it strictly carpenter-tomboy with some Timberlands. I would've done something in the middle, of course; sneakers, chapstick.

"Hi babe," she said, "How was your day so far?"

"Good," I said. "Weird." We settled onto our stools.

Michael, the white-haired bartender who always pretended to have never seen me before glanced and then turned away; I was the only person in the bar without a drink, and he acted as if I wasn't needing anything.

"I've gotta pee," Georgie said, and slid off her stool and slunk into the even darker back of the bar. I knew those bathrooms well. The toilet's porcelain was degraded, the stall was narrow, but I didn't mind that feeling of being locked in with my body, swaddling via bar bathrooms.

Michael didn't rush to me, he didn't seem bothered to help me, as I eagerly anticipated my first drink of the day. I put both my forearms on the varnished wood and leaned forward. He asked me what I wanted with a gesture.

"A boilermaker with a Bud please," I said.

He didn't have to move far to grab a shot glass, fill it up, and get the beer open.

I glanced at my phone.

2:35 PM	Lydia

i promise Mom.

Do as mother says.

yes mami

Today 2:35 PM

YOU PROMISED TO CALL ME BACK, BITCH

I STILL WILL CALL U BACK, BITCH

Nothing from Ezra.

"Did you see Ezra earlier this morning?" I asked Michael.

"No, I said," Georgie said, returning to her seat.

Michael delivered my drinks. "You know, the guy I'm always with?" I pressed him.

"There are always guys," Michael said. "That's seven dollars."

"You can put it on my tab," Georgie said.

"Last name?"

"Delvalle, one word," Georgie said, with a tinge of vocal fry. Georgie was a Valley Girl, born and raised in the San Fernando.

I clinked my shot glass gingerly against her pint, tapped the bottom of it on the bar, and took the shot. Georgie, always a little physically affectionate, rubbed the flat of her hand on my shoulder blade. I wanted her to wrap her whole arm around my shoulders and squeeze me a bit, but I didn't know how to ask for that.

Georgie and I had sex once, years ago, when she was femmeier. I'd driven to her house with a bottle of rosé and three pre-rolled joints; she'd ordered Los Burritos, nachos and enchiladas, and we'd watched her old DVD of *Now and Then*. Stoned and a little drunk, we'd cried when Gaby Hoffmann nearly drowned in a sewer while a young blonde Thora Birch scrabbled impotently at a heavy manhole cover, and rain like we'd never seen pummeled them both into oblivion; we had earthquakes and fires yes, but neither of us really understood how easy it was to be killed by rain.

"Are you anxious about Sunday?" Georgie asked.

My beer was disappearing fast; my throat was full and wet.

"I feel like, anticipatory sadness. I want to really celebrate Miggy's life, but I'm worried I'm going to wind up in a bathroom, sobbing my eyes out."

"If that happens I'll get in the bathroom with you and we can cry and pee," Georgie said. "I'll bring you bathroom wine."

This was a good enough excuse to hug Georgie, so I did, and she squeezed me like I wanted.

"Bea's coming," I said, "I can put our shit aside for the night. We were both so close with him."

Georgie nodded, sipped, wiped beer foam off her lip. She picked up her phone and pointed it at me, I twisted my beer so the label could be caught on her camera, then licked at my lip in a way I hoped was cat-like. Georgie laughed and took the picture. She turned around her phone to show it to me. I looked squinty and a little deranged, but sexy enough.

"Post it," I said, and she fiddled with her phone, getting the filters right.

DONT TEXT BEA

Maybe everything IS fine.

Today 2:41 PM

georgie says hi, she's excited to see you at miggy's thing

Bea's response came superfast.

DONT TEXT BEA

Maybe everything IS fine.

Today 2:41 PM

georgie says hi, she's excited to see you at miggy's thing

You're with Georgie?

You guys are talking about me?

"What do you think?" Georgie said. I looked up from my phone, put it down, took hers. She'd filtered me graciously, and added the caption and tagged me: "cheers from your best american girl, @sleeve." There were already three likes on it.

I giggled, "I look like a sexy squinty drunk babe."

"Add it to your Tinder profile," she said.

"Oh god," I said. "Is it time to go back on?"

"Eventually you're gonna run out of friends to rebound-fuck," Georgie said.

"Not yet though," I said. "What are you up to tonight?"

Georgie shrugged, "Going to Chelsea's party, I suppose." She drank. "What's going on with Ezra?"

I wanted to give Ezra the chance to tell the story in his own time and in his own way, but the riptide of two drinks on an empty stomach was too strong to swim against; so I recapped Ezra's breakup, our late night together and his radio silence since, the unusual and extended gap in our conversation. I censored my own actions here and there, tried to seem calm about the whole thing, excluded my manic visit to Ezra's empty apartment. But even so, Georgie saw through the gaps in my storytelling, to the anxious knot I was pulling at. She saw my unraveling.

She didn't want to scare me, so avoided hitting it head-on, "Did you guys talk about Miggy last night?"

Georgie knew intimately about the frantic day, one year ago, that I'd spent trying to track down Miggy. Ezra was in New York for work and I hadn't heard from Miggy all day, nothing from him on my phone, nothing at all, until I went on his computer and signed into his Find My Phone and followed the beacon it provided to a motel room in Palm Springs, and

I banged on the door so long that the manager finally came. She wouldn't let me go in until she got consent from her guest; she opened the door and went in herself, and so a stranger found his body instead of me. I lost some time then. Later, a police person or someone who worked for them told me they couldn't let me drive home in the state I was in, and so I had to call someone, and I cried so hard into the phone to Georgie that I could barely get any words out at all. I can't remember how I told her, I can't remember how she knew to come get me, I can't remember the hours between calling her and her car rocketing into the motel's parking lot; she found me on the asphalt behind the hotel, screaming for Miguel's ghost to speak to me, my face sunburned and my lips chapped. I remember the slam of Georgie's car door, two slams actually, Nozlee and Georgie loading me into Georgie's car to take me home, and Nozlee whispering in my ear, *"His ghost isn't here, Eve."*

Days later, Ezra was with me at the Drawing Room when my phone lit up with the first afterlife text I'd gotten from Mig:

Miggy

Sorry but it's v chill that even in death I can text u

I'd frantically destroyed that phone, flinging it into the dirty toilet in the narrow bathroom stall. I'd flushed over and over again, but my phone was too big to go down, lingering dead and waterlogged at the bottom of the basin. Ezra'd found me, my sobs were making me heave so hard he'd thought I was vomiting. I let Ezra take care of me; I left my phone to get shit on. I didn't have a phone for two days.

Georgie gently tapped on my upturned palm. "Are you worried about Ezra?" she pressed.

"I can't even think like that," I said to Georgie. "Plus Ezra has never exhibited signs of suicidal ideation."

"He hasn't. He might just be really sad this weekend. A lot of bad shit all at once. Maybe he put his phone on Do Not Disturb and he doesn't even know how worried he's making you."

"Probably," I said, even though Ezra had never, to my knowledge, put his phone on Do Not Disturb and knew how bad this weekend was going to be for me, so why would he leave me to stand alone against the crush of my memories?

"Did you text Noz?" Georgie asked.

"Fuck her, how would she know where he is?"

"They do have a tendency to fall back in after breakups."

"Not this time," I said. "I saw her at Woodcat this morning, alone."

"Did you text everyone else?" she asked.

"I'm going to wait at least twenty-four hours before freaking everyone else out." Probably none of my not-as-close friends would take my panic seriously, and even if they did, I knew Ezra best so they probably couldn't help me anyway.

Georgie sucked on her lip. "I'm not saying this Ezra thing is like Miggy, at all, okay? But I think it would've been better for you last year if you'd called someone else when you were worried about Miggy. Not that you could've saved his life. But you didn't have to be alone."

I took the last sip of my Budweiser instead of saying something. I tried to wave Michael down, but he either didn't see me or pretended not to.

"You've had a really rough year," Georgie said. "We all know that, we all tried to help you through that. But so did Ezra, and maybe it's just coming to a head right now."

I gestured again for Michael. He came over at his usual glacial pace. "Did you see Ezra this morning?" I asked him again. "The guy I'm always here with."

"I wasn't here until noon," Michael said.

"Who was?" I asked. "Do you think I could call him? I'm worried about my friend."

Michael fixed his full attention on me for the first time. He'd lived, like all bodies do, through broken bones and sinus infections, cutting fingers while cooking, rope burn. At this bar, he'd seen worse than me. He could see ghosts.

"Does your boyfriend drink?" he asked, skeptically. He was probably used to wives coming in, asking him to spill the whereabouts of their alcoholic husbands, but it was always a surprise when people didn't read me as gay. I looked really dykey on purpose.

"He's just my friend and I can't reach him. He's not a drunk."

"The guy who was working here this morning, he's a fucking idiot," Michael said. "I could ask him, but I wouldn't rely on him."

"Try him anyway?" I asked.

I turned back to Georgie and she was looking at the floor like a hole had opened up in the linoleum leading straight down to hell.

"You okay, Georgie?"

"Yeah," she said, like she'd been startled. She shrugged, she sipped her beer. "It's a bad weekend for all of us."

My phone lit up. Work was calling, my supervisor.

"Work," I said to Georgie. I scrambled to plug my earphones into the audio input hole, and answered.

"Heyyy, Eve," Jeff answered, the connection was glitchy and he sounded distracted, "Did you send your report from this morning to me and James Danielson?"

"I'm so sorry, I should've flagged this to you earlier, I'm having some technology issues this morning. My phone wouldn't transfer any images from my computer, and I tried upgrading everything, then I had to call Apple Care and wait on the line. Finally got it all sorted out but I'm a little bit behind."

"It's no problem, just try to loop us all in when you're going to be behind, or log into Slack so we can get in touch with you quickly."

"Absolutely. Sorry Jeff. Won't happen again."

"No problem. Let's touch base again in a few hours."

I took out my earbuds. "Georgie, I'm sorry, I've gotta go. I'm late sending in my report."

"I'll close out," Georgie said, finishing up her beer.

"Thanks for meeting me for a minute," I said. "I'm sorry I'm so tunnel vision right now."

"It's okay, we can talk about me next time," Georgie said.

I'd spent a million hours in this bar and others, talking about myself, hearing my friends talk about themselves. The things we told each other were important, but I'd forgotten so many of them. I deal daily with the absence of things I've forgotten—smaller things, mostly, like my third date with Bea and what Georgie's brother's name is—but at bars I'm most used to forgetting to close my tab. It is not unfamiliar territory for Ezra and me to forget to close out, then spend a night wandering through bars looking for the credit cards we left behind, getting happily giggly drunk together.

"Hey Michael," I said, "Can you see if there was a card left behind, last name Levinson?"

Michael handed Georgie her receipt to sign and thumbed through his box of unclosed tabs. "Yup," he said. Michael handed me the card, with a receipt wrapped around it. I examined the receipt: two whiskeys and two vodka cranberries, total twenty-eight dollars. The time on the receipt, marking when it was printed, was 9:32 a.m.

I'd left Ezra's house in the early morning, still dark, and though I was no longer a witness to his movements or an in-person interpreter of his thoughts, I could picture them as clearly as if I'd been invisibly hovering over his shoulder the whole time: He hadn't been able to fall asleep, he'd been restless, the day starting and heating up. He sweated into his sheets, thinking about Nozlee. When he couldn't stay in bed any longer he'd gotten up, gotten dressed, and driven to the Drawing Room, where he'd gotten two whiskeys; suddenly, somehow, a woman was with him, someone who ordered vodka cranberries. She'd been at the bar when he arrived, maybe, and pretty enough to drink with. Sometime before 9:32 a.m., he'd finished his last whiskey, probably gone to the bathroom, and left. I was five and a half hours behind him.

Friday, 3:00 p.m.

Even absent, Ezra was at my fingertips. In the long backwards scroll of my Instagram grid: there was his hand wrapped around a margarita glass from last weekend; there he was across the table from me at El Condor, his biggest doofy smile; sitting on a couch on Georgie's porch, surrounded by all of our friends, waving at me in a continued loop because I'd used the Boomerang setting to take the picture; there he is sandwiched between Noz and me in a booth at The Holloway, Noz's left arm reaching away from us to hold the phone that took the pic; Noz, Ezra, and me out in Joshua Tree, posing next to a rock where we'd stopped to take pictures because someone had graffitied the words "Sick Boy" on it; Ezra and me in the pastel outdoor chairs in the back garden area of the wine bar Tabula Rasa, Ezra staring at the camera and me looking somewhere off to the left; Ezra's arms outstretched, under a bright pink sunset; Ezra in a bar with Nozlee, her face scrunched up and him sticking his tongue out; Ezra sitting on Lydia's floor, mid-conversation; Ezra looking grim at the beach; Ezra in the park; Ezra outside his building; Ezra in a Dodgers hat. The quicker I scroll the more he blurs into unrecognizability, until he is nothing but shapes and color. At the bottom of the scroll there is a picture of me, Ezra, and Miggy. They have their arms around me and we all look happy.

Friday, 3:20 p.m.

I didn't want to go to my bungalow, which would've been stale-aired in the heat, so a few blocks before I reached my street, I flicked on my turn signal, swerved into an empty parking spot, slid my credit card jerkily into the parking meter, and dashed across Sunset at the crosswalk. I pulled on the heavy doors of my favorite spot in Los Angeles, Taix.

Taix is one of the last Old Hollywood restaurants, living LA history. It's cavernous and ninety years old and sells soup in tureens, bottomless as Olive Garden's breadsticks, enough to satiate a full table of underpaid creative kids eking out enough money to pay rent while freelancing. The restaurant has white tablecloths and the servers in the lounge are neighborhood girls with good braids and clear skin; the patrons are a mix of cool kids and older couples and groups of female friends in their sixties. Taix has free Wi-Fi.

My favorite booth in the lounge was free, isolated in a corner, and Happy Hour was on. I ordered a well gin martini with a twist from a familiar waiter and opened my laptop; it flickered on and there came all of yesterday's open tabs I'd left unread: reviews of the new Rihanna album, a no-nonsense breakdown of all the bad things that were going to happen to me specifically as a result of Trump's new executive order, a new profile of Kristen Stewart from the latest issue of Italian *Vogue*. Each of them semi-magnetic, perhaps enough to inspire a burst of procrastination, but instead I attached my phone to my computer via its USB cable. While the photos uploaded, Messages loaded up my most recent texts. All my unanswered pleading to Ezra's inbox's deaf ears. My screen flickered, and my message chain with Miggy once again appeared.

Miggy

He'll text you back when he's ready

Today 3:39 PM

do you miss olive garden?

I MISS THE CHEESECAKE FACTORY IN BEVERLY HILLS WHERE I ONCE SAW LAUREN CONRAD EATING A KALE SALAD

i'm at taix do you miss taix

I miss you

I'm going to forgive you being a bitch to me earlier, ok?

thanks

i guess you love me

I guess I love you

i love you too, The Ghost of Miguel

I scrolled back up, to Ezra.

EzraIsTexting

jus tell me if you're alive out there bc i have a bad feeling

if u don't answer imma come over to your place

ezra please i'm getting so stressed

Lydia

YOU PROMISED TO CALL ME BACK, BITCH

I STILL WILL CALL U BACK, BITCH

I'M BEHIND ON WORK BUT IMMA HIT YOU BACK, BITCH

Miggy

i guess you love me

I guess I love you

i love you too, The Ghost of Miguel

i haven't heard from ezra in hours.

i told him i was scared and still i haven't
heard back

if he was dead, would you know

I think so

I don't think he's dead

thanks bb

My Photos program dinged, the shots from this morning, all the #glassbricks uploaded and ready to insert into my PowerPoint format for my daily report. I catalogued each possible stop on the next walk, each possible piece of history our loyal user base would hungrily absorb.

The glass bricks thing was getting a little passé, a little untrendy. This was the kind of red flag I used to pass on to my bosses when I was first hired: to highlight glass bricks would be to telegraph to the world that we are behind the turn of the cycle, on the wrong side of the trend. This was before I was given access to the user metrics of our LA by

Foot app, which showed me that while we had a strong 19ish percent of users in the twenty-four to thirty-five range, the vast majority of active users were in the forty-five-plus demographic. These were users who didn't want the hottest thing, they wanted the most interesting but also established ideas. Glass brick appreciation had reached enough of a cultural saturation level to appeal to the over-forty walkers, the slow staircase climbers, the seekers of a breathtaking view over a tony neighborhood near their own tony neighborhood. They were ready for a walk among the glass bricks of the late eighties early nineties, to gawk at their own history in the same way they giggled at their own prom haircuts and puffy-sleeved wedding dresses. Sometimes I took a walk in the days right after it was added to the app, to look for them, lean and gray-haired, stopping in front of a house I picked, reading things I'd written. I watched their bodies, looked for ways to know them better.

At the bottom of the scroll of my uploaded pictures, I clicked through the images of the dilapidated house, the sign for the realtor who used to date Ezra, the crumpled Rams Bud Light can. It was strange, seeing an image of Paris Montgomery's face, seeing another one of those commemorative cans that Ezra and I had been drinking last night, before he tried to sleep and couldn't and got up and had drinks with someone who ordered cranberry and vodka. I zoomed in on my shot of the crumpled can; I didn't know what I was looking for. A message from Jeff slid into the upper-right-hand corner of my screen, *Can you send me an ETA for when we can expect that report?*, and I didn't answer him but I did stop looking at the picture of the can and return to my PowerPoint. I

finished it up, and sent it on to Jeff, with another apology for
its lateness.

The waitress came back to my closed computer and empty
martini glass, her bun a tight knot on her head.

"Are you hungry?" she asked.

Was I?

"I need a second," I said, even though the service is languid
at Taix and if you send away a waiter you might not see them
again for a solid twenty minutes.

My phone lit up with an incoming text, I looked at it on my
computer.

Lydia

> I STILL WILL CALL U BACK, BITCH

> I'M BEHIND ON WORK BUT IMMA HIT
> YOU BACK, BITCH

Have you eaten?

I decided I wasn't actually hungry but I couldn't remember
when I'd last eaten. A bag of gummy bears at Ezra's apartment,
and then what?

Miggy

I think so

I don't think he's dead

thanks bb

All you've had to eat today is an
espresso and shot of whiskey and a beer
and a martini.

whoopsie.

I agreed to meet Lydia at El Condor, which years ago had been a restaurant called El Conquistador, with purple walls and queer customers, then had been rebought and redecorated and renamed. I miss the tchotchkes that used to decorate the walls, and the old, faggy Mexican waiters who'd lewdly hit on Miggy in suggestive Spanish, which he'd mostly understood and translated to me over fishbowls of sticky margaritas, even though he didn't have enough of a grasp of Spanish grammar to respond. We'd made lots of good jokes about glasses with salted rims and rim jobs. The longtime Echo Park gentrifiers, like me, still come to El Condor, but now we mingle with Instagram influencers and fitness bros and Silver Lake moms who take their colicky babies everywhere despite the nonstop screaming, instead of the old regulars, who like the waiters had been in their fifties and Mexican and gay. I don't know where those guys congregate now; all their bars have been gentrified away.

Miggy

going to Condor now are you jealous again?

Can't get your ass eaten when you don't have a body

a truism worthy of including in those suicide prevention brochures they pass out at the LGBT Center

You really need to start volunteering for the Trevor Project

i'll volunteer when i'm dead

How about when I'm dead?

I stopped at home to take off my bra and change into my good tank top with little holes in it, just sheer enough that the girls at the bars wondered if they could see my nipples. I couldn't stop myself from thinking about how Ezra used to joke with me that the shirt made everyone around me feel like a big pervert and the way he valued naked desire and his deactivated Twitter (gray and blank) and his all-day absence and the shifting and turning of my mind towards him and also the blank spaces where he used to be. All my empty text message fields. I guess he could've been fucking the girl from the Drawing Room, on and off all day, social accounts off because of Noz. But that didn't explain his sinister lack of communication with me.

When I arrived at El Condor, Lydia was already sitting at a small table among other small tables, kept separate by only the narrowest of aisles that the waitstaff passed precariously, turning sideways to squeeze through, hands full of plates of enchiladas. It was like the worst parts of the New York City restaurant scene: no room, everyone screaming. Lydia was on her phone, swiping. Lydia used to use Tinder like Serena Williams played tennis. Since she'd gotten her boyfriend, she had turned that ferocious energy to BarkBuddy, "Tinder for adopting dogs." It looked like it was going to take her as long to find a perfect small dog as it did to find a good boyfriend.

"I ordered margaritas for us, and queso," Lydia said, while I awkwardly tried to scoot into my seat at the same time as a waiter put our drinks and dip on the table.

She was wearing a red bandana in her hair and her usual Friday-night look of a white t-shirt with rolled sleeves and high-waisted black jeans, which arranged her curves into a neat hourglass and emphasized the ampleness of all of her: ass, tits, thighs. Lydia had a cascade of naturally auburn hair and a thick speckling of freckles over the most perfectly symmetrical, angelic face I'd ever seen. She was a little bit famous online for being the first high-fashion teen plus-size model and for an essay for the *Atlantic* that had gone viral about what it felt like to find an old webpage with a countdown clock to her eighteenth birthday. When she found it, the comment section had been long since abandoned, and she'd aged out of being that particular kind of object of obsession.

I sat down and sipped on my margarita. It was smoky, made from mezcal instead of whatever well tequila. "Thank god," I said. "You always know what I want."

Despite not eating I wasn't really feeling hungry. Despite not feeling hungry I dipped a chip in queso and ate it. I felt warmed by it, at least.

Lydia set her phone on the table, face down. "Cheers," she said, and we clinked, and we sucked in a few good sips. "So," she said, "What's with you today?"

"What's with me how?"

"You didn't call me back, but you went to drinks with Georgie, and then G told me you'd been running around all day looking for Ezra."

"She said that to you?"

"Was she not supposed to?" Lydia asked.

"I told her I didn't want to get everybody riled up this weekend," I said.

"Well if you're actually worried—"

"I'm not worried, like, Miguel-style worried. I don't want everyone to freak out and then get pissed at me when Ezra is just like . . ." I shrugged. "Somewhere."

Ezra wasn't just "somewhere." I could feel a black cloud of something wrong, but I was anxiously certain that no one else would feel it or understand it or understand him or understand me. This absence was somehow about me, somehow for me. I wanted to be as smooth and unbothered as a starless night, but when something feels wrong I'm incapable of the stillness of "wait-and-see."

A waitress with long, crystalline acrylic nails crouched near our table so she could hear us well enough for us to order two plates of *pollo* enchiladas and another round of mezcal margaritas.

I lifted my phone turned on portrait mode and Lydia lifted her mezcal margarita and struck a practiced pose. It was impossible to take a bad picture of her, especially under the glow of El Condor's neon accent lights; my iPhone picture of her looked like a select from a *Vogue* editorial spread.

In the loud restaurant, we were surrounded by people around our age in pairs or fours, drinking margaritas from glasses similar to ours, wearing a new pair of trendy jeans and shifting uncomfortably because the denim hadn't stretched out to fit them yet, taking Boomerang pictures of all their friends' hands as they cheers a round of tequila shots, all the girls' nails painted; or couples on a second date, explaining the mechanisms of their job, talking, talking, everyone can always think of something to say, even me, especially me, as the ghost of El Conquistador—a slutty 1920s serial murder victim, my favorite ghost in the city—vibrated over the heads of the bartenders and waiters, giggled happily in the bathroom, creeping on all the guys' dicks.

"When was the last time you heard from Ezra?" Lydia asked.

"I hung out with him last night until late and haven't heard from him since," I said.

"Where does he go when he's depressed?" Lydia asked.

"Sometimes to the Huntington Gardens but he always Instagrams like a billion flowers, and then his face near a rose bush." I said. "I tried some of his places."

"Where?"

"The Drawing Room," I said. I certainly couldn't tell Lydia about going into Ezra's apartment, she wouldn't understand.

"Okay, well like isn't Chelsea doing her half-birthday drinks thing tonight? Ezra told me on Thursday he was going to go," she said.

We handed the waiter our empty goblets, exchanged them for ones that were full and new, their contents sharp and campfire-y from the mezcal smoke.

Lydia continued: "So you'll see him tonight, then, and you can ask him then what the fuck he's been up to today."

"He's not going to come," I said.

"Are him and Chelsea fighting again?"

"No, I mean like he wouldn't not text me all day, then just randomly show up at a party."

"Who says?"

"I says."

"Ezra loves you," Lydia said. "But sometimes people fuck off and it's not about you. Whatever Ezra is doing right now, it's not about you, and you need to let him do it."

I didn't want to say to Lydia, because I knew how it would sound, that even though it wasn't about me, by blanking me out Ezra had made it about me too. He knew me well enough to know I'd be uncertain and therefore frantic. He was letting me dangle, and I hadn't done anything to deserve it. If he'd sent me just one text, I could calm myself down and let him do his thing, but he hadn't, so he was letting me panic on purpose.

The food runner came back, holding our plates of enchiladas with napkins. He put Lydia's down first then said, "Hot plate."

"Thank you," we said. He put my plate down.

"Hot plate," he said.

"Thank you," we said.

When he turned away, I touched the plate with the sides of both of my hands. Whenever a waiter tells me a plate is hot, I have to touch it. I want whatever heat anything is giving off.

Lydia made an eating noise. "Are you doing anything before Chelsea's?" she asked.

I shook my head.

"Come with me to my sound bath meditation thing at the crystal store after dinner," she said. "This shaman who works at a meditation center in the desert is coming out to lead the class today, it's a special event."

"No way," I said, "You know I always hate that kind of thing, I can't sit still, I disturb everybody, I spend the whole time thinking about sex and it messes up everyone's energy." I took a very big bite of enchilada. I always felt like I should be good at that kind of witchy ritual, but I wasn't, like a fish that couldn't swim.

"You're obviously frantic," Lydia said.

"I'm regular."

"You're not," she said, "You're nothing like I've ever seen you, except that one time last year."

"Could you please stop bringing up Miguel."

Lydia didn't know I could text with him, so she had found my initial dramatically intense mourning, then sudden recovery, very suspect; she assumed I was repressing, she bought me crystals that were supposed to aid grieving and hid them

was not hurting. Months and years from now, when I scrolled back in my feeds, would I remember how I'd actually felt, or would I remember this vibrant image that I had placed on top of my feelings like a shroud?

Normally on Instagram, I scroll through the images before watching the stories, but I saw Noz's round icon at the top of my screen, first thing in my video feed. I put my headphones on and clicked to watch her story.

The first thing I saw was Noz's pale brown arms and her raw cuticles, nibbled on, peeling because of a dryness she couldn't shake. It must've been worse where she was, heading away from the water, into the deep desert.

Her first clip was a driving video, her arm out the window and fingers rolling through the whipping wind. Out her windows, the sky was bleakly bright and huge. Her radio was playing music loudly, a Bluetooth connection to her phone, the Priests song "JJ": *I thought I was a cowboy because I / Smoked Reds! / Smoked Reds! / Smoked Reds!"* The video was from five hours ago.

The second fifteen-second clip, also from five hours ago, I watched from Noz's perspective as she walked into a gas station. The video broke, a Godardian jump cut, picking up in a third clip moments later, with a new human subject: an awkward looking gas station attendant who seemed unsure about whether or not to wave. Nozlee's voice: "Can I get a pack of Marlboro Reds?"

The fourth clip was from four hours ago, Noz's hand outside the car again, a Marlboro Red between two fingers, the smoke drifting up in a picture-perfect coil.

Her videos jerked to a stop, stalling me in a still image,

finally something with Noz's face. Her cheeks shapely and full, her bleached hair fell artfully along the curves of her face, her eyes bright and shining, her parted lips revealed an inviting cavern of a mouth; there was a pink tongue in there, waiting for someone. I could see only its pale tip.

This was Nozlee, driving into the desert, projecting fun, projecting silliness, unbothered by the heart she'd squashed mere hours before, what a fun perfect little life, this desert babe, a liker of good music, a pretty face, a good sense of humor, a real treat to know. Fuck her for all of it. If smashing my phone could've destroyed all evidence of her *superfun* Instagram story, I would've sacrificed it, smashed it against the floor, dunked it in a pint of beer, let it fizzle to death. But there was nothing I could do to wipe the internet clean of her.

I can have fun too, bitch. I posted the pic of Lydia, captioned it "Dinner Date."

Lydia came back so I took out my headphones.

"You ready?" she asked.

"I just have to tweet this thing," I said.

I typed:

i'm a bad boy because your nice day makes me mad at you

I showed Lydia, "Is this a good tweet?"

Lydia read it, "Who is this about?"

"I'm speaking in general," I said, "about all videos of peoples' nice days."

"You need to let people be happy."

"Happiness is a construct just like everything else," I said.

"That's what you should tweet," Lydia said.

She was right, so that's what I did.

We reached my car first. Lydia stopped to hug me even though we were driving to the same place. She broke the hug but held onto my arms with her hands, her palms' skin was so soft. "I know you've had a hard year and I've tried to give you a lot of leeway."

"Leeway?" I asked. I didn't know what she was getting at.

"But I don't think I'd be a good friend if I didn't say: You need to get ahold of yourself."

I decided to interpret it as loving and overprotective. I touched her where she was holding me. "You don't have to worry about me, I'm managing."

She stopped touching me but smiled and said we'd see each other in a few minutes, and she walked away from me.

Friday, 6:30 p.m.

The meditation thing was in a crystal store, Sacred Light. When we arrived, it was filled with very skinny women of various ages and one or two other women who weren't skinny; most wore stretchy athleisure pants, one of the younger women wore a linen jumpsuit which made her look trendy instead of dowdy. She slipped her feet out of shoes I recognized, she'd bought them from Everlane. Their white bottoms were lightly scuffed. Lavender-scented smoke pumped out of bamboo oil diffusers and on all sides, massive crystals were arranged in color-coordinated energy grids. Lydia embraced the lineny-ist woman and handed me a thick Mexican rug and square cushion, muted colors. We set up in rows like a yoga class.

I looked around the room and neither saw nor felt the presence of any gathering ghosty. I could even feel the faint pulse of my own cell phone, which had a bit of spirit energy as a result of all my texting with Migs, but normally I couldn't feel it because there was so much haunted energy everywhere on earth; everywhere is a place where so many people have died. Sacred Light was an unusual hush, a lack of energy, like the opposite of a TV show's racist fantasy of an Indian Burial Ground that's dense with mad ghosts and bad juju. Generally, botanicas and crystal stores—even the whitewashed new ones capitalizing on trends, like Sacred Light—attracted a dense cloud-cover of spirit energy. The quiet was unnerving. I glanced around looking for answers and saw only the glint of light bouncing off a cluster of rose quartz points.

The woman Lydia had embraced, who evidently was the owner of the store—excuse me, the space—gave the annoying "housekeeping" notes that precede every class of this type ("please silence your cell phones, don't disturb the energy of those around you, but feel comfortable to express whatever comes up for you"). Then she vaguely praised the visiting shaman, who worked not at a desert meditation center but coincidentally at the expensive spa hotel Two Bunch Palms where Nozlee had planned to take Ezra before smashing his heart. The space-owner told us we had two minutes to get ready and then we all started murmuring again, while she walked into the corner of the room to confer with the shaman. I realized with a jolt that the shaman was Witch Colleen.

The meditation leader stepped to the side of the room, where she turned off the music and adjusted the light levels. I sprang up and hurried towards Colleen, cornering her away from the group.

"Hi," I said. "It's Eve, from Brooklyn a while back, maybe you don't remember—"

"I remember," she said, cutting me off, twisting a strand of dark hair in her finger. She was in her early fifties by now, with a smattering of wrinkles around her eyes and a sun-worn look to her skin that I didn't remember, but that might be a function of being in LA; a healer who looked like she didn't do any plastic surgery or Botox was rare in Los Angeles.

Witch Colleen, in her sharp mentorship style, had warned

me of the various dangers of telling anyone that I could see ghosts, constantly reminding Noz and me and our fellow students of the burning, stoning, and hanging of witches, of the turn-of-the-century women chained to the walls in dirty asylums, the lobotomies, of modern institutionalizations—more humane now, sure, but still traps, still rooms with locked doors that isolated witches from the rest of humanity.

So, with so many people around, we couldn't be perfectly candid. Tongue-tied, Colleen not inattentive but not speaking to me either, I was awkward. "I didn't realize you were working in LA. I think about you, but I didn't know how to get in touch."

"I have to keep my energy clean for my work out here," Colleen said, again not turning away from me, but offering me nothing.

"It feels calming to me. I often feel very psychically attacked and this place is just nice and quiet," I said. "Maybe the owner put a lot of Cascarilla round."

Colleen's eyes narrowed, "Well you would be familiar, wouldn't you?"

"What does that mean?"

"You're doing a bad job," Colleen said, more meanly than I anticipated.

"What does *that* mean?"

"I tried to teach you how to appreciate and use your gifts, not how to squash them."

"I have to—" I tried to protest, but she cut me off.

"Cascarilla is a way to banish the past without dealing with it." She looked right at me when she said it, accusing me of something. "You're supposed to embrace the past, no matter how rough, work your way through it and come to a peace."

"I just use it to protect myself."

"No, you use it to hide from yourself," she hissed. "Don't bring that energy into this session."

"I'm not!" I wasn't! This woman couldn't know the ways in which I suffered, and couldn't know who I was.

"I'd ask you to leave, but you probably need this more than anyone else in the room."

"That's actually super rude," I said, and took a step away from her. Her wrinkles, her knotted black hair, suddenly looked witchy to me, in that bad horror movie way: hooked nose, warts, eating children. "I paid like forty dollars to do your dumb meditation."

"If you wanted to be coddled you shouldn't have come over here to talk to me when I could still feel Cascarilla seeping out of your pores." She grabbed my shoulder, suddenly and hard enough that I stepped back, trying to get her out of my space, but she danced forward with me and pulled my ear towards her mouth. "I can read your aura, Ghost-Seer," she said in a harsh whisper, "You need fixing."

I swiveled as she walked away from me, watched her fast transform back into the placid leader of a meditative sound bath, asking everyone to lay on their back in the most soothing of voices. That bitch thought she'd won, but I'd show her.

I stomped back to my rug and flopped hard onto my back, nestled in next to Lydia.

"What was that?" she whispered.

"Colleen and I don't see eye-to-eye on matters of the spiritual realm," I said. "I'll show that bitch."

Lydia rolled her eyes, "Meditation isn't supposed to have anger as a driving factor."

"Revenge, not anger. Let me find my motivation wherever," I said.

"Let's turn our third eyes inward," Colleen said loudly, "And close the other two."

Lydia schooled herself into a good student's perfect posture, but when I felt Colleen turn away, I squinted my eyes open. I saw her pick up a large, caramel-colored alchemy bowl and run a short wand along the inside. The bowl rang, a pleasant drone, and Colleen sang a chant in a language I didn't understand. All the ladies settled down to meditate; Colleen turned her eyes on me again, sharply, noticing my squint. I smirked, closed my eyes, gratuitously tensed all the muscles in my body, then dramatically relaxed. I pantomimed serious devotion to a meditative ritual.

At first I was as twitchy as I always was in meditation. Both sides of my nose itched and I suffered as I tried not to scratch, suffered as I tried not to shift my body from side to side to find the exact right positions for my arched back, my squished ass, my hard heels, my whole foot. I tried to listen to the chimes, to focus on the fire that made me want to prove Colleen super fucking wrong about me.

In the lavender-scented air, soothed despite myself by the echoey chimes, my mind wandered into my body; for a while, for maybe as long as ten minutes, my thoughts leveled into something pleasant and pristine. For whole moments, I didn't miss Miggy or worry about Ezra's whereabouts and motivations. That was nice, but as always when I attempted to meditate, my mind eventually turned to daydreams about sex. Not exactly the sex act, not the various forms of licking or penetration that characterized most of my sexual encounters, but the shapes of bodies that I liked. I like the outer curves of hips, the way knuckles curve and bump like a mountain range, the look of tufty pubic hair when a woman takes off her underwear in front of you for the first time.

Though I rarely fuck them anymore, I do also appreciate a really sexy guy. Miggy always looked really good to me, showing off his well-shaped but lean biceps in his endless collection of pastel and sky-colored tank tops; his well-manicured moustache that made him look like the guy who got the most ass in San Francisco in 1976; his one crooked canine that he would lick at, like a husky; his long, long torso. All of this was dead, now, but I had my memories. Like that time he was housesitting for his boss in the Hollywood Hills. It was a hot afternoon, and we swam and ate dinner, then decided to moon bathe and night swim. We decided to skinny-dip because we could, because it was just our small core group, just Miggy, Ezra, Nozlee, and me. That was the first time I saw Noz naked. I was trying not to watch her even though I'm hungry to see any naked body I've never seen before, so I was glancing around a lot, looking at Migs more than I normally did maybe, and accidentally turned my head at just the right moment to see Noz take off her underwear. Her breasts were out already, tan-lined, nipples taut, and as she peeled away her blue underwear she revealed neatly groomed, dark hair on her pussy, the color the hair on her head had been before she'd started bleaching it out. She saw me looking, wiggled her eyebrows at me, and laughed.

"You doing this?" she'd said.

I pulled my stretchy bra over my head and tossed it at her like a bride throwing a bouquet. Had Ezra and Miggy seen us flirting? Had they seen us fall into a pattern of female homosexuality that's designed to appeal to a heterosexual male gaze? Had Ezra saved his memories of our public flirtation for the next time he'd jerked off? I'm not sure. I remember only Nozlee, that she'd laughed and told me my little tits were better than her big ones, and we'd been bathed in the blue neon lights from the swimming pool, and that soon we were in, and swimming.

I held onto the image of the blue glow of the lights, clenching and unclenching my thigh muscles because I needed to move in some way and I was trying to appear still; I was as deep into the meditation as I was going to get. Then unbidden, I slipped into a different memory, from sometime last year, Nozlee, Ezra, Miggy, and I walking down Sunset Blvd in Silver Lake as the sun set; our footsteps in synchronicity. In that moment, I'd felt like part of one big feeling of love that we all had for each other, radiating from one body to the next. But now the memory was one of love and closeness lost, Miggy leaving me and Nozlee blowing up the small pocket of love I had left. The meditation had sunk me so deep into my own feelings I could feel sadness knot itself into fear and the fear burn into anger. The anger didn't transform, it just turned my body to fire.

Witch Colleen had taught all of her students who were "post-cognitives" (her very nineties-era term for people who see ghosts) to find the point of origin inside their body for their "sixth sense" (another truly lol turn of phrase that she'd been using from way before the movie came out, but that I could never dissociate from a prepubescent Haley Joel Osment whispering *I see dead people*). We were to discover or decide the "location of emanation" of our ghost-seeing, as a way to manage and control it. Like probably 99 percent of our class "discovered" or, more likely, *decided* that their location of emanation was in their Third Eye. Typical. Nozlee and I considered ourselves a cut above the rest, so our places in the body had to be unique. She choose the swell of her bottom lip. I chose the palms of my hands.

Slowly, so I wouldn't attract attention from the other meditators, I turned my arms over so my hands faced upwards, and I sought a ghost. The meditation space was still serenely free of ghostly energy, so I pushed myself in a way I normally tried to avoid; I searched the sidewalk outside the crystal store. I searched the street. I stretched, and it ached, like taking a really deep yoga pose that you have to hold for a very long time. Lingering half formed on a corner, I found a young woman, who was reaching out too. I didn't know what she was thirsting for, but I would give her something wet to eat.

Come on, I coaxed it. Come find me.

The half-ghost sparked, started to re-form, drifted down the street, towards the crystal shop, with barely any coaxing. The ghost drifted all the way to the entrance of the crystal shop, then stalled, its body coalescing and then fading out over and over again, like a heartbeat.

Please, please, I begged it. Please come here.

It couldn't get in I realized. Something that rude meditator had done to the space was keeping it clear of ghosts; unfortunately for her, I was both more powerful and pissed. I psychically felt around for the corners of the witch's spell, and when I found one, I peeled it away with my mind's fingernails, like peeling packing tape off a box from Amazon. I picked and picked, while the woman ghost scraped on the other side. My attention was making her strong, her face was formed enough that I could make out her features; she was looking more and more familiar.

Finally the hole in the protection spell was big enough for

the ghost to somersault through. She pulsed and her body came into focus; it was the ghost from my walk on Silver Lake Blvd this morning, the one who had waved at me.

I sat up onto my forearms and thought in her direction, *Are you following me?*

"So what if I was?" she said, drifting closer to me, her eyes white and wide.

The rest of the room was still, the women on their backs, Colleen softly playing her sound bowl with her eyes closed, the sound waves making the ghost vibrate like waves on the surface of a pond.

Leave me alone, dead bitch.

"*Please, please. Please come here!*" she said, her voice mimicking my unspoken pleas from a few minutes before.

I didn't know who I was calling.

"You should be more careful, witch," she said. She hovered right above me and her teeth grew sharp.

I didn't flinch, Why are you following me?

"Somebody asked me to follow you," she said. She reached out with one pointer finger and her fingernail grew long so she could scrape it along my cheek.

Who told you to follow me?

"Wouldn't you like to know?" she mocked.

TELL ME WHO WAS—

"Sit up," a voice said, panicked. The woman who owned the studio. Her eyes were wide, but searching. She could feel the ghost but not see it. And then I couldn't see her either, she let her body fade into nothing. I felt her, lingering, but receding from me. The whole room stirred, women doing what their leader had told them to do. Lydia swiveled her neck to get out the kinks. Colleen glared at me, knowing what I had done.

"I think that was a little shorter than normal," Lydia whispered to me conspiratorially.

"Please, everyone, sit up," the store owner said, still sounding like someone had set her house on fire. She wasn't sure what to do.

"It's not a big deal," I said, not loudly, but I knew Colleen was hearing me. "It's just a small disturbance."

"It's a big deal to me, I paid forty dollars," Lydia said.

Above me, I heard the ghost cackling. Maybe the store owner could hear it too.

I looked at Colleen, and she was looking at me. Her face was stricken. Her unbothered students were starting to stretch and chat softly to each other about how good they felt, post-meditation. Colleen looked only at me.

"Let's get out of here," I said to Lydia. "I need a drink."

Friday, 9:09 p.m.

We arrived at the party already a little tipsy, ready to be friendly to everyone. A Chairlift song I liked was playing off an iPhone plugged into the speaker, and my friends were spread throughout the familiar living room, the narrow kitchen, and the porch where everyone's discarded couches provided ample, if weather damaged, spots to sit and smoke. The group was slightly smaller and friendlier than it had often been over the past year; when she and I were still together, Bea had always invited a small pack of her scary cool dyke friends to my group's parties, and everyone had fun flirting with each other, but sometimes they had been cold and distant and mean. I squeezed Lydia's shoulder to signal that I was splitting off from her and she responded by pulling me into a sideways hug and whispering in my ear that she loved me, to make sure that any rough edges from our tiff at dinner were smoothed to softness. I told her I loved her too and then she was able to leave my side; she pushed into the crowd at the kitchen door-way, saying hello to everyone, and I ducked into the corner with the iPhone; I added three trap songs to the Spotify queue.

While I'd always been closest with Ezra, Miggy, Lydia, Georgie, and even Bea, every person around me sparked warm

Georgie

Today 10:53 AM

woman, you were ful of a smoky scotch
whiskey and spouting inanities, are you
feeling filthy & disgusting this a.m.?

Today 9:11 PM

Did u just go to dinner with Lydia?

I'm in Chelsea's bedroom, I need to talk
to you.

i'll make my way back there

I hugged everyone who was nearby and asked about how
their weeks had been, got caught up on the small moments
in all my friends' lives. I felt a hand wrap around my wrist
and turned towards the new person; it was Tommy, who lived
in the house with their girlfriend Chelsea. They squeezed my
arm in manic little pulses, which meant they had coke and had
done some already.

"Hiya babe," I said, turning to wrap them in a hug. They
made a druggy sort of purring noise in my ear. I'd fucked
Tommy once, when I'd first moved to LA, we were maybe
twenty-two, but no attraction remained, at least on my end.
There was little attraction to begin with, truly; even before
Tommy's gender presentation had shifted from futch to mas-
culine-of-center, they'd had markedly masculine energy. They

were lanky and beautiful with their Doc Martens and rolled t-shirt sleeves, and though I understood them to be widely desired all over the LA scene, pheromonally I didn't respond to them.

"How are you?" Tommy shouted over the music.

"Pretty okay," I shouted. "Have you heard from Ezra today?"

"Yeah!" they shouted. I must've looked at them with some kind of bug eyes, and they looked startled in response.

"What did he say?" I shouted.

"He texted me and Chelsea together, to say he couldn't make it."

"When?"

"Like an hour ago?"

So, after I'd locked his phone. And to text he would've had to unlock his phone, and see the message I'd left him to get in touch with me. But, no, he could've been texting on his computer. As much as it felt like Ezra was letting me stress, there was a chance that he just didn't know I was looking for him. I wanted to believe that if he knew how hard I was looking for him, no matter what, he'd hit me back. If I could see his texts to Tommy and Chelsea, I could maybe tell if he'd sent them from his phone or his computer based on whether some words had been automatically capitalized. Maybe he'd dropped his phone in the toilet at the Drawing Room.

"Can I see? Did he say why?"

Tommy shrugged, "Come to the back room! I think Chels texted with him more!"

Tommy grabbed me by the wrist again and pulled me through the singing crowd to their back bedroom, pictures of cacti and surfers on the wall, all taken by our friend Gabe, who was in the living room singing somewhere.

"I was going to ask you to come back here anyway," Tommy said. The song from the living room, something by Frank Ocean, sounded tinny and tiny in the bedroom with the door closed. Chelsea was sprawled on the bed, wearing a gauzy birthday dress; Georgie was curled up in the chair, her knees up, pissed-off body language. The mirrored end table was cleared off except for several long lines of coke and an uncurling one-dollar bill.

"Eve!" Chelsea squealed.

"Chelseeeeee," I squealed, and sloppily pressed my body into hers for a hug.

"Here you go honey," I said, pulling a sealed envelope out of my bag and handing it to her. Like a raccoon, she scrambled with her little hands to get it open. She opened the card and watched her present drift out: a personal check, for one million dollars, cut in half.

"If it was your full birthday, you'd get the whole check," I said.

Chelsea cackled.

"Don't try to cash it," I said. "It'll bounce."

I sat next to Georgie, then gestured at the coke on the table, "Do you mind?"

"Of course," Chelsea said. I pulled a ten-dollar bill out of my pocket and tried to hand it to her but she waved it off. "You got us last weekend," she said.

I shrugged and did a line. *U Up?* "I did some yesterday, so I'm not going to do too much."

"Very wise," Chelsea said, took the rolled bill from me and leaned over the table.

She passed the bill to Tommy, then they passed it to Georgie, and then we were all up. The coke made me more panicky, but it also made me happy, and for the first time all day my frantic energy inside seemed in tune with the world outside my body. I was relieved by the sudden symmetry and loved everyone around me fiercely. I deserved to bask in something good, for a change.

The muffled music turned to buzz, probably something from that 2010 era when fuzzy guitar rock took over the California indie music scene, something we could all be nostalgic about together.

"So babe," I said to Chelsea. "You texted with Ezra today?"

"A bit," she said. "So what?"

"What did he say?"

"That he wasn't coming."

"Did he say why?"

"He didn't answer that question, which I definitely tried to grill him on. Do you know how hard it is to grill that motherfucker via text? He just ignores."

"I know," I said.

"Did he tell you?"

"No," I said.

"Very interesting, unless you're lying, you're not lying right? No, of course not, what reason would you have to lie? Unless Ezra was being shitty about me throwing half-birthday parties. But no, he says that kind of shit to my face. So what is it?"

"He didn't tell me," I said.

"I heard he and Noz broke up, it's probably that," Tommy said.

"Who told you that?" I said.

"The woman herself," Chelsea said. "Noz texted us last night."

"I saw online that she's still going to the desert, though," Tommy said.

"Probably she wants to wallow a bit." Chelsea said.

"Why?" I said. "She was the perpetrator."

Chelsea shrugged. "Doesn't mean she's not feeling some kind of way."

I rolled my eyes.

"Not on her side?" Tommy said. "I thought you guys were close."

"I just don't get why she'd break our darling Ezra's heart for no good reason," I said. "Anyway she chose to take a solo vacation to the desert instead of celebrating you, Chelsea, so you should maybe be mad at her too."

I waited for someone to respond. For a long second—especially long-feeling because we were all amphetamined—but no one did.

"Please baby," Chelsea said, finally, "No more hateration in this dancery. Georgie, come over here for a moment please."

Georgie stepped over me and I felt stepped over.

From across the coffee table, Tommy gestured to me, curled their two fingers, *come here.* Thank god for that, for something nice and warm the second I was feeling cold. I scooted away from the couch and around the table; Tommy wrapped their arm around my shoulders and pulled me into their chest. They leaned their mouth to my ear and whispered:

"You doing alright? I know this is a rough weekend for you."

"It's a rough weekend for everyone," I said. I felt them squeeze me, felt them shake their head.

"Sure, we're all fucked up about Miguel, but we all know it's extra-hard for you and Ezra. We can all tell. Not in a bad way!

Just, we see how you've been wilding out and we want you to know that we're here to give you as much room to wild out as you need."

I squirmed and when Tommy didn't immediately let me go, I elbowed them a bit.

"Sorry," I said, scooting a few inches away. "I know you're just trying to be nice, I just don't want to think about Ezra or Miggy right now, okay?"

"I get it," Tommy said. "You didn't have to physically attack me." They were trying to be light and it wasn't working.

"Do you mind if I do one more?" I said, gesturing to the lines on the table. Tommy nodded so I bent down, inhaled through my left nostril, then wrapped Tommy into a big apology hug. "Thank you, I'm sorry."

Tommy patted me on the back, and then I stood up, intending to drift back into the crush of the party.

"Eve."

Georgie sat up on the bed, staring at me with big eyes.

"Yeah . . ."

"I have to talk to you. Remember?"

"Oh yeah, sorry, I'm sorry, G," I said. "This stuff makes me stupid. Let's leave these lovebirds to their canoodling and go pee." Tommy had crawled onto the bed and was halfway into wrapping Chelsea in a cuddle.

Georgie stood up and we slipped out of the bedroom and into the nearby bathroom, locking the door behind us. The floors and walls were all white tile and the mirror was very tall and long, broken into three segments so you could see the back of your head if you angled it the right way; it could be a very intense space, full of echoing mirrored versions of yourself, but both Georgie and I instinctually pushed the mirror into its flattest position, checked our nostrils for stray clumps of white powder or unruly boogers, then turned away from our single reflections to look at each other.

"Did you go to dinner with Lydia at Condor today or was that a tbt?" Georgie asked.

"Yeah, no, it was from today," I said.

"Look!" Georgie thrust her phone into my hands, her text convo with Lydia open. "I know you're going through it today, but I need you to look at this."

I scrolled up searching for the start of the conversation.

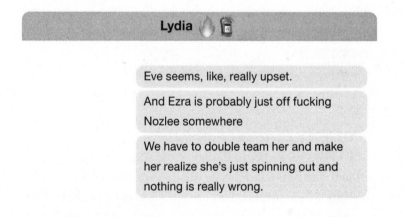

Lydia

Eve seems, like, really upset.

And Ezra is probably just off fucking Nozlee somewhere

We have to double team her and make her realize she's just spinning out and nothing is really wrong.

"Thanks for that, friend," I said, showing Georgie her own screen. "I'm spinning out?"

"I'm sorry! I didn't mean to hurt your feelings or anything! I said basically the same thing to your face in the bar, didn't I? I did."

She hadn't, really.

"Anyway it's not the point," Georgie said, "Scroll down."

It wasn't a bad enough comment for me to stay mad, I was feeling so coke-happy anyway, I scrolled.

Lydia

> And Ezra is probably just off fucking
> Nozlee somewhere

> We have to double team her and make
> her realize she's just spinning out and
> nothing is really wrong.

> Wanna grab dinner?

> I'm hungry for tacos

I think I'm gonna stay quiet until chelseas
thing tonight

I'm tired and I must recharge

"Okay," I said, "So obviously she lied."

"Did you invite her to dinner or did she invite you?"

I hated to be so deep inside the mess of someone else's relationship, a key witness. Did I protect Lydia or Georgie? Gun
to my head, whose back did I have when I couldn't have both
backs? Georgie was plaintive, and she'd been so sweet to me in
the bar while Lydia had riled me up at dinner, and she was just
trying to hold on with both hands to love she had thought she
didn't have to worry about losing.

"She invited me," I said. "I didn't know she'd texted you
this, I swear."

"Fuck," Georgie said. "I told her to talk to you, so I thought
maybe, you know, you'd reached out and she'd taken the
opportunity. Fuck."

"She probably just got a second wind and decided to do what you'd asked," I said.

Georgie plopped herself down on the closed toilet seat and ripped a big piece of toilet paper off the roll on the wall. She blew her nose so hard her eyes watered.

"That's bullshit and you know it," Georgie said. "Lydia is bullshitting me, I can't take it from you either. I feel gaslit as fuck right now."

"Sorry," I said. "I just don't know."

Georgie stood up fast. "Don't tell her we had this conversation, okay?"

"I'm not going to lie to either of you."

"Okay fine, if Lydia directly asks you if we had a dramatic conversation about her texts in a bathroom you can tell her the truth, but could you at least not volunteer the information?"

"No, of course not, I would never."

"I'm still trying to figure out what I want to do."

Georgie's hands looked shaky and I reached out. We hugged hard, her chin digging into my shoulder. "I need a minute," she said, stepping out of my arms.

"I'll just be outside if you need to talk or get weird or whatever," I said.

Georgie nodded, already her gaze was turned away from me, to her own reflection. I left her with it, whatever it was she had. When I was back in the hallway, I heard her lock the door after me.

Instead of heading back into the party, I slipped back into the bedroom. Tommy and Chelsea were gone, back into the crush of the party to chat with their guests, the coke cleaned up and taken with or hidden somewhere so people couldn't just wander in and devour it. I glanced around the room. I was

looking very specifically, and I was lucky: Tommy had left their
phone behind, on the nightstand, plugged into a charger. If
they'd been playing with it within the last ten minutes, it might
still be unlocked, I might not need to put in a passcode; I was
lucky again. I swiveled so my back faced the door and my body
blocked Tommy's phone, so I could pretend I was coke-addled
or just checking the time if someone caught me. I opened their
messages app and scrolled to their exchange with Ezra:

CHELSEA AND EZRA

Today 2:54 PM

Ezra:

Heyyyy guys sorry but I can't make it out
to the party tonight

Have a shit ton of fun without me

Capitalized first letters of each text probably meant auto
caps, which probably meant he'd been texting from his phone,
which meant . . . what? He'd unlocked it and still refused to
text me? My hands shook a little; maybe I was just freaked and
paranoid because of the coke? I knew I shouldn't have done it
when I was already anxious, but when I'm already anxious it's
hard to resist doing anything.

I went immediately to find a drink in the kitchen. I took a
shot of tequila out of a familiar green shot glass shaped like a
cactus that said Tucson, AZ, on it in garish colored lettering. I
held onto the glass cactus while the tequila burned down my

throat and my mouth watered ungracefully, trying to remember where I'd last seen and held and drunk from this small cup. At Miggy's apartment, I remembered; it had been his. An echo of every single drink Miggy and I shared, warm and communal, a bright pattern abruptly halted; my solo shot could be a version of many past moments with him, but no future moments.

I wanted to see Miggy at forty-five, black hair speckled with gray, still with that seventies mustache but not trendy anymore, dad-like in an uncool way, like badly fitting shorts. I imagined all of us at this house, but more subdued in our old age, grilling instead of getting fucked up, laughing together on the back porch. If he'd survived, if that scene could somehow come true, his laugh might've been genuine, or it might've been a laugh signaling a single moment's respite from the constant tug of his depression, dragging him down into a dark abyss that, from inside, felt like an inescapable cage. Left alone for one second, Imaginary Old Miggy could deflate with the weight of his own black depression, the way Real Young Miggy had done, probably a lot, though I'd only caught him a small handful of times. Maybe he was happier as my phone ghost, but fuck him for leaving anyway. So many people try to kill themselves and are caught, saved, 5150'd, living on. Why did it have to be my best friend who beat the odds and made it happen?

I resisted texting Miggy "Fuck you for leaving me." But I couldn't be in the kitchen anymore. I fished a fresh-cracked can of Bud Light (the regular kind, not a Rams can) from the fridge, and ducked into the narrow hallway off the kitchen that led back to the bathroom. It was unoccupied, Georgie having apparently finished her solo sulk, so I went in, shut the door, cutting off the sounds of my trap music and all the girls talking to each other and grinding on each other on the dance floor.

I peed, then sat dripping on the toilet; I opened Instagram. We were all thirsty, we were all giving each other pictures of our faces, and with the pulse of tequila and beer coursing through my body, I was so grateful to get to see all my friends' faces. My friends are so beautiful; flawed and messy, angry at me sometimes, angry at each other, but beautiful; they are looking to live a ripe life. We try to live inside our own nice pictures. I suddenly felt like they'd posted them just for me, for a moment I couldn't see the absence of Ezra.

Standing, I felt a disorienting tilt of dizziness, I steadied myself with a hand on the wall. The lights got soft, then sharpened. I felt the pucker of my mouth drying out, and after washing my hands, I slurped water out of them; water would take my edge off. I teetered out of the bathroom.

I pushed my way through a small crowd that had gathered in the kitchen doorway, through the kitchen, outside, in the cool night air. I saw someone sitting alone on the far corner of the porch, where no one usually sat because the couch there was the worst. I knew Clara by the back of her head, her unruly cascade of pale tangled hair, under the tan baseball cap she wore frontwards during the day and backwards at night. She swiveled and I saw the empty cup in her hand; she tapped her fingernail against the glass; she was alone; a male ghost who was so weak he couldn't even tell living humans were around hovered unnoticed over her head.

Clara had gone to Barnard with Noz and me and I'd had a devastating crush on her freshman year, from one drunken weekend after finals when she'd tugged me into a stranger's dorm room and kissed me once on the mouth. After that, she'd seemed as far away as a cloud, running with a crowd of fine arts major straight girls who wore stylish glasses and talked theory in the cafeteria. I thought she thought she was too cool for me, until about two years ago, when she'd moved back to Los Angeles and I realized she'd just had a raging social anxiety disorder; she'd broken up with her live-in girlfriend four months before Bea and I split. I'd invited her to sleep on my couch for a few nights, which she didn't accept, but which unexpectedly was one of the things that ultimately did Bea and me in. I didn't really understand what had made Bea so angry about me offering my couch to Clara, she was usually into helping out one of our friends when they were having a rough time.

I knew Clara liked whiskey and being alone, but I decided to respect one preference more than the other. I ducked back into the kitchen and filled two clear plastic cups with an overshare of scotch, then hurried back out to the porch and plopped into the empty seat next to Clara. She jumped then, oh yes, smiled when she saw it was me and that I was thrusting a newly filled cup towards her.

"I was starting to think I was desperate enough to go back into the party," Clara said, her voice husky and low from smoking cigarettes, and shouting all day at her elementary school teaching job, and organizing the crowd at her community action events focused on ending homelessness in Los Angeles, and singing in her band that was getting more gigs at Hi Hat and Lot 1 and other venues all around the east side of the city. She was wearing a white t-shirt and a thin gold chain hung down her chest, between the small slopes of her barely there breasts. The fabric of her shirt was too thick for me to see if she had a bra on, or if her nipples were hardened in the chilled air.

"Eve to the rescue," I said, knocking my plastic against hers. "What the fuck is up? How's thotting it up in Highland Park?"

"How's fucking your way through West Hollywood?"

I gasped with mock outrage. "I hooked up in West Hollywood *one time.*"

She leaned forward and sniffed at my neck, "And I can still smell the men's cologne all those butches wear."

"How *dare* you," I said, darting forward and tickling her briefly, gently, under her left arm.

Clara giggled, yelped, scrambled back, spilled scotch on her fingers, and tried to lick it off while laughing.

"Stop it," she said, "Stop it. I'm trying to sit alone in the dark and you're ruining my vibes."

I shrugged, sipped my own cup.

Clara went quiet again, bit at her cuticle, shook her hand under the light and I could see that she was gnawing herself raw.

"You're having a bad week?" I phrased it like a question. Her breakup had been weighing on her, and everybody knew it.

"The kids are restless and it's stressful. And all of our friends are being so sweet to me, which is somehow excruciating, much worse than if everyone was being shitty to me."

I nodded.

"I want to, like, hug everyone and talk and hang out," Clara said. "But I hate everything too much. Every time someone's nice to me, I experience it as an attack."

I nodded.

"Then I feel shitty and guilty and it's my fault because I'm the shit one."

"You're not," I said.

"And I try to will myself into being nice and I look like a fucking psychopath," she said. She flashed me a truly terrifying forced smile that did in fact make her look like a psychopath.

"Stop it," I said, joking gently. "I brought you liquor, I don't deserve this."

She softened into her real smile, laughed a little while looking down, then looked back up to me, then scooted closer. We hadn't so much as kissed since that first year of college, but now, our thighs were touching.

"I'm sorry," she said, and the way she said it, I knew she was flirting.

Clara would've heard that Bea and I broke up, she would know I was free to do as I pleased with whomever wanted it. Though my head was still full of Bea, there was no reason why I couldn't have this one thing, for someone I'd had a crush on to look at me and see that I wanted them, and, after years of me wanting, to finally want me back. I wanted Clara's desire, and I didn't care if she was only feeling it now because she was adrift and I was familiar. Her interest meant that people could go away from you, but then come back.

"Do we need to get you out of here? For the safety of yourself and others?" I kept my tone light, giving her room to push back or to transition the vibe into something more familiarly platonic. She licked her lips, and the spit on them shone in the moonlight.

"Let's go to Hermosillo?" she asked. "Get a quiet glass of wine?"

It was within walking distance. "Sure," I said.

We smashed our plastic cups against each other again and took the rest of the nice scotch as a shot, then ghosted the party. The residential streets were barely lit; all downhill, our footfalls were loud. On the seven-minute walk to the bar, Clara recited the plots of her favorite scary movies in a successful attempt to terrify me. We held hands and stumbled together, giggling, equally drunk, the edges of all the leaves blurring into one dark green blob, the motion sensor lights in front of nicer houses blinking on as we stumbled by. David was working the door at Herm, we hugged him as we went in.

We ordered beers from a bartender named Jason, pints of light beer from Highland Park Brewery, and we could barely hold them steady, sloshed beer all over our fingers and the floor as we pushed through a small clump of people to a recently vacated table near the door, still covered with other people's empty glasses. Clara sat a friendly distance away through half a pint, then finally, finally she put a hand on my thigh, as low as you could get without just touching my knee.

"Am I going to fuck up our friendship?" she asked.

"What friendship? I've just been trying to get in your pants." I scooted closer to her, which made her hand go far enough up my thigh that the tips of her fingers were underneath the hem of her jean shorts, and the gentle rub of her fingertips against my skin made my cunt pulse, just once. "No," I said, seriously. "We're both single, and you're beautiful. In the morning we'll go back to normal."

"Okay," she said and she kissed me, which I guess I'd been waiting for.

We Lyfted back to her apartment, and I unbuttoned her shirt, one by one. The whole time we'd been chatting on the porch, flirting over pints of beer, she hadn't been wearing a bra. My lizard brain interpreted her bralessness as a deliberate gift and made me shudder, pulse. I wanted a chance to touch every part of her body, which was warm and semi-naked and most importantly here with me, not disappeared somewhere, like Ezra, leaving me with only an impression of him trapped inside my useless idiotic lump of an iPhone.

Clara sat on her couch and I straddled her, put my glasses on the hexagonal side table. She grabbed at the fabric of my tank top and pushed it aside, so she could get her tongue on one of my nipples. She said, "Fuck, I love this shirt."

As we kissed I worked one hand into her black jeans, trying to snake low enough into the unforgiving denim to reach her clit, and all my failed attempts I think felt to her like a tease; I could smell her, she was getting wet.

"Do you want to go to the bedroom?" she said.

"Sure," I said. I got off her. Clara left her shirt in a crumple on the couch; I followed the twin mountain crests of her shoulder blades into her bedroom. The room was dim, a little bit of light from outside coming in through her high long windows, and she turned on one of those pink Himalayan sea salt lamps, a muted glow. She had the typical LA-apartment architecture: the closet stretched along one entire wall, closed off from the bedroom with sliding doors that were also floor to ceiling mirrors. It made the room stretch long. Clara's bedsheets were decorated with a print I recognized from IKEA, but otherwise everything in her room looked thrifted. All the plants in her apartment were leafy, not succulents, which meant she could take care of them.

I kneeled on the bed and helped Clara unbutton her jeans. Her underwear was pale and damp, I touched her and tried not to catch sight of my own reflection in my peripherals. Nothing is as unsexy to me as seeing your own body contorted awkwardly during sex, the way I had to scrunch my belly unflatteringly to get my mouth around one of her pink nipples while my fingers still worked gently at her clit, over her underwear, smelling and feeling how she soaked them. I remembered from our friendly conversations about sex, over margaritas somewhere, that Clara did like to be teased a little.

We moved apart and together again (then apart and together again) as Clara took off my top, my pants.

"Get over here," I said, even though she was close enough to touch.

Her legs were long underneath me as I pulled her underwear off finally, and I could smell her better then. She watched me as I put my fingers back on her clit, she closed her eyes as I circled there a few times. She didn't let me stay there long.

She opened her eyes, flipped me so she was hovering over me, her eyes glowed, she nudged two fingers at my cunt to see if I was wet, and of course I was, I was ready.

"Is this alright?" she said, before going anywhere else. I nodded.

She fucked me with one finger, then two, curling up towards my g-spot, asking a few times if it was there (no), if it was there (no), until she gave up on finding it, and moved her fingers to my clit where she flicked a little too hard. She was so used to fucking someone else, she couldn't fuck the body that was under her; she didn't try to pleasure me, she tried to pleasure the girl that had left her.

"I'm good," I said, grabbing her hand to stop it from moving anymore and before she could get too in her head, I guided her onto her back and went down on her. It took her a while, as I tried to interpret her small noises as guides to how I should adjust, but eventually she came with a gush and a shudder. We nuzzled, got under the covers, smelling each other in the air.

"We're okay, right?" she said.

"We're great," I said, touching her cheek and giving her a kiss, so I could remember what her lips felt like. We probably wouldn't ever kiss again.

"Okay, I'm going to turn over."

She drifted away, to sleep, and I got up for a minute, went to the kitchen and got us a glass of water for the morning, got my phone.

I put the water on the side table next to Clara, where she'd be able to blindly grope for it in the morning, she was drunker than I was. I lay on my back and held my phone up. I tapped Georgie's name.

Georgie

Friday 11:59 PM

Where are you?

Lydia

Have you eaten?

Where are you?

BEA SHOWED UP

Are you okay with that or did you flee?

i left before Bea showed

went home with Clara

don't tell

Lydia was giving, caring, loyal, but a gossip. If she was still at the party, and she probably was, then Bea would find out I went home with Clara before she went to bed. If Bea had gone home already, she'd find out from someone at brunch the next morning; her hair would be frizzy, up in a big bun, her eyes would be squinted even behind her big Crap sunglasses. She'd pretend in front of other people not to care, but I'd wake up with a nasty text. I would be happy, waiting for her response.

I opened Instagram and waited for a second while it loaded; even though I hadn't posted last night, I saw I had a hearty crop of notifications since the last time I opened the app, almost three hundred red hearts according to the small red bubble that popped up at the bottom of my screen. Find out who's liked you, figure out why. It wasn't a mystery that was hard to solve; I didn't even have to tap my notifications button, the culprit was at the top of the screen: a new post from Ezra.

It was a picture I recognized and remembered, Ezra and Miggy and me, in a hot tub at a Palm Springs Airbnb rental, taken on a trip three years ago, the sun setting pink, and behind us the big mountains, the bigger sky. Ezra's caption said, "We're missing our boy tonight." With me in that picture, did that "we" include me?

EzraIsTexting

> jus tell me if you're alive out there bc i have a bad feeling

> if u don't answer imma come over to your place

> ezra please i'm getting so stressed

Today 2:22 AM

for real you post that pic but you won't
text me back?

Did the "we" stretch to include the woman who had taken
the picture, Nozlee in her red bikini?

Fuck him. I prepared my own post, of the crushed Bud
Light can from my walk this morning, the special Rams logo
fully visible despite the aluminum's crumple. I picked the filter
called Juno because it made the blue on the can lighter but kept
the metallic shine of light bouncing off metal. I typed the caption: "A violent crime! If anyone has any clues about how this
buddy's life was taken from us, please slide into my DMs." I hit
post and watched the screen for a few seconds while it loaded,
posted.

Then, disgusted suddenly with my entire cell phone and
everything it contained, I turned off the screen, stuffed the
phone under my pillow where it would be safe, and tried to
fall asleep.

Saturday, 7:37 a.m.

I knew I was hungover before I was really awake, my body heavy and disjointed, my location unfamiliar, the headache building in the bones between my eyes and my nose, the acid taste of last night's last drink lingering in the back of my throat. If I could prevent myself from fully waking up, I could slip back to sleep and ride out at least half of my hangover in sweaty unconsciousness.

With a burst of sound loud enough make my headache pulse, Clara's air conditioner window unit chugged on. For five terrible seconds, the noise was intense enough to kill me. I felt it forcing too much blood into my brain, felt my brain on the verge of explosion, felt the nausea swim through my throat and cheeks, I was absolutely going to die. As my last act before definitely dying, I moved my limbs haphazardly, like trying to climb out of a volcano while it was erupting; Clara's sheets were soft but in an unfamiliar way. Then, I realized that if I could hold on a little bit longer, I could get used to the noise of the air conditioner and it would fade into a tolerable buzz. I willed my body to still and for the air of my breath to go in and out of my nose, to avoid tasting my hangover breath.

Then, the air conditioner turned off. The air was still and

everything was quiet and I could feel my body settle again, and breathing wasn't such a difficult task, and neither was closing my eyes, and neither was slipping gently away to wait out my hangover in pleasant unconsciousness. The air conditioner jolted on again.

It was somehow louder, and metallically sharp, as if with the noise it was coming apart and little pieces of metal were stabbing me in the temples, and eye sockets, and either side of my nose, and in the skin underneath my eyebrows that is so close to the bone. Like someone suffering from severe brain damage, Clara slept through the assault without waking. The air conditioner turned off. I turned over to watch her lay peacefully in the temporary quiet, her hair matted onto the side of her face, her mouth slightly parted in sleep. I liked this soft and unkempt version of her face, the fact that after years of looking at her I got this private view. It was better than actually sleeping with her to know that I had slept with her; I will take any and all intimacy freely given. I could fall asleep again maybe, ride out my hangover, use her mouthwash, wake her up, eat her out for a couple of hours, go get brunch. Think of things to say to her to make her like me more.

The fucking air conditioner jolted on again and she didn't even twitch. Nothing in her face changed, but it lost its rare and inviting quality all the same. We were just two stupid drunk people, and if I stayed she wouldn't like me any more than she ever had. That was enough of Clara's house.

I spotted my underwear in the opposite corner, remembered flinging it there with abandon the previous evening; not all the details were there, and many which remained were ringed with fuzz, but I recalled my tossing of my own underpants. I stood up, my head swam, I retrieved and put on my clothes with practiced quiet. But when I opened the door, I heard Clara moan, finally stir. The on and off of the air conditioner couldn't rouse her, but someone leaving did. I got out of there before she could fully regain herself.

Clara lived in Echo Park like I did, but south of 101, in the pre-gentrified zone, where high-rises painted disgusting Kermit greens had just begun sprouting in between liquor stores and auto body shops. The apartments were nice and cheaper in Clara's zone, but crossing the 101 presented some challenges. To get to my nice home, I had a few options: pay for a quick Lyft and be forced to make small talk with an annoying man in the early and terrible morning, take a very long walk around the 101, or use the pedestrian overpass above the 101, which was the shortest way but very loud and hot and sometimes populated by the homeless men who considered it their territory. None of the three sounded doable while my body was in an in-between place where nausea had taken it over but actual vomit was not yet forthcoming; I had only one option, to induce the purge. Luckily, Clara had a half bathroom off her impossibly bright living room and I didn't have to venture back into her bedroom to use the en suite; I had the blessed opportunity to vomit in peace.

The half bath was speckled with indigo blue like the rest of her apartment, blue in the towels, blue in curtains. I locked the door so if Clara rose and came to find me, she wouldn't interrupt. I knelt before the toilet, I checked the pointer and middle fingernails on my right hand for embedded dirt and finding them clean, I delicately inserted them into my mouth and buried them snake-like into the hot wet of my pulsating throat. The gagging came easily, the retching came quickly, and I threw up only the fizzy aftermath of beer and liquor, barely a hint of enchiladas, eaten so long ago they were a non-factor. I felt better than I had all morning in the throes of my purge, the nausea faded out, my body cleaning itself, de-poisoning itself, taking care of me, making me ready for a new day. When it was done, I stood shakily and gripped the sink, turned on the faucet. I sloshed some water around in my mouth, rinsed once, rinsed twice, then swallowed a few gulps. The nausea was temporarily abated; it would be back for sure, but I had enough time to get home before it got bad again.

Out of the bathroom, my phone and keys laid carefully on the coffee table as a helpful gesture from my past drunk self to my current hungover self, my boots in a little pile near the door, out the door, down Clara's small staircase, past her gate, and out onto Cortez Street. I walked past the gated liquor store, turned onto Belmont, and hurried onto the overpass, to get this part of my walk over fast. The narrow overpass was blissfully empty save for discarded shoes and crushed beer cans and a thick layer of graffiti tattooing the concrete edges. The cars whizzed down the 101 below me, taking advantage of a rare moment of low traffic congestion. Their noise was beastly, I was hot all over, and in the final patch of garbage near the end of the overpass, I spotted a crunched up Budweiser Rams can. Like a bad omen, I ran from it.

I scurried down the pedestrian staircase and landed at the base of Echo Park Lake, already swarming with families and runners and people lounging in the shade with their dogs and Mexican men selling ice cream, hot dogs, pupusas, and churros. Nearby me, a baby started crying, but I couldn't spot where the baby was exactly, just heard its nightmarish squeals, as if the sound of impotent sobbing was coming from the very air. As I hurried up the path around the lake, a large dog waddled over to me and slobbered all over my knees, while its owner tugged and apologized; but with her spidery arms, she was no match for the dog's heft. I darted away from the dog's grasping tongue.

Normally, I love the clamor of the park, its oasis-like quality, the way the downtown skyscrapers glimmer mountainous above the palm trees. But hungover, it was a hall of mirrors. I had to get out of there as fast as I could.

Several long and horrible minutes later, I made it out to the clamor of Sunset Blvd, then up Echo Park Avenue and into the oasis of my little bungalow. I slammed the windowed door behind me and locked it fast, as if chased by the noise and the sunlight. I dropped my blackout curtains and fired up my own quiet air conditioner; I lit my lavender candle; I peeled off all my clothing except my underwear and plopped down in my luxuriously cold and empty bed, the sheets a familiar softness. Sleep didn't come immediately, though, what with the remains of that small bit of cocaine swimming around somewhere behind my eyes, and the nausea spins gently returning. I thumbed at my phone like a life preserver as I tried to distract myself long enough to feel drowsy, instinctively clicking on Instagram. Maybe the gentle flow of art-directed images would soothe me.

First thing I saw was a crop of heart notifications, indicating that fifty-four people had liked an image, and remembered posting the crumpled Bud Rams can. I remembered suddenly that after a full day of absence and panic, Ezra had emerged digitally: he'd posted on Instagram, he'd texted Chelsea and Tommy, but still hadn't texted me back. There was nothing wrong with him physically, he wasn't hurt or blocking out the world, he was just refusing me. It was a black panic, not knowing why. I wanted to drain the anxiety out of me, somehow, as easily as I'd emptied my own stomach. But I didn't know how to by myself, without Ezra here to explain my crimes and absolve me. Maybe there was gossip about it and somebody else could tell me. Maybe I would feel better if I screamed about it to all my friends.

I texted my group chat with Georgie and Lydia:

BABES

Today 8:14 AM

did you guys see Ezra's Instagram post last night?

I asked in case only I could see it, and Ezra was dead, and he was stretching out towards me, confused in the afterlife, the way Miguel had via text messages. Instagram has a messenger, if he was dead I could still communicate with Ezra, and if only I could see the post then I could play off my text to Georgie and Lydia, I could say I was still drunk when I woke up. I remembered that if Ezra was dead and Instagramming, Nozlee probably would be able to see it too, and they could sext behind my back for the rest of Nozlee's life.

I noticed, in the corner of my screen, a red circle indicating someone had DM'd me through the Instagram messenger. I clicked and at the top of my messages feed I saw the unread one, bolded, from someone with the username ParisInThePM. I clicked on the feed and read:

PARISINTHEPM

Hey I don't know if you remember me, this is Paris Montgomery, I used to date your friend Ezra.

I saw that post of the Rams can.

Was that outside the house I'm selling? You would've seen my sign in the yard.

This is super weird but if I'm right can you text me? 818-976-4545

I'm worried about Ezra.

Anxiety and nausea are a nasty pair, together they make the mind swim and the body move without considering the situation or consequences. I texted Paris back feverishly.

818-976-4545

hey this is Eve

i'm worried about Ezra too

what's going on

I watched the phone for long seconds, but response bubbles didn't appear right away, so I let it go dark and dropped it to the bed. I turned on my side, drowsy finally, probably from the mental exertion of the anxiety rush, and stared at my dark phone. It didn't light up, and I felt myself drifting.

Saturday, 12:49 p.m.

818-976-4545

hey this is Eve

i'm worried about Ezra too

what's going on

Today 8:55 AM

Can you meet me up later?

I woke up slow and ragged, but the spins had stopped and my hangover was all but gone. The blood was hot and fresh in my head. My text message inbox was ripe and full like a fruit tree, some lemons still hanging, others gone splat on the lawn and jagged sidewalk.

[818-976-4545]

what's going on

Today 8:55 AM

Can you meet me up later?

sorry I fell asleep, when can you meet up?

BABES

did you guys see Ezra's Instagram post last night?

Georgie:

I saw it

Cute for Miggy, but he still didn't text you back, I take it? That's so fucked up.

Lydia:

i admit i assumed you were making a mountain out of a molehill yesterday when you said something was going on with Ezra, but obviously he's okay and obviously not texting you. i'm sorry i was

> skeptical, and i'm so sorry he's being a
> dick, especially this weekend.

Lydia was texting long and with no caps, so she must've been typing from her computer, probably from bed, probably updating her still-popular Tumblr with pictures of her body in various flattering outfits, inspiration for her still-fervent followers, equal parts thirsty men and other stylish plus-sized women. I imagined her swathed in her striped Mexican blankets; it was a comfort to imagine myself next to her, curled up in her colorful bedroom, her rubbing my back like my mother used to do when I was sick, like Lydia had done after so many breakups. When a friend had been wronged, she was a natural soother, and I liked to be swaddled and soothed when wronged; this was one of the ways that she and I fit together.

BABES

Lydia:

> i admit i assumed you were making a
> mountain out of a molehill yesterday
> when you said something was going on
> with Ezra, but obviously he's okay and
> obviously not texting you. i'm sorry i was
> skeptical, and i'm so sorry he's being a
> dick, especially this weekend.

Lydia:

> so while i was right that he isn't hurt or dying anywhere, something is going on.

thanks Lydia

my feelings are hurt

Georgie:

> Are you going to confront him?

if i can find him!!

Lydia:

> he'll be in Palm Springs with all of us on sunday right?? why not just wait and confront him then, or monday morning?

i appreciate the sentiment but I need to talk to him before sunday

he's not some random asshole

he's my best friend

he got broken up with exactly one year after our other best friend passed away

and now he's not answering me

As I was typing my next text to the group chat, the text

notification bubble popped up at the top of my screen, some-thing from Miggy. In case it was important, I stopped typing and clicked the bubble to read the message from Migs.

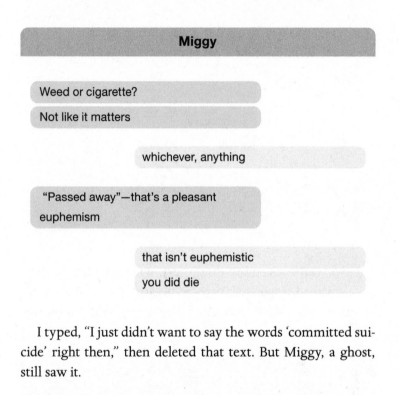

I typed, "I just didn't want to say the words 'committed sui-cide' right then," then deleted that text. But Miggy, a ghost, still saw it.

> It's not an easy thing to say

> But it IS the thing

> > sorry

> > you know how i get

> Scared.

> > i'm not scared

> > i'm just . . .

> Euphemistic

> Mea culpa

I switched back to my group text, where neither Georgie nor Lydia had responded, perhaps because they had seen my typing ellipsis bubble earlier, and they were giving some space for my next texts to come in.

BABES

> he got broken up with exactly one year after our other best friend passed away

> and now he's not answering me

> even if he's physically okay, there could be something really emotionally wrong with him right now

Lydia:

and if there isn't?

if he just needs space?

if you need space, become an astronaut,
don't be friends with me

I waited there, in that chat window, for something to happen. For the ellipsis bubble to appear, for Lydia to comfort me, for Georgie to comfort me, but nothing happened; the vibrant thing in my hand went inert. The blocks of text, gray and blue, were ordered neatly now, and I thought of them calcifying into bone, the bone manifesting muscle and blood, the muscle and blood necessitating skin. What would my texts look like if they grew a body? Would that body look tall and messy like mine? Or would the body look like someone I fixated on, like Ezra when he was mad, his mouth parted to express is instinctual disbelief that anyone would do anything he didn't like? Or Nozlee, even, the lines of her long fingers, the curve of her breasts in a stretchy top that made them look as buoyant as buoys, scowling at me from across brunch tables all across Los Angeles when I had to count on my fingers to calculate a tip? Why did I imagine my texts in the bodies of my friends when they were at their most annoyed?

Miggy

i'm just . . .

Euphemistic

Mea culpa

This is all kinda fucked up, isn't it?

fucked up how?

Shouldn't you give your friend space if
that's what he wants?

maybe if he asked for space, he'd get it

I love you so much, but you know that's
never been your vibe

You don't like to let something percolate

You are frantic to get rid of any bad
feeling

speak for yourself

Okay we're the same

But that doesn't mean that you're not
going down a bad road right now

Texting Miggy back would only give him more permission
to say rough things to me; it was okay to like closeness, to be
suspicious of space, in the right context. Anything stripped of
context would sound pathological, and it was annoying for
him to throw my normal reactions in my face and twist them

so they seemed problematic. I closed my message box and went in search of other notifications that needed my attention. My phone's apps were speckled with red circles adorning their upper-right-hand corners, each circle filled with white numbers: fifteen on Twitter for something clever I'd written drunkenly and promptly forgot; an alarming fifty-six on useless Facebook (why didn't I have the wherewithal to delete my account or at least remove the app from my phone?); a reasonable ten on Gmail, probably all spam from online clothing stores I bought from once and now pursuing me probably forever and ever with their desperate newsletters: "Half off everything. Seriously." "These boots will change EVERYTHING." "Your make-an-entrance dress is here." "The softest t-shirt ever! Try it for free!!" Despite the thirsty and impersonal subject headings obviously awaiting me, I opened Gmail first, craving the satisfaction of swiftly deleting and decluttering. I found the expected solicitations, but nestled between them was a personal email, and I thought maybe I read it wrong as I scrolled, but no, there it was, an email from Nozlee. Subject heading: Please Don't Immediately Delete.

I very much wanted to immediately delete. Nozlee couldn't offer me absolution, just complication. To read the email would be agreeing to allow her perspective to influence mine, and I didn't want to feel empathy for her. I wanted to prioritize my own terrible emotions.

But the subject heading was so indicative of our intimacy, she knew me to my bones, and I felt the pull of our attachment. Delicately, I clicked.

Hi Eve,

I'm writing to you from Desert Hot Springs, and it won't cool down even though it's the middle of the night. I'm typing this on my phone, I'm lying in the dark directly under an air conditioning vent.

I was so hurt when you, especially you, immediately dismissed me after I broke up with Ezra. I know how close you guys are, and how much his friendship means to you, but we are friends too. You are basically my best friend, and I love you, and I've been figuring some things out in my life that directly relate to our friendship, that directly relate to why I broke up with Ezra. I knew you'd feel betrayed, but I thought I'd at least be able to have a conversation with you. I deserve that conversation. But because it seems like you obviously won't give it to me, and because you've obviously blocked my cell phone number, I'm going to tell you everything in this email where you can't avoid it, I won't let you avoid it like you avoid everything else you—

On protective reflex, I quickly clicked the Trash icon at the top of the screen and got Nozlee's presumptive bullshit out of my face. Nozlee knew what it would take to get me to open an email, but she didn't know what it would take to get me to keep reading one; I could avoid whatever the fuck I wanted. I wasn't required to be confronted by anything I didn't want to know; I didn't have to sit with any feelings I didn't want to sit with.

The email wasn't completely gone, of course, it was lingering ghost-like in my Trash folder. As I navigated to the Trash folder in my sidebar, before I could permanently delete the email, a text notification popped up at the top of my screen. Paris.

818-976-4545

Today 8:55 AM

Can you meet me up later?

Today 1:17 PM

sorry I fell asleep, when can you meet up?

I can meet you now if you want?

We texted back and forth to coordinate time and location. I needed a little time, I had to shower, I had to walk back to Daniel's to retrieve my car. Unfortunately, Paris lived in downtown Los Angeles, where parking was impossible and everything smelled like New York City. I suggested Clifton's Cafeteria, before she could insist on some lesser institution. It was an old bar, full of ghosts, and I'd have to snort some Cascarilla to be steady in there; even though I'd promised Miggy I wouldn't, I didn't want to deal with him pushing on me so much.

As we texted, I puttered around my bungalow, getting my shit together; I opened the curtains, I took two Walgreens-brand ibuprofen over the sink with water straight from the tap, wincing at the taste of LA's ratty swamp water. I threw on my summer jeans with the holes in them and a shirt that one of Bea's creative, intimidating friends hand-printed; I rolled the sleeves. I noticed that I'd left my lavender candle burning all night, without even putting an intention on it, and it was now gone, burned down to the aluminum bottom of the wick, the glass bottom of the candle holder scorched, and with my nice candle all gone my entire apartment should've smelled like a lavender bush, but it didn't. Or maybe it did, but I'd been inside the smell so long that lavender air read as normal in my brain. Either way, it felt like I'd lost something, no more candle, and no smell to savor.

Behind the scorched glass thing that used to hold my candle, I'd left a small ziplock baggie full of white powder, labeled with Sharpie: C for Cascarilla. I couldn't remember why I'd bothered to label it, I'd never confuse it with cocaine because I purchased that in much smaller quantities. I picked up the bag, I rubbed at the thin plastic, the C wasn't in my handwriting. I remembered that Noz had dropped off the bag for me a couple of weeks ago. She'd started grinding her own eggshells like I did, she'd wanted me to test out their effectiveness; I'd forgotten about the task. I didn't care about completing it now, but I wasn't picky about the materials I was going to use to blank out, to be alone in my head and as empty as I wanted. I grabbed for my phone.

Miggy

Okay we're the same

But that doesn't mean that you're not going down a bad road right now

i miss you so much

i don't know what to do about anything

> i wish i could take the cascarilla and get rid of all the ghosts except you
>
> i'll text you when i'm on the other side

Seriously Eve?? You're going to shut me out AGAIN? You promised you wouldn't do any at all this weekend, and now you're going back for another round? Isn't this supposed to be my fucking weekend?

> you don't own this weekend just because you decided to die on it

That's so fucking rude.

I never call you out on your bad patterns, and I thought we'd get to spend this weekend at least a little bit together, and all you've done is snort ghost-blocker drugs and freak out about Ezra.

I threw my phone away from me, onto my bed, so that I don't have to feel guilty anymore. Off the top of my bookcase, I pulled down the coaster I'd stolen from an Airbnb in Rosarito during our Mexico vacation, a single Mexican tile, deep blue background patterned with orange and yellow flowers, slick and perfect for doing lines. I brought it to my bed where I sprawled next to it and poured a bit of the Cascarilla onto the tile. As I was arranging two lines with the side of my credit card, my phone lit up, a phone call from Noz. The fucking *nerve*. If that bitch wanted me, she would get me.

I swiped to answer the call, I turned on speakerphone. "What the hell, Nozlee?" I said, continuing to arrange my lines.

"Miggy texted," she whispered. Who was she trying to keep from overhearing? She'd probably gone to the desert with one of her *Shahs of Sunset*–style friends, the Iranian Jews she ran with, friends she kept neatly apart from her Eastside white writer friends. "He said you're about to snort a boatload of Cascarilla. I thought you promised not to do any this weekend?"

"Firstly, I'm taking a tiny bump for practicality, because I have to meet someone at Clifton's and you know that place is crawling with the desperate ghosts of dead actors."

Noz started to respond, but I cut her off; I had the upper hand because she couldn't shout. "Secondly! You lost the right to comment on my lifestyle choices when you broke Ezra's heart for no good reason."

"I did have a good reason!" Noz said, harshly but still whispering, she didn't even want her friends to overhear this part of the argument. "Did you look at your email today?"

"I deleted it without reading it," I said.

"I hate it when you act like such a fucking brat. Read your email. Listen to me. Firstly, you know I'm not a stranger to snorting eggshells when you're like, on a family vacation to a Civil War battleground and you don't want to see gross ghosts, but right now you're cutting off your best friend on the anniversary of his death for the sake of your own convenience."

Nozlee paused, accidentally gave me the floor.

"Before you go on," I said, not shouting now in order to keep the high road for myself, "You breaking up with Ezra hurt me because you were breaking apart the last bit of our friend group, which Miggy had already broken in half last year. And you didn't have a reason to leave us."

The air in my apartment felt prickly. My eyes stung like when I had allergies; the water in them felt hot and poisonous and ready to spill. If I'd been allowed to just live how I wanted, I wouldn't have been forced to feel sad right now. I can't do anything when I'm sad, and I have so much I need to do. I heard Nozlee breathing into the phone, I could hear her breath but I'd never again get to hop in the car for a spontaneous road trip to get dim sum for breakfast, or wrap my arms around her neck on the dance floor and shimmy while the DJ played "Return of the Mack," or pass out in the same bed in Palm Springs as the sun came up over the hotel's swimming pool, or get high and wander around the Americana mall, trying on all the jeans and ordering lychee martinis and pork soup dumplings at Din Thai Fung. She broke up with Ezra, didn't give him a reason, and didn't care that by breaking up with him, she was also leaving me behind.

"I don't want to leave you, Eve," Nozlee said.

"You have a funny way of showing it," I said, and hung up the call.

My Cascarilla lines were done, all white and neat, cut to exactly equal length. I opened my text chain with Miggy and typed with my thumbs:

Miggy

That's so fucking rude.

I never call you out on your bad patterns,
and I thought we'd get to spend this
weekend at least a little bit together, and
all you've done is snort ghost-blocker
drugs and freak out about Ezra.

> if you wanted to "spend this weekend
> together" you could've fucking tried not
> killing yourself. you and i both know,
> death is something that happens to the
> people left alive, not the people who've
> died.

Then I took the lines, then I left the house.

Saturday, 1:45 p.m.

I drove from the twisting hill streets above Echo Park down into the gridded, super-urban zone of downtown Los Angeles. Around me, the air thinned out, making room for the towering apartment high-rises and office buildings; most neighborhoods in Los Angeles were bound by regulations that dictated that buildings stay short enough to accommodate the sky, but downtown they block it out with metal and mirrored glass. This part of the city glistens. It's beautiful to look at from above like when you're on a hike in Elysian Park, but from inside DTLA, the buildings make me feel claustrophobic and cut off, like I'm not even in Los Angeles anymore. As I started to look for a parking spot, I passed a sporty gold Maserati that was parked neatly in the intersection of two metered parking spaces, rendering them both useless for other parkers, obviously done so that the owner of that gaudy piece of trash wouldn't get any scratches on his delicate fucking bumpers. All I wanted in that moment, stronger even than my desire to find Ezra, was to be legally allowed to ram my car into that asshole's dumb vehicle in punishment for keeping me from a parking spot that was rightly mine. Over and over again, I circled back to the Maserati, because certainly the fuckhead who'd committed this crime against the social contract wouldn't have done so for an extended period of time. I circled the cloying streets for almost twenty minutes waiting for justice to be served, waiting to get the visceral satisfaction of spotting a parking ticket below his windshield wiper, waiting at least for him to move his goddamn car.

I gave up, and pulled into one of the public lots that charge an atrocious twenty dollars for any stay longer than fifteen minutes. I begrudgingly parted with my money.

I'm on my way in

Walking, I navigated the thick-for-LA foot traffic, stopped to hand off a few dollar bills to a homeless guy who crossed my path and asked for the money, waited at the light, darted across the street, and arrived at the doorstep of Clifton's Cafeteria. I went inside, and into another world.

The bottom floor of Clifton's was designed to look like a Redwood forest, picnic tables nestled between actual Redwoods and plastic re-creations, booths nestled into the rock that covered all the walls, chairs arranged in a semicircle next to the tiny waterfall that emptied into a little pond that glowed with the green neon lights nestled into the sides. A plastic Redwood tree with a fireplace carved into the base towered above me; three floors of bars encircled its plastic branches.

I looked at the small crowd of daytime drinkers but didn't see Paris sitting at the nearby bar, or in the leather chairs artfully placed near the Redwood or the glass cases with the taxidermy mountain lion and Buffalo. I looked at my phone.

818-976-4545

parking was a nightmare

i'm on my way in

Meet me in Pacific Seas

I went up the side staircase, stopped at the seven-foot-tall mirror, resettled my curls and hiked up my jeans, and pushed on the left side of the mirror. It swung open, a hidden door. Inside, all woven bamboo and sunset murals, was Pacific Seas, the tiki bar. The light was dim and the music was crickets and ukulele.

I saw Paris right away, alone at the slick wooden bar, hunched slightly over her phone and bright blue drink-in-a-fishbowl, ice melting; I slid onto the stool next to her and hung my bag on a hook under the bar. Looking up from her phone, Paris blinked at me, then registered who I was, then leaned forward to hook one arm around my shoulders into the kind of awkward little hug that acquaintances often share when they unexpectedly run into each other at a cocktail party. I hadn't liked Paris, but I hadn't disliked her either; we were different species of women. The entire time she was with Ezra, we hadn't found one topic to talk about, we didn't even watch the same reality TV shows. I had always wondered why someone who loved me so much could've also been interested in her, and assume she'd regarded me with the same mixture of uncertainty and skepticism.

Compared to the messy frizz of my hangover hair, Paris looked artfully put together with her mermaid-long extensions, pointed red acrylic nails, and perfectly even liquid eyeliner; her only blemish was a cluster of pimples on her chin that were so tiny, they practically disappeared into her otherwise smooth and glimmering super-dark skin. Despite the half-finished boozy-looking drink sweating on the bar beside her, Paris looked clear-eyed and solid. She did, however, grip the rounded glass with the intensity of a terrified child holding fast to her mother's hand.

"So how have you been doing?" Paris asked, useless small talk, at the same time as a sexy, freckly, redheaded bartender brandished a menu in my direction, with a nerdy gentlemanly gesture style used only by the least-cool butch dykes who had just come to the city from some square Midwestern place and hadn't adapted to the cold vibes of the LA lesbian scene yet. This bartender was too hot to be so dumb. "Do you need to look at our cocktail menu?" she asked.

"No," I said. I didn't say "nope" because "no" was sexier. "I'll have a Penicillin."

She smiled, "Coming right up," and busied herself with the glassware and ice and rum, at a station right next to where Paris and I were sitting. We watched the bartender do her work in silence, a mutual and unspoken decision to hold off on our conversation until we were more alone. After the tiki drink was in front of me, after I'd opened a tab, after the bartender had gone down to the end of the bar to clean something or look at her phone, I spoke first, to keep from having to endure any useless small talk:

"You saw Ezra on Friday night?"

"Friday morning," Paris said apparently as ready and as willing to skip the small talk as I was. She liked being the one with something to say, a story to tell. "You know I can't sleep?"

I nodded, familiar with Paris's insomnia. Women like to talk about their afflictions.

"So on Friday at like sixish, Ezra texted me."

"That must've been weird," I said, "You guys have been broken up for a while."

"Not really," Paris said, "I mean like, we still text all the time."

This was news to me, Ezra and Paris texting this whole time, while he was with Nozlee? Learning something new about Ezra's patterns unsettled me; I drummed the stubs of my fingernails against my glass and took a big swig.

"Oh it wasn't like that," Paris said, "we only got drinks once or twice and we never did anything physical when he was with Noz."

"Sure sure," I said. What had these texts been like? Cursory, checking in, hi how are you, did you read that article that's been going around, did you see any movies this week? But how could you sustain that kind of bland contact with an ex, how could Ezra sustain a slog of nothingness? Their texts must've been meaningful, maybe about problems he was having with Nozlee, the same things he shared with me? And Paris, to him, talking about men she was seeing, the two of them shifting from lovers into friends with a uniquely insightful perspective on each other's romantic situations; that would probably be fine, I'd feel okay about that. Or maybe they'd been sexting, not cheating exactly, just reminiscing one night about a tryst that morphed into some kind of steady exchange of flashes of sexual fantasy, deleted the next morning to hide from whomever. I couldn't get my head around it, I didn't like the thought of Ezra looking for something outside of what he already had, didn't he get enough from his relationship with Nozlee and his friendship with me? Didn't we cover all the bases for him? Unless he just wanted to get laid, what was he looking for at 6:00 a.m. with Paris that I wouldn't have been happy to wake up and provide?

"I was awake, as usual," Paris said. She was picking up her story at six o'clock, when Ezra had texted her.

I interrupted with, "Sorry, but can you tell me the exact time?"

"Like 6:30."

"No, like, can you check on your phone?"

She raised her eyebrows like I was being weird, when she was the one that had reached out to me on the basis of just an Instagram post, but she pulled out her phone to check timing without verbal comment.

"Uh, 6:23 a.m.," she said.

"Okay," I said. I'd left around 4:00 a.m. and he'd gotten at least a few hours of rest, maybe sleeping, maybe unable to sleep but lying in bed while Bonnie hovered nearby like a controlling spouse. Then, he'd texted Paris. Only interrupting herself once, to order another Blue Hawaiian, Paris recounted her relatively brief encounter with Ezra.

She'd been lying on her back, bored out of her mind and too exhausted to be excited about any of her usual television shows or the YA novel she'd been reading, *Grace and the Fever*, so when Ezra texted she felt saved. *(Oh yes, sweet phone and glorious late-night texter, yes I was up!)* Ezra told her about the breakup, probably with some version of the texts he'd sent me on Friday after midnight, "u wanna come out for an early drink at the Drawing Room?" then in a second text, "Noz broke up with me last night." Was Paris just the early-morning version of me?

Though Paris would've loved to live a normal orderly life, a life all her friends lived, with spin classes before work, and happy hour drinks, but never getting drunk the night before a big meeting, Paris's persistent insomnia pushed her into a strange shadow world populated by food service workers and the weird population of thirty-year-olds who made their money writing for or doing things on the internet, a population of people who did the things they wanted to do at whatever time they wanted to do them. Like her coworkers, like her friends, Paris put on trendy athleisure when she left the house before 7:00 a.m., but while they went to Yoga Works or Soul Cycle or Bar Method, she parked in front of the Drawing Room under a pink rising sun, and went into a bar where the sun didn't matter.

Ezra was there when she arrived, looking ragged from his haircut, sagging from lack of sleep, but he still looked good, Paris noted; why, even when she could see that he looked like shit, did he still look good to her? Paris didn't understand her

attraction to Ezra, didn't know if it was chemical or psycho-
logical, didn't know how she could think of herself as a basically good person when the first thing she thought, when she
saw Ezra sitting at the bar, was that if Ezra said he and Nozlee
were really over for good, that she'd be willing to go into the
men's bathroom of that dark dive bar and lean over the sink,
so she could watch it in the mirror while he fucked her. It
wasn't unusual for Paris to give me this kind of visceral detail.
I remembered we did actually have one point of connection
when she was dating Ezra, a frankness about sex; we both preferred it when we knew exactly what was going on in all of our
friends' bedrooms.

Ezra put Paris's drinks—vodka cranberry? Yes—on his tab;
he told Paris he didn't know what to do, should he try to get
Nozlee back? Should he follow my advice and let the rocky
romance finally and fully end? He was wearing a white t-shirt
that had just the barest hint of sweat stains in the armpit, which
Paris thought was a little bit sexy, combined with his obvious
anguish. Why, sometimes, does another person's heartbreak
make us want to fuck them? Paris tried to be a good friend.
She asked him a lot of questions to try to help him find his way
through his own mind, which was twisting in on itself, trap-
ping him in a maze of repetitive thoughts, of unending dead-
ends. Sometimes he characterized Noz as an uncaring bitch,
sometimes he was the asshole that pushed her and pushed her
until she had no choice but to break free of him.

This man needs something he's not getting, Paris thought
while Ezra spoke. Is it because no one is giving it to him, or is
it because he can't see it when it's right in front of him?

After they ordered their second round, Ezra apologized for
being messy and upset. Paris scooted her barstool a little bit

closer to his, and hugged him, one of her knees slid in between his knees, and when he hugged her back he also squeezed her leg with his; she felt the hug like a current through her body. She felt strong, like she was the only thing holding him upright, like he was a churning stormy sea and she was a rocky cliff, the only thing stopping him from raging too hard and too far; together they were a beautiful natural thing. It felt like time didn't exist inside the Drawing Room, everything was so hazy, and Paris felt needed and wanted and loved.

They were quiet for almost ten minutes while Ezra looked at his cell phone. He'd gotten an upsetting text from Nozlee, and was texting back furiously, demonstratively. He was arguing with Noz right in front of Paris, but there wasn't anything for her to overhear; she watched his shoulders hunch and tighten, she watched his mouth screw up into a frustrated scowl, she saw him freeze all over his body after he sent a text and waited for the response. She looked at her own Instagram feed while Ezra texted and when she looked up, his phone was facedown on the bar and he'd shifted from sad to actively fucking angry.

Ezra took a big sip of his fresh glass of whiskey, he didn't wince. He told Paris that a little more than a year ago, if you'd asked him, he would've said that his life was alarmingly close to perfect. He and Noz were in a very loving phase, and he had two perfect best friends in Miguel and me, and when all four of us were together it felt like he'd found the place where he was supposed to be. "And then, you know," Paris said, stuttering around Miggy's death like so many people did, "what happened with Miguel kind of blew things up for him, he said." Then Paris looked right at me and then right away from me, and I could tell she was going to say something I didn't already know.

"He was sounding a little tipsy at this point," Paris said, "Not incoherent or slurry, just like, he was saying things he wouldn't normally say. And what he said was, after Miggy died, he felt like things slipped out of place a little for you guys too."

"Me?" I said, stupidly.

"Yeah," Paris said, "He said you got weird, secretive. He felt guilty that your style of mourning was hard for him."

"My *style* of *mourning*? What the fuck?"

"Just that you really freaked out at first, and then it was like nothing had happened at all. Like you got out all your sadness in one huge, really fucked up burst, while all the people around you had to go through the normal, slow, mourning process and you left them behind. Left him behind. Started spending all your time with Bea, even though your dynamic with her was really fucked up."

Who the fuck was he to speak about fucked up dynamics!? I felt hot all over, suddenly, a fresh ripe anger burst into bloom inside of me. I felt so close to that anger, like the way people on most reality TV shows must have a deep oil well of it inside, one that is tapped and always gushing to the surface.

"Goddamn it, that is so rude and reductive."

Paris shrugged. "He seemed very hurt by you."

Paris had never liked me, though. She had been inclined against me since the moment she'd started dating Ezra, as if I were a romantic rival. No matter how often I paraded Bea in front of her, she'd acted like every time Ezra and I got stoned and went to the movies, or dressed in suits and went to Dan Tana's, or stayed up all night watching the first season of *Alias*, that Ezra was somehow stepping out on her. Intimidated, as if I had any kind of sexual power over Ezra, which I obviously did not; possessive, as if his best friend shouldn't have special and intimate access to his life. Despite their apparent continued closeness, I refused to believe she could know him well enough to understand him. She was probably interpreting what he said incorrectly; and I was taking her viewpoint too seriously.

"When Miguel killed himself," I said, choosing the phrase *killed himself* deliberately, "We all went through hell. Ezra is allowed to *seem* whatever way that he wants, when it comes to Miguel. We all deserve that latitude, I think."

Paris shrugged again. I sucked my Penicillin and crunched on crushed ice.

"Do you need another?" the hot bartender asked, suddenly right near us, gesturing at my empty fishbowl, and then Paris's, but secondarily, less interested in refilling Paris's drink than she was in refilling mine.

"Sure," I said.

"Yeah," Paris said.

We looked at our separate phones while the bartender busied herself with big ice cubes and cocktail shakers and eyedroppers of bitters. I opened my Messages app and saw Miggy appear at the top, then disappear, then reappear when I reloaded the app; my Cascarilla was wearing off.

"Look," Paris said, after the bartender had placed our fresh drinks in front of us, "I didn't mean to say that to make you feel shitty."

"I don't feel shitty," I clapped back immediately.

"Whatever. Okay. I just was telling you that he got heated, he got upset, he wanted to leave, get out of that dark place."

Was she talking about something emotional, or the physical darkness of the Drawing Room? I didn't ask. She kept talking:

They had left the Drawing Room, stepped out into the
light, blinking, it was only 9:32 a.m. and they both felt out
of time, the way you do at an airport. Paris suggested they
go hang out at the house on the hill she was selling; she'd
just done an open house, so the pool was full and cold. On
the way, they stopped at Ezra's apartment, where he'd filled
a tote bag with Bud Rams cans and grabbed his swimsuit.
They drank the beer poolside, under the beating sun. While
I'd been sleeping through a cocaine hangover, Paris was floating on her back, wearing her bra and underwear as a bikini.
They made out, finally, sitting on the tiled pool steps, staying partially submerged to stay cool. Ezra took off Paris's bra,
her nipples had been tight, she could've rubbed them against
his chest for the pinpricks of stimulation that would've given
her, but she didn't. They were too tired to fuck. They floated
again, Paris still topless, sometimes reaching for each other's
bodies.

Around noon, Ezra had gotten a text from someone; something happened on his phone that took his attention away
from Paris and their little oasis. He'd said he had to go, and he
promised to text when he got there, and kissed her once on his
way out, thanking her for being such a good friend, for being
there for him when he'd needed her most.

"He promised he'd text," Paris said again. "And when an
hour had passed, he hadn't texted me back, so I texted him. I
still haven't heard from him. I'm worried, and until he posted
that Instagram I honestly thought he could've died."

A part of me knew that feeling, a certainty around doom.
Another part of me wanted to mock her for jumping so quickly
into the idea of life-ending disaster. I knew Ezra couldn't die,
because Miggy already had. I couldn't survive a second loss.

"He deactivated Twitter and Instagram. I kept waiting for him to just, be there, but he wasn't, he still isn't. You haven't heard from him, right?"

"Not directly," I said. "But I heard he's texted other people. Just not us." Carelessly, I threw us in together, and then suddenly I did feel like we were together, ignored together.

"Who has he been texting?" Paris sounded scandalized, as if the very thought of Ezra having other friends shocked her. What had she thought? That every time he opened his text message app, her number was at the top of his list, and he always texted her back first, and always texted her whenever he thought about texting?

"Who did Ezra go see?" I asked.

"What? When?"

"You said, at the house, he got a text and left, did he say where he was going?"

"I'm not sure, I mean, he said who he got the text from," Paris said.

"Who?"

"Your girlfriend," Paris said, "Bea."

"What the fuck!?" It slipped out, loudly enough to startle the bartender, and make Paris choke a little. I coughed.

"My ex," I said.

"What?" Paris asked.

"Bea isn't my girlfriend, she's my ex."

"Oh, I'm sorry," Paris said. The bartender was maybe pretending to listen, looking at her phone but not really moving her fingers.

"What is there to be sorry about?" I snapped.

"That's what you say when someone has a breakup."

"Maybe I broke up with her and I'm happy," I said.

"Well then I'm sorry for assuming you weren't," she said, but not nicely.

I excused myself to the restroom with as much dignity as I could muster, which in fact was none at all, but I decided to be okay with shitty energy replacing decorum in this instance. There was nothing worse than being shamed/ashamed in front someone who was not anonymous enough to be a stranger but not close enough to be a friend. In order to regain my composure, I needed to separate myself from her physically until I could pretend the conversation had gone down in a different way, one that left me with more of my dignity intact.

The bathroom had tile floors and good mirrors and was extra-dark. I sat on the toilet, but couldn't make my body need to pee. Usually, when I had as little as a single glass of water in me, I could sit on a toilet and eke out at least a trickle; today I sat dry. I used to know what I was looking for.

I thought I was looking for Ezra, his body, and the groundwork we'd laid over years of friendships, a mutual unspoken rule that even if it hurt each other we'd tell each other everything about our lives, we wouldn't spare the details. Ezra and Miguel had once gone to Mexico on a boy's trip with a bunch of our friends, a trip that had taken gender segregation so seriously that even I wasn't invited, and when they got home they spent an hour discussing the trip minute by minute, so that I would have a history, a memory, of those moments in his life they spent without me. That used to be the way it was.

When had that been taken from me? And was it my ex-girlfriend that had plotted to take it from me? And even if Bea had felt the need to explode my only remaining close friendship, why had Ezra fallen for the bullshit? What possibly could she have said?

When I got back to the bar, Paris was signing her check. When she looked at me she looked me right in the eyes, in an intense police-interrogator kind of way, and I realized she was looking to see if I had been crying; I was so glad I hadn't been crying, that I hadn't even been able to produce enough liquid out of my body to pee. I was like a cactus, conserving all of my water inside my body, surviving a desert because I could ration all the hydration I needed. I wanted to text this to Miggy, and I could imagine his response, *you're a cactus because you're fucking prickly,* except he was mad at me and I couldn't text him anything.

"Ezra didn't mention you and Bea had broken up," Paris said, maybe an apology. I resolved to be calm and collected.

"Can you close me out?" I shouted in the direction of the bartender. I didn't even care about how she looked anymore. I responded to Paris: "It was only a few weeks ago."

"It's weird Ezra didn't mention it to me," she said.

I allowed my resolve to be calm and collected go out of my body like birds scattering from a tree.

"You guys were together for what? Almost a year?" she was saying, while I was untethering my angry impulses.

"What's weird is your interest in my personal life," I said, looking right at her.

"Huh?"

"What's weird is you trying to pry little details out of me. What's weird is you expecting Ezra to tell you anything at all! About him or me!"

I saw my check waiting for me in its little leather folder thing. I hadn't noticed the bartender drop it off.

"What's weird," I continued, snatching my check and signing it furiously, "is you continuing to keep up with Ezra after

you broke up! What's weird is you telling me all about how
you still want to fuck Ezra! What's not weird at all is Ezra not
divulging the personal and emotionally difficult details of my
life to you, practically a stranger!"

As I was storming away from Paris, thundering down the
staircase, I realized I was storming out of a bar, something
I'd never done before, and I lost track of myself for a disorienting series of seconds. In order to keep myself emotionally
coherent, I tried to summon a memory of watching a friend
storm out of a bar, but that doesn't happen often in real life;
instead of storming out people linger hoping for a happy reso-
lution to a difficult moment, lingering long enough to be hurt
more. So, as I descended the final steps, I tried to think of a
scene in a movie or television show where a character I liked
had stormed out of a bar, but I couldn't think of a single indi-
vidual scene or person; instead, the idea of storming out of a
bar came upon me like I was reading an entry on TVTropes.
org, an idea of what storming out meant, an amalgamation
of so many moments that no single one was distinguishable,
like when you mix all the colors together and they become a
murky brown.

I burst through the doors, squinted, the sunlight suddenly
everywhere. I was uncomfortably illuminated. I pulled out
my phone and ducked into the shaded doorway of Clifton's
so I could see the screen clearly, unconcerned at the idea that
Paris might walk through the doors soon, having already paid
her bill and been stormed out on. I had messages, like a flood,
all at once.

Miggy

if you wanted to "spend this weekend together" you could've fucking tried not killing yourself. you and i both know, death is something that happens to the people left alive, not the people who've died.

Today 3:15 PM

i wish so badly you weren't dead

I know, honey, but I am.

I was enough absorbed in my phone that I would've missed Paris had she left while I was texting. It didn't matter if she saw me lingering.

Miggy

i talked to Ezra's exgf paris. they made out on friday morning and then according to paris, he left her to go talk to bea

Shiiiit

> But listen girl, any contact with Bea is a
> bad idea for you right now

> I wouldn't recommend following this trail
> any further

>> i plan to disregard your advice

One thing that had drawn me to Bea immediately was how available she made herself; to me, in particular. We had long dates that started with a good boozy brunch and ended up curled up in the huge seats at the ArcLight Hollywood, wrapping her hand around my wrist to claim me. She made herself available on a bright Thursday afternoon when she skipped a weekend away with her crew to hang out with me, stroll with me around Echo Park Lake, and make out at the wine bar El Prado and eat cheese pupusas from the cart outside the bar Little Joy, that Thursday when I knew I loved her. She made herself available to me more and more often, sometimes five nights in a row at my apartment, practically living with me.

To the rest of the world, she made herself available online. Almost all of my friends lived online, but she gave herself over to the internet the most; she'd started at thirteen by dipping her toe into AIM chat rooms, and finding the temperature of the water perfect, she'd dived in, and stayed in that pool the rest of her life, always wet. She'd been active and well-followed on Myspace; her LiveJournal, which has been allowed to remain online for posterity, was an obsessive chronicle of her high school years; in college she shifted to Tumblr, discovered reaction GIFs and memes and other forms of internet-specific humor, and discovered that she was also uncannily good at creating the right GIF for every occasion and developing memes that struck a chord. She was on Twitter and Snapchat before anybody and she'd made an Instagram account so early that her name on the app was just "Bea." Bea was a consumer tech reporter, of course, working her way up through BizBash and TechCrunch; while we were dating, she had gotten a big new job as the technology editor at *GQ*. All this to say, to find Bea, I didn't need to tediously text her and wait some agonizingly long minutes for a text back, all I had to do was check online.

Though I'd unfollowed her on everything, there was of course nothing stopping me from searching her, she was unlocked, unblocked, available. I searched her name on Instagram and there she was again; if I scrolled down I'd see happy versions of myself doing fun things with my girlfriend who loved me, but that version of myself was hidden by a ton of new pictures. The most recent one was from less than an hour before, Bea with four of her friends, all of them in outfits, all of them posing, on a wooden porch; even if she hadn't geo-tagged it, I'd recognize the scene, Verdugo Bar in Highland Park. One Saturday a month, Verdugo hosted a lesbian nineties dance party called The Grind, and when Bea went, she stayed all day with her crew of cool scary lesbians, sipping pints of craft beer, dancing until she was wet with sweat, available. All I had to do to get to her was show my ID at the door.

Saturday, 3:59 p.m.

Verdugo sprawled, a huge dark interior with black leather booths and craft beers on tap, and an equally large wooden deck, which would be blasted with afternoon sunlight at this hour. The air inside vibrated slightly from the bass; the DJ was playing a remix of "No Scrubs," which is a song that didn't need a remix. As always during The Grind, the booths inside Verdugo were packed full of girls who wanted to be present but were too timid to dance, and a few regulars sat at the bar watching the Dodgers play the Giants, whooping every time a boy in blue got a hit, no matter if it was a home run or base hit or a foul ball or a fly out. The manager Julian was lingering behind the bar, which was lucky for me, because he loved me and perked up whenever I came in and immediately poured us shots of tequila.

"Hey Eve," he said, all excited, getting the shot glasses out without even asking me, I'd never declined a gift from Julian.

"Hey Jules," I said, "how's Matilda?" His daughter recently had surgery for a cleft palate.

"All she does is cry," he said, "but she won't remember anything when she grows up, which is good."

"Therapist Lauren thinks early traumas affect the person forever."

"Therapist Lauren was referring to the kind of emotional trauma you rightly received for being such a nerd in high school." Julian balanced a slice of lime on top of the full shot glass and slid it across the bar to me. I waited for him to put the bottle of Espolòn Tequila away, then we picked up our lime slices and clinked shot glasses and tapped them on the bar and took the shot and bit the lime.

"Matilda," Julian said, "will know that sometimes the people who love us the most have to be the ones that make us suffer."

I left Julian with his glasses to wash and limes to slice and his bartenders to order around. I walked past the dykes lining up for the women's room and trans guys lining up for the men's (Verdugo doesn't have gender neutral bathrooms) and took my first tentative steps onto the sunlit porch. The dance floor was packed and everyone was moving as much as they could, everyone was sweating. I probably knew or had fucked or had partied with half the crowd; I surveyed everyone: baby dykes who had just graduated from Cal State, recent transplants from Brooklyn (they decorated our dyke nights the way smog made our sunsets such beautiful oranges and pinks), women in their early thirties who had just started dating women and leaned so hard into their lesbianism they acted more like TV characters than people. All these unfamiliar faces, all their unfamiliar limbs mixed in with the people I recognized, an overwhelming mash of queer people rubbing their bodies against each other, this is where I used to live; I had years and years of plowing through this world before I settled into my domestic thing with Bea, the smells of their spicy sweat were as familiar as the smell of Bea's pussy. All the lives I've lived were being performed here under the blistering LA sun. I elbowed through the crush.

I stumbled, my arms prickling with my own sweat, up two small stairs into the DJ booth. Naomi greeted me with a one-armed hug and a lipsticky cheek kiss; I immediately wiped the waxy red lipstick off my skin. She was wearing a look I knew she had aped from Cara Delevingne: high-necked t-shirt and no makeup except red lipstick; she was twenty-three, still looking at icons to guide her. Naomi held up a single finger—*hold on one second*—and fiddled with something on her computer. She was playing LL Cool J, *I'm going back to Cali, Cali, Cali, I'm going back to Cali*, and she started mixing in Biggie, *Going back to Cali, strictly for the weather, women, and the weed.*

I surveyed the crowd from my modest perch, two crooked steps separating me from the group, and if I waded back in I'd be absorbed, I'd be one of them.

I saw a flicker in my peripherals, a figure distinctly unlike the dancers, unlike us. A fully bodied ghost sat on top of the ten-foot wooden fence, happily watching the women dance below. It was the ghost who'd been following me, the one in the Silver Lake hills and in the meditation space, but now her body was so crisp and present. I remembered the freaky way her mouth had bled when we last met, and for a dramatic moment I thought of running away from her, but then she did a little grooving dance with her shoulders which made her look cute and fangless. She seemed to like "Going Back to Cali," *But that don't mean a nigga can't rest in the West / see some nice breast in the West / smoke some nice sess in the West.* Maybe it was a coincidence that she was here; a thought I was only able to hold onto for a few seconds, until she looked right at me. She cocked her head like she was checking me out, she beckoned to me with one crooked finger like a lover; did she expect me to climb the fence?

"I'll come talk to you later," I shouted above the heads of the living crowd, and the ghost heard me and she nodded. She pointed at me and narrowed her eyes playfully, *you better not be an LA stereotype and flake out on me.* Did ghosts know about new stereotypes? I've watched them float through the world all my life and I still don't understand what they know or see.

"What did you say?" Naomi shouted.

"I said I could come back later!" I shouted back.

"No wait! Hold on!"

The music smoothly transitioned into "Tomboy," a Princess Nokia song that everyone played at every single lesbian party in all of Los Angeles, and all the women on the dance floor screamed when they heard the familiar opening beat and dropped into sexy wide-leg squats and popped their hips, *WHO THAT IS, HOE? / THAT GIRL IS A TOMBOY! / THAT GIRL IS A TOMBOY! / THAT GIRL IS A TOMBOY!*

I grabbed Naomi's shoulder and pulled her ear close to my mouth. I shouted, "This song isn't from the fucking nineties!"

Naomi pushed a little at my shoulder and shifted her head, so her mouth was now near my ear. "The album it's on is called *1992 Deluxe*," Naomi shouted.

I leaned away from her, looked her straight in the eyes, and gave a dramatic eye roll. She raised her eyebrows and gave an equally dramatic shrug. It didn't matter that I was right, she was the DJ so she won. Princess Nokia played on and all the women shouted the lyrics, *Who that? / Who that? / Who that? / Princess Nokia, Baby Phat / I be where the ladies at!*

Naomi gestured for me to lean in again, so I could hear her.

"Are you okay!?" she shouted.

We swiveled our heads, so I could speak into her ear.

"Why!?"

We swiveled back again.

"Bea's all over some girl!"

"Who!?"

Instead of responding, Naomi grabbed my shoulders and turned me around so I was once again surveying the whole scene of women dancing, and she pointed deep into a shadowed corner of the porch, at a bench pushed up against the wall to provide seating for any dykes feeling dizzy from too much tequila and gyrating, and at first I didn't see anything, and then I saw all of Bea's intimidating friends—the sommelier, the model, the film academic who had been a jury member for the Teddy Award at the last Berlin International Film Festival, the one who had briefly dated Hayley Kiyoko—and then I saw two people kissing and then I saw that one of the people was Bea and then I saw that the girl she was kissing was Georgie.

At first, the press of their lips didn't seem real, the way Georgie rubbed her hand up Bea's thigh was a fantasy; Bea broke the kiss and her smile was so big, and then it was real. Bea has eyes as big and blue as wading pools, and when she smiles at someone it's like they're in the sun, she makes people come to life like a field of cacti bursting into bloom after a rare desert rain. When we'd first started dating, I felt like I'd been woken up from a long slumber; one gloomy June morning, about a month after we started getting cozy, I lay next to her in my bed and I told her how much she made me glow. She'd kissed the side of my face, all tender, and she'd said, "You're my

Sleeping Beauty," and for almost a year that's what she called me. She addressed my birthday card "S.B." and in so many 2:00 a.m. Lyfts from a party or a bar to my bungalow, she'd press up against me and call me "Beauty." She never stopped calling me that, even when we got tired of each other, even when things got bad; I wondered what she would call Georgie.

Horribly, I was going to cry. My skin and eyes prickled. I was helpless to stop them from shredding my heart, in fact the damage was already done; I didn't want the pain but I didn't know how to purge it. It was like being smacked in the head with a brick, there was nothing I could do but sit and suffer until the dizziness receded.

I counted the sins committed against me: Georgie was fucking my ex-girlfriend, Nozlee had broken Ezra's heart and our friend group, Ezra had disappeared remorselessly, and Miggy was dead.

"Don't you know that bitch!?" Naomi asked.

I jerked; Naomi shouldn't have been allowed to watch it all with me, fascinated and unemotional about the whole mess.

"Yes!" I tilted my head back to shout in Naomi's ear. "That's my very good friend Georgie."

"That's fucked!" Naomi shouted.

I maybe heard Naomi shouting, but I couldn't quite hear her, I didn't want to hear her, I wanted to cut through the crowd. Two steps down and I was with the people dancing, I was pushing through them; I wanted to be able to push right into Georgie and Bea, to make them look at me, I wanted them to stammer, trying to explain. I wanted Georgie to be particularly spooked, because Bea and I were broken up and technically Bea could fuck whoever she wanted even if her choices were hurtful to me, but Georgie was supposed to be my best female friend, she wasn't supposed to do things to me. I wanted to watch Georgie perform contrition, I wanted her to literally fall on her knees and beg me for forgiveness.

As I weaved around the elbows and gyrating hips and popped asses of the dancers, at the last second, I changed my course, not bursting into the carved out area where Bea and her crew were sitting, but moving through the crowd just on the edge of Bea's zone. I made sure to seemingly accidentally nudge a few of the girls around the edges of Bea's crowd and shout "Sorry!" loud enough so they could hear it, but Bea probably could not. I did this a few times, then watched with carefully controlled glee as one of Bea's closest friends, Nicole, turned around to see who had bumped her, then saw me, then her eyes widened, then she turned away and dipped deeper into the crowd of Bea's friends, and then I quickly made my way off the porch into the bar's dulled and dark interior. I flung myself onto a barstool. "I need another shot, Jules!"

He raised his eyebrow like I was taking advantage of his hospitality.

"I'll open a tab," I said, "But also I just saw my best friend kiss my girlfriend, I mean, my ex-girlfriend."

"Oh fuck, girl," Julian said. He poured me the shot and took my card. "The shot's on me but I'm gonna charge you for a beer."

"Budweiser in the bottle," I said. I didn't care about the cheapest pint or the most well-balanced IPA, I wanted something comfortable from my childhood, I wanted the beer bottles I saw in the fridge when I was growing up, I wanted the simplicity of Budweiser's bright and familiar red.

"Ezra and Bea are hooking up?" Julian asked as he popped the top off the Budweiser.

"What? No, not Ezra. My best friend, Georgie. That pretty soft butch I run around with," I said.

"That makes more sense," Julian said, "Still fucked up though."

"Still fucked up," I agreed. I took the shot, just as a laughing group of women arrived in the bar area, flipping through the beer list and examining the cocktails listed on the chalkboard. Julian patted my hand, then left me for them.

The ghost from outside was sitting in a shadowed corner at the very end of the bar; she had a ghostly beer bottle that she sipped from.

"Come over here," she said. She was a welcome distraction, something to do while I waited for Bea or Georgie to seek me out. If I was talking to her, I wouldn't have to sit with any of my feelings.

I got up and took the barstool next to hers, angling my back to the rest of the bar, so that none of the normal people would see me talking to nothing. She was wearing a long jacket with big front pockets, tailored pants, and huarache sandals; her hair was puffed up into a big pompadour thing; her lips were very dark red.

"I'm Babs," she said, with a light accent I couldn't place.

"I'm Eve," I said.

"I know," Babs said, laughing, like she knew more than me, which she did. Babs pulled out a ghost cigarette case and lit a ghost cigarette. The smoke curled towards the ceiling, the way it must've done when the cigarette was alive and people were allowed to smoke in bars. I would've liked to be alive with Babs in a bar decades ago—I wasn't sure exactly when she was from, maybe the forties or fifties—passing a cigarette back and forth while we flirted, hiding our attraction behind the pretense of friendship.

"Have we met before?" I asked, like I was picking up any girl from The Grind.

Babs laughed like that was a line some woman would've used to pick her up in the 1940s. Or maybe she'd just heard it from years of hovering over lesbian daytime parties. "We have a mutual friend," she said. "Nozlee Rostami."

"I wouldn't call Nozlee a friend anymore."

"That's a shame, she still calls you a friend."

"Did she tell you to follow me?" I asked.

"Yes," she said.

"Why?"

"She said when you're mad at people you talk to ghosts because you don't consider them people. And that you were going to be mad at her."

"For the crime of premeditated heartbreak, yes."

Babs cocked her head, I'd confused her. I felt a hand on my shoulder and immediately jerked it off, caught.

"I'm sorry," Georgie said, like a reflex. I swiveled, I faced her, I was sitting on a stool and I realized my posture was probably very hunched; I sat up straight. I didn't want her to see me make my body small.

"Bea said you would leave but I knew you wouldn't," Georgie said.

I hadn't even considered leaving, and Bea and I had dated for a year, lived together even, what had she even learned about me during that long time?

"I guess I know you better," Georgie said. Without asking if it was alright with me if she sat down, Georgie took the seat to my left; Babs the Ghost was still on my right, I saw her watching out of the corner of my eye.

"Who told you? I mean," Georgie scrubbed her eyes like she was tired. "I wanted to be the one to tell you, or Bea did."

"If we must talk about this, can we go to one of the booths?" I asked. I didn't want to be overheard by someone Georgie couldn't even see; I wanted to be able to speak my mind without one of Nozlee's friends overhearing me.

"It's quieter over here," Georgie said in a low voice, as if to prove her point. The timid booth girls were loosening up, they were doing shots and wrapping their arms around each other's necks; some girls who were going to kiss each other eventually.

Babs smiled ghoulishly, her teeth a little whiter and her smile a little wider than a living human's would've been. All ghosts were ravenous; Babs was a thirsting for the dyke drama. Babs reminded me that even the nicest, hottest ghosts were still the hungry undead, transformed from human into creature if they smelled a meal.

"I know this place isn't ideal, but can't we talk now before it festers? You didn't leave."

Though I'd courted this conversation, enticed Georgie into coming to speak to me, her actual presence somehow swapped the power dynamics, so that the conversation belonged to her now and I was forced to submit to something. But I didn't want to bottom to anybody. The motions I would have to go through to leave (stand up, head for the door, pretend I didn't hear Georgie calling after me) were so familiar I could've done it on autopilot—because I'd already done it so many times this weekend.

Leaving was an effective way to reclaim power, but it wasn't my own option: Nozlee once told me she has her moon in Cancer and that meant she was sensitive and nurturing and when she felt she hadn't taken care of someone properly, she got really guilty. I'd spill everything then, where Babs could hear and report back, to her. I'd throw open all my emotional curtains and shine light on all my raw nerves, and Noz could bathe in her guilt. Georgie, too, could potentially be punished in the same way. If I was going to be forced to speak, I'd let them all know how bad they'd hurt me.

"Okay," I said to both Georgie and the wide-eyed ghost with her toothy smile, "Let's fucking talk then."

"I'm sorry."

"I don't care, I don't forgive you. Like, what the fuck, Georgie! You're supposed to be my friend."

"Let me just explain, okay?" Georgie had her drink with her, she gulped from it. "It didn't start while you guys were still together."

I hadn't even—but of course I should've worried about that, about them sneaking, cheating, meeting in secret. But then, Bea and I had spent the last weeks of our relationship together for a painful amount of time. We spent a month pushing on a bruise, unable to spend more than a few hours apart, addicted to hurting each other and being hurt. Bea wouldn't have had anywhere to put a dizzying love affair when we were too busy beating each other up.

"I know," I said. I didn't say anything else, I made her keep talking to me.

"We ran into each other by accident the day she moved out of your place. We've always gotten along—"

"You've always gotten along!?"

"Yes, I mean, I liked hanging out with her—"

"So you had a crush on her this whole time!" I said. "All the times we hung out together, you were just laying down a primer, waiting for the very first second our relationship went bad."

"No, I—"

"No!? What then?"

"Let me get a fucking word in!" Georgie shouted. I was stunned, Georgie never shouted.

"You act like I'm your best friend and I owe you the fucking world!" she shouted again.

"You *are* my best friend!" I shouted back. The music was loud enough that no one around could tell if we were shouting angrily or happily or drunkenly. They left us alone.

"I am *not* your best friend, this is such bullshit, Eve."

"Well, you're—"

"No, you let me talk. I'm your best friend when it's convenient for you, when you're mad at Ezra or Noz for some imagined slight."

"Best friend is a category, not a title," I tried to say, but she talked right over me, and Babs's big eyes grew even rounder and shone. I saw blood in the spaces between Babs's teeth.

"You don't see other people's side of things. I mean, like you never see my side of things," Georgie was saying. "I'm always there for you when you're having a hard time but you never see when I'm having a hard time."

"You never tell me!"

"It's hard to tell you when you make every situation about what's going on with you."

"I never pay attention to myself. I'm always thinking about other people and what they're doing," I said. "I'm always focused on other people."

"You might be focused on what other people are doing," Georgie said. "But you're the one that writes the emotional narrative."

"What does that even mean?" I asked.

"It means, you decide what everyone is feeling, and if they try to contradict you, you think they're wrong or lying."

"I don't do that," I said.

"You do that, always," Georgie said. "I've been depressed, did you know that?"

"Of course I did!" I sort of did.

"I needed someone and Bea was there. I deserve a big romance, too. I deserve to be loved by someone decent. Bea got completely fucked up emotionally by your relationship."

"We were bad for each other, that's not my fault," I said.

"I'm not blaming just you," Georgie said. "I heard all about it from both of you. You were awful to each other and it's better for both of you that you're done."

She was winding down, all her angry steam was gone, she was slumping, she made me want to slump. If Bea had told Georgie her side, if Bea'd given her an unfiltered truth that she filtered for me, because of me, like water through a Brita filter, all the toxins taken out—if Bea had given Georgie something real, then maybe Georgie knew more about my relationship than I did.

"I feel guilty," Georgie said, "and I hate myself for doing this to you, and I'm sorry you had to find out on the bad weekend. I didn't want it to be like that. But I'm always going to be a second-string friend to you, and Bea is someone who might love me, one day. Even if not, I have to stop making my life decisions based on how they're going to make you feel."

"I didn't know you were doing that," I said.

"I knew that by dating her I was going to lose you and you know what I felt? I felt like, even if Bea and I broke up, our friendship wasn't worth not trying this relationship out."

"Why?" I asked. I was looking at all the little bubbles in my beer, because if I looked at Georgie's face I would start crying.

"You don't know how to be good to people," Georgie said. "I know you were closest to Miggy, but he was my friend too. I loved him, and he loved me, and he made me feel loved, and I feel wrecked without him. And this weekend, you've run around acting like you're the only one who is carrying this tragedy with you every day. All weekend, you haven't answered my calls, you haven't asked how I am, you've acted like you're the only one that is devastated. I'm devastated too."

"But this thing with Ezra," I said. I sniffled, I was crying even though all I could see of Georgie were her beautiful long fingers. "It's bad timing, I would've been there for you."

"The point is," Georgie said, "No matter what the circumstances are, you expect other people to be there for you. But you aren't able to give people that same treatment. It's lopsided, and it's hurting me."

"I'm sorry," I turned my head to the right so that maybe Georgie wouldn't see that I had tears coming out of my eyes now, hot and spilling, but when I turned I saw the wet pad of Babs's tongue, like a cat slurping out of its bowl. Her gums were dripping with blood now, her eyes were as big as her cheeks; ghosts are real, ghosts are terrifying, I had to turn my back on her.

Georgie was crying too, her cheeks were blotchy and she was chewing hard on her lip.

"Oh god, Eve," Georgie said, "I had to break the cycle somehow."

"You should've told me, I would've tried," I said. "I didn't know I was doing so bad."

"I was scared, I'm sorry," Georgie said. "For what it's worth, even though you're not in an emotional place where you're capable of being a good friend, I don't think that's permanent. You need to figure yourself out fast, though."

I shoved my fingers under my glasses to wipe at the tears, scowling to try to stop from crying. "Listen, I'm not trying to poison the well," I said, I lied maybe, I couldn't tell what I wanted to do, "but Bea's been texting me a lot. She tries to get me to come over at night. I do too. We've fucked a few times since she moved out."

"I know, I know," Georgie said. "She shows me."

"She fucking, what, shows you my private texts to her?" I said, angry again, sparking. From behind me, Babs chortled and spit and suddenly my arm was covered in ghost blood and I had to wipe it away furiously even though Georgie couldn't see it, but she didn't see because she'd turned away from me, embarrassed.

"I haven't acted right," she said.

"It was a *fucking violation*," I said.

"I know it was a violation."

"The things I said to her, those were supposed to be mine."

"She said she's going to stop," Georgie said. "She promised."

"I want her to stop."

"She's going to. I'm not going to let her be bad to me the way she was to you."

That made me cry again, I sobbed before I could hear it coming.

"I love you, Georgie," I said. "I wanted to be your friend for the rest of my life."

"I loved you too," Georgie said.

We hugged each other tight, she a liar, me a maniac who doesn't care who I flatten with my rampage. Her palm was hot against my back, her arms felt strong around me and smooth like a boa constrictor, I felt the whole weight of our friendship in the press of my body against hers, maybe the last time we'd hug or be friends with one another. I knew that once I let go she'd wipe her face and go back out onto the sunny porch and immediately put a big smile on her face, and no one would see that she'd just been crying and no one would know that moments ago she'd ended a friendship, because Georgie never lets anyone know if anything is wrong; so I didn't want to stop the hug, but it didn't matter what I wanted, Georgie leaned back and let go of me and we were done and she was gone.

She left her drink, I downed it without tasting what it had been, it was just wet and alcoholic and inside me. Next to me, the ghost panted. I could do a little bump of Cascarilla and she'd be gone but then, but then, my phone lit up.

Miggy

I wouldn't recommend following this trail
any further

i plan to disregard your advice

Today 4:39 PM

> Oh honey, I'm so sorry.

> Good people sometimes lose track of
> themselves and do bad things.

> You're not a monster, you're just a
> person, and it's okay.

> I love you.

I took off my glasses and dug my eyes into the crook of my elbow so I could shake and sob unnoticed. I was, though, mostly focused on the heave of crying, somewhat surprised that no drunk/kind/turned-on-by-crying lesbian tapped me on the shoulder to ask what was wrong; I was making a spectacle of myself in a bar that I drank at a lot, and it was going unnoticed, as if I was as ghostly as Babs. I got myself together eventually. Or, I'd only cried for thirty seconds, but each second had been terrible, and that had made the short time stretch.

Babs the ghost was bloated and laughing, blood dripping out of her mouth and pooling on the bar floor, like someone's spilled beer, except unseen and unslippery.

"Hey bitch," I said, "Fucking pull yourself together."

Babs shut up and stared at me.

"You're having your period all over the place and it's disgusting," I said.

Babs blinked, she shuddered, she shrank, the blood on the floor disappeared and her smile returned to a normal size and there was no blood in her mouth as she sat on a barstool, smoking her ghost cigarette and sipping on her ghost beer.

"You know, I can't really help it," Babs said.

"That doesn't matter to me, because I know you get pleasure from it," I said, sipping my own beer.

"Nozlee understands," Babs said.

"I'm not as nice as Nozlee," I said. "She has her moon in Cancer."

"You don't deserve her," Babs said.

"Ohhhh I see, you have a little crush on her!" It was nice, after all that heavy sadness, to just be pleasantly mean to someone who deserved it.

"No!" Babs insisted, in a way that plainly meant yes.

"Too bad you're dead."

Suddenly, I wanted to know how Babs had died, and what her life had been like. Had she been born in Mexico, or Puerto Rico maybe? Did she kiss and fall in love with another girl, and if she did, did that girl dress like her, in tomboy pants and a pompadour, or did she wear her hair down and long like a woman's? But with Georgie's admonishments ringing in my ears and the pulse of bass vibrating through the bar to remind me how close that drama was to even my physical body, I couldn't waste my time talking to Babs about herself, I was burning with the need to talk to her about me.

"Did Nozlee ever mention the night we went night swimming?" I asked.

"Oh you're going to be nice to me now?"

"I was mad about you feasting on my misery, but I'm over it now and I want to be friends," I said.

Babs chewed her fingernail, deciding.

"I could've taken Georgie into the bathroom to talk, but I did it here instead," I said. "For you."

"Bullshit," Babs said, but weakly, relenting.

"Please?"

"Night swimming, you said?"

"Yeah."

"I don't think so."

"We were skinny-dipping at this house in the hills," I said, trying to jog her memory. "It was just the four of us."

"You stayed up all night, just the two of you?" Babs asked.

"Yes!"

Babs lit another cigarette. It didn't matter how much she smoked, the dead don't get lung cancer, or have a sore throat in the morning from bumming a lot of Newports, or have to get their dress dry-cleaned again because the smell of smoke was still clinging to it the next morning.

"Noz only had two Adderalls. She followed you into the bathroom and gave you the other one. The guys fell asleep in the master bedroom and the two of you went into the other room and stayed up all night talking, until the sun started to come up."

"Did she say what she was mad at Ezra about?"

"I don't understand the question."

"She gave me the Adderall because she was mad at Ezra," I said.

Babs shook her head.

"She could only get two Adderall, so the other one must've been for Ezra, but she got mad at him about something and gave it to me."

"No. She could only get two Adderall and she didn't mention them to Ezra at all, and she gave one to you because you're the one that she wanted to spend the night talking to," Babs said.

Someone opened the front door and the whole dark bar was

flooded with sunlight; it was still daytime in Los Angeles, and the sun lit everything up.

"Why did Nozlee ask you to follow me?"

"She just wanted to make sure you were okay," Babs said.

DONT TEXT BEA

You're with Georgie?

You guys are talking about me?

Today 4:49 PM

im at the bar, can you come talk for like 10 mins tops

i think you owe me

I texted Bea, and sat alone at the bar. Babs dissolved into nothing. While I waited, I checked Instagram and saw that Ezra had posted on his Stories, a picture of a strange cactus and his bare feet. His toes were gnarled, but elegant somehow.

And then Bea sat down next to me and I smelled her, peppery and familiar; she'd been dancing so hard in the sun that her hair was matted and her tank top's armholes were damp.

"If you're gonna yell at me, can we at least go out front?" she said, maybe she wanted to provoke me, but I was beyond that.

"I just have to ask you something," I said.

I forced myself to look at her, and when I did she looked away from me, and when she looked back I instinctively looked down, and that's what our relationship had been like the whole time.

"Did you text with Ezra on Friday morning?"

"Yeah . . . ?" she curled her lip, confused.

"Why?"

"Can't you just ask him?"

I wanted to scream at her for being so fucking annoying and not giving me what I needed, like how she'd *never* given me what I needed, but if I screamed she'd walk away and not tell me anything.

"He's not answering his texts," I said, my voice as calm as I could make it.

"He was just asking if I'd pick up Leslie when I drove up on Sunday, because he was supposed to give her a ride but he decided to go to the desert early with Nozlee, which obviously you know," Bea said.

It was obvious, now, that he'd gone after Nozlee, and I didn't know why, even though I'd been told it was a possibility, I'd never really entertained the idea. He'd posted a picture of a cactus and I still needed Bea to say it out loud to believe it, taking in bad news slow and direct. I didn't want to look in Bea's eyes, and the reticence made me feel unlike myself.

"Why?" Bea asked. "Is something going on with Leslie?"

"It's fine," I said. "I just wanted to make sure she had a ride."

"Was that really it?" Bea asked. She swiveled in the bar seat, stood up but didn't leave. She was waiting for some kind of confrontation but I didn't have anything for her anymore.

"That's it," I said.

And she gave me a funny look, but she left; I watched her as she walked away but didn't miss her when she was gone.

Saturday, 5:01 p.m.

The light was a little brighter than it should've been, outside the bar. I switched from regular glasses to sunglasses. I drove back to my bungalow. Inside, I switched from sunglasses to regular glasses and spent an empty, quiet moment fingering the leaves of the spider plant that hung just inside my door. The leaves should've been a rich, deep green, but instead they were pale, bleached by the sun. The indigo tapestry that had hung on my wall was also fading out, waning like the moon. The canvas bag with a zipper I took to the beach or the desert and otherwise left hanging on a hook by my desk was both wine-stained and faded out from the sun. Is that what happened in LA? The sun beat down on everything until it either disappeared or burst into flames?

EzraIsTexting

Yesterday

if u don't answer imma come over to
your place

ezra please i'm getting so stressed

Today 1:11 AM

for real you post that pic but you won't
text me back?

Today 5:05 PM

i know where you are and if you don't
text me back in 10 minutes, im driving to
Two Bunch

After unloading so much at Verdugo Bar, transitioning from the loud crush of girl-bodies into my quiet apartment where everything was mine, I felt a strong calm and self-possession. These were heightened moments and I could allow myself heightened responses.

I unzipped the canvas bag; I packed my black one-piece, my blood quartz hand stone, and a toothbrush. I packed everything I would need for Sunday. I took off my glasses and washed my face with cold water and shivered. I changed into my striped shirt. I looked at my phone. Nothing from Ezra, nothing at all, the whole world gone as still as in the moments before an earthquake.

I drove to the glowing blue Chevron at the corner of Echo Park and Morton Avenues and picked out one big bottle of water and one little Topo Chico sparkling water and a bag of Haribo Twin Snakes gummies for the ride. At the counter, I asked the familiar clerk, a slow and fat man, for a pack of Marl-

boro Reds, like Nozlee had a few days before me, in a different
Chevron, an echo of this Chevron. *I thought I was a cowboy.*

I couldn't tell if I was angry or sad or restless or desperate.
While the slow man charged me for my supplies, I opened my
Messages app.

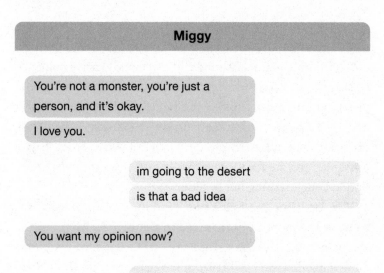

> **Miggy**
>
> You're not a monster, you're just a person, and it's okay.
> I love you.
>
> > im going to the desert
> > is that a bad idea
>
> You want my opinion now?
>
> > yes

This, no playfulness, no avoidance, this could maybe be my
apology to him, if he was willing to take it.

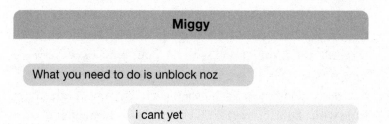

> **Miggy**
>
> What you need to do is unblock noz
>
> > i cant yet

> like, emotionally

> Then proceed at your own risk

> warning signs noted

The man handed me back my card and I gathered my various items into an unruly bundle in my arms; I barely managed to carry it all back to my car and get the door open without dropping anything. I tossed my items on the passenger seat and sat for a few long seconds in the car, stuffy, baked from the heat; I let it warm me inside. Then I ripped open the bag of gummies and ate four snakes really fast, until the sweet taste flooded out anything hot or bitter.

The last time the four of us were in my car, the sky was so blue, the palm trees flickered in the breeze, Miggy sat in the front seat, and Ezra stuck the AUX cord into his phone and controlled the playlist from the backseat, ignoring Noz's suggestions for songs to add, smoking out the window. I was barreling down the highway at like ninety miles an hour on my way to Miguel's house-sit in the Hills, and Miguel was shouting at Ezra to roll the window up so he could roll a joint, and Noz was shouting that she had a vape pen in her purse, and Miggy said he wanted to smoke actual cannabis flower, and Ezra and I were singing out loud really loudly to the JEFF the Brotherhood song he'd put on: *I know everybody stays up late / I know everybody stays up late.* We were so loud, but we could all hear each other, each one of us perfectly in tune with all the others for that bright loud moment. If Nozlee had given Miggy that Adderall and stayed up with him, would it have helped him even a little, maybe just enough to keep him from killing himself the next weekend? If Nozlee had given Ezra the Adderall, would they have fused together their bond that night, laying a strong enough foundation that they wouldn't have broken up a year later? Nozlee picked me, she followed me into the bathroom, our hair was still wet from swimming, and we took the Adderall together with sips from the faucet, and then we stepped out of the bathroom into the master bedroom, where Ezra and Miggy were already lounging on the bed, and they pointed at the big picture window and we all saw the lights of Los Angeles spread out below us. "Look at that," Ezra had said, and we all did. Then Nozlee said, "I want another beer," and I said, "I do too," and she and I went into the kitchen and then into the bedroom and didn't come back and didn't see the boys again until the next day.

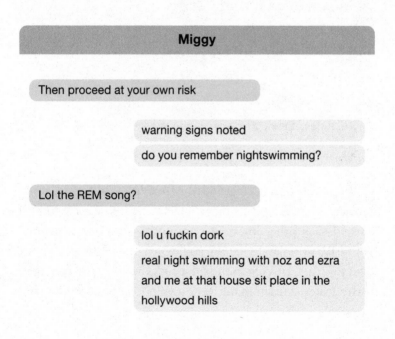

Miggy

Then proceed at your own risk

warning signs noted

do you remember nightswimming?

Lol the REM song?

lol u fuckin dork

real night swimming with noz and ezra and me at that house sit place in the hollywood hills

I remember.

noz gave me an adderall and she and
stayed up all night together

I know

We talked about it after

did you love us then?

i loved all of you guys that night

it felt like it could just be the four of
us forever and that would be the best
possible life

You can't build a moat around the things
you like and live there

It doesn't work

I know, I tried

I loved all three of you so much

But it wasn't enough to keep me alive

We could romanticize our romantic friendships. We could
replace sex with the stronger feeling, desire. We could curl
around each other like a litter of kittens and bite at anyone
who tried to separate us. We could have the best night of our
lives together, singing in the car, drinks at a bar, swimming in
warm water at night in our very own pool. But none of it, and

maybe nothing, was big enough to keep Miggy alive, to keep Nozlee and Ezra safely together. Safe for who? Safe for me.

EzraIsTexting

> i know where you are and if you don't text me back in 10 minutes, im driving to Two Bunch

> im not kidding

> i will drive to two bunch right now

I twisted the key, I put the Honda Fit into drive, and I made the few familiar turns onto the highway. I didn't need to turn on my Google Maps, I knew by heart how to get to the desert.

Saturday, 6:17 p.m.

A few years ago at an industry party with Noz, I met a wonderful old hippy cinematographer with a big white beard who told me what Two Bunch Palms was like during the Summer of Love years. (When I mentioned Two Bunch he said "Ohhhh" with all the weight of Los Angeles's history in his exhalation. Only people that really belong in/to Los Angeles know how heavy and simultaneously light our long history is).

In the sixties and seventies, this cinematographer told me, no one wore clothes at Two Bunch. They stepped naked from their spa-side bungalows (if they were richer or luckier) or desert-facing rooms (if they were on a budget) and descended unencumbered into the tubs and pools pumped full of water from the hot springs. Everyone got very tan under the desert sun, and no one had tan lines, their white bodies were brown and crisp. I didn't ask him if there had been any black or Mexican people at the hot springs then, in my mind it was like a very porny version of a Linklater film, which meant there was one black guy—but no black women—integrated in the scene, and he got to say a few lines and hook up with a few of the hot girls who didn't have any lines themselves.

On the 10, an hour outside the city, I imagined a 1970s version of Nozlee, Miggy, Ezra, and me at Two Bunch, lying on pool chairs in a neat row, passing a joint down the line, browned, Nozlee's and my public hair ungroomed, bushy and puffy, us naked together, our eyes closed to keep from burning our eyeballs on the sharp yellow sun, at night we'd walk barefoot around our suite, Ezra would cook steaks on the grill with meat tongs in one hand and a cigarette in the other, Ezra's hair would be luxuriously long, Miggy would pour red wine into four glasses, and after dinner Nozlee would follow me into the bathroom and she'd tell me that she could only get two Quaaludes and that she wanted me to have the other one and after we took them, we'd go into one of the bedrooms together and lie on our sides, looking at each other as our eyes flickered and clouded over, and in our heavy downer daze we wouldn't want to move or turn over so we'd spend hours looking at each other's faces, memorizing the bumps and the lines, memorizing the shape of each other's nostrils, memorizing the arch of each other's eyebrows, memorizing the pink tips of each other's tongues.

On the road, I thought only of these fake versions of my friends, and swiped away any thoughts of the real ones and what they might think when they saw me in a place I wasn't supposed to be.

The entire drive to Desert Hot Springs is unearthly beautiful, but the best part is the last forty-five minutes. First, the 10 winds through a desert mountain range, red and camel colored, made of rock that seems precariously close to crumbling; after the mountains, the highway bursts into a blustery valley, where LED signs warn about the gusty winds; then the road continues through a field of gigantic white wind turbines, mining the wind for energy, looking like future technology, like what Tomorrowland is supposed to make you feel, but doesn't.

I turned off the 10 onto the CA-62, a desert road that took me from the highway-side wind machine spectacles into the real heart of the desert landscape: rock formations in the distance that look like a giant child was making towers out of stones; spindly Joshua trees that puff and prickle like cacti; sandscape as far as the eye can see, and the eye can see very far, the skyline is uncluttered and vast and very blue. It's like driving on the moon, and at this point in the landscape, I was almost there.

The road leading to Two Bunch is called Two Bunch Palms Trail; the trail dead-ends at the guarded gates that protect the entrance to the historic, exclusive spa. A man in a sand-colored polo shirt walked out of the guard stand and approached my car; he had a clipboard. I rolled down the window and the hot breath of the desert air exhaled into my car.

"Name?" he said.

"I'm not staying the night," I said. "I'm just visiting some friends."

"Well, yes, they would have put down your name as their guest."

"Well, no, actually, I wanted this to be a surprise."

"Perhaps you can call them and they can call me here at the guard stand to let you in?" he said.

"I just said, I want it to be a surprise," I insisted.

"Unfortunately our hotel and hot springs are not open to visitors, just guests of guests," he insisted right back.

"You have to buy a hotel room to get in?" I asked, trying to sound scandalized.

"We welcome guests on a day pass to the spa," he replied, with perfect snobbery.

"How much is a day pass?"

"Our day rate for use of the hot springs use only, no food or spa treatments, is fifty dollars."

Ridiculous. I handed over my credit card; I didn't even consider calling Ezra, who probably wouldn't answer, or Nozlee, who it seemed would definitely answer, but that would mean unblocking her number, which was something I still couldn't do. The guard, having won, happily retreated to his little station to steal fifty dollars from me so I could be allowed to enter.

The guard smugly handed me a different, smaller clipboard. "Sign here."

I signed and wrenched my card out from under the metal clamp.

"Follow this road to find our guest parking lot," he said, now kindly, now that I was officially a guest. "You must always be wearing a bathing suit at the public pools." The times, they are a-changing.

I rolled up my window with only the barest mumbled thank you. He lifted the gate and I was allowed to drive inside. Immediately, I was swallowed into a totally different atmosphere, the vast, dry, empty desert gone. I was surrounded by vegetation: palm trees, cacti so big they towered over me, olive trees creating pockets of shade, even grass. The roads were graveled with white rocks that sparkled and reflected the sun. I drove slowly inside this elegance, I parked where I was supposed to, I slammed my door shut. It was a million degrees outside and sweat sprung out of my face at my hairline, I knew that the part of my forehead under my bangs and the part of my nose under my glasses frames would soon be soaked.

Though it should've been impossible to deny the fact that I'd driven into the desert to crash Ezra's weekend and force him to speak to me, the heat made everything simmer like a mirage and my choices seemed unreal to me. I trotted down to the public hot springs, with the energy of an invited friend whose arrival was eagerly anticipated. I didn't, couldn't, entertain any other vibe.

Two Bunch is all about the springs, and they sprawl and twist, with lots of semiprivate areas shaded by the dozens of towering palm trees; the light was all dappled, everywhere I glanced. I wove around the kidney-shaped concrete pools, and the oval baths, and the wooden tubs with tarnished silver faucets that guests could fill with whatever desired combination of hot and cold spring water, to lounge in like a water lily in a pond. The guests themselves were plentiful and relaxed-seeming, all wearing as little as possible, pale beige linen or blue-and-white-striped bathing suits. I was looking in every pool, at every lounge chair, circling and doubling back, when I got semi-lost in the maze of tubs and seating areas, and I kept accidentally making eye contact with people I didn't know who were all taller and prettier than me, and I was still wearing my jeans and my tan Timberlands, and the Timberlands especially looked insane in the context of Two Bunch, and I was sweating out the drinks I'd had at Verdugo and maybe they could all smell it on me. The air was so dry I felt my lips chapping at the edges and I knew that, especially with all the coke and eggshell I'd been snorting all weekend, I'd eventually get a bloody nose. I looked insane enough to feel self-conscious, which is unusual for me, and since I hadn't made a friend of the security guard, I was a bit paranoid about someone alerting the staff to the frantic sweaty girl running around like she'd lost her child. Now, finding Ezra and Noz had become a necessity, and I started to feel frantic in my search; my strange presence wouldn't make sense without them.

I scurried over to the gravelly road/path that ringed the Two Bunch compound like a moat, and I looked more normal there, like I was the kind of person who would go on a desert hike while the day was still hot—this insane kind of person does exist, must exist. The sun was starting to set over the desert rocks, the glare of the sun was getting close to eye level, which made me squint even behind my sunglasses. Not even a single thread of wind disturbed the stillness of the leaves on the olive and tamarisk trees as I walked by them, underneath their partial shade. The ghosts of Two Bunch all hummed happily.

I turned right, down the first of many side roads that grew off the main path and led down to hotel rooms and bungalows and villas. I wandered towards a grouping of four hotel rooms. Outside the first was a stranger smoking; outside the second a bathing suit I didn't recognize was drying on a deck chair; the curtains were drawn on the third and I watched an unfamiliar woman put in an earring; I walked up to the fourth and knocked on the door. I tapped my foot like Sonic the Hedgehog, until I heard someone moving inside the room. The door opened, I saw a sliver of an arm first, dark brown, then the whole body of some black hipster dude wearing tortoiseshell glasses and a faded MTV Spring Break tank top that he'd probably paid eighty dollars for at the good thrift store in Highland Park.

"Sorry," I said fast, before he'd even gotten a good look at me, "Wrong room."

I turned and hurried back up the path.

"Who was that?" I heard a higher male voice ask.

"Wrong room," the guy replied, and the door clicked shut.

I looked down while I walked the next stretch of path, to keep the sun out of my eyes. The next side road led, twisting, down to the Casablanca Suites, a villa, the most expensive accommodations available at Two Bunch and big enough for four; no way they would've rented it; if they had rented it, no way Ezra wouldn't have mentioned that newsworthy fact when he first told me he'd planned a Two Bunch trip for this weekend. The sun continued menacing me, following me down the path. I imagined the possibility that Noz and Ezra had decided, last minute, to stay at some other hotel, and pushed myself to walk faster, heart and lungs pumping. I was scorched and the sun didn't care about me.

The third side road led past a small parking lot; Noz's red Fit was parked there. I examined the car, maybe it was someone else's red Fit, but there were the scratches on the left side from when she tried to pull into a compact spot between two badly parked SUVs in the overstuffed parking lot of the Hollywood Arclight movie theater on a Saturday night; I peered into the hatchback trunk and saw her pink yoga mat and that lime-green hoodie she wore over crop tops when we decided to stay up into the dark cold hours of a Los Angeles winter night.

There were only two doorways to choose from in this little cluster, which meant Ezra had booked a suite-sized room for them. I'd seen pictures of them online, they had decks out back that were maybe private enough that people could fuck out there late at night, like coyotes, under the speckled desert sky. I stood in front of the two suites, their front walls were glass. The one on the left had the curtains drawn open, that room was empty; the one on the left had the curtains snuggly closed.

The choice stopped me in my tracks and despite the heat, I felt jolted suddenly into the reality of my situation; that I was so frantic to get rid of my bad feelings that I'd driven all the way into the desert; the only indication I was doing so, a text to a number that had probably blocked me.

"Are they in there?" I said out loud, to whatever desert spirit might be listening, perhaps happy enough to provide guidance to someone on a quest. If I stayed long enough in this place would the trees start to talk to me like in some bad movie? Or would I sour all the ghosts with my presence, making them frantic and homicidal?

"Someone tell me," I said to a nearby tree, "should I knock?"

Nothing answered. Contented spirits don't give a fuck, or maybe they served only that shaman. I'm so fucking embarrassing. I knocked on the door, and Nozlee answered.

"Fuck," she said, "Oh fuck."

"I texted," I said, which was technically true.

She turned away from me, looked over her shoulder—she spoke, "What do I do?"—and when she turned I could see around her body to the rest of the room. Ezra was sitting on the couch. Ezra ran his hands over his shaved head the way he used to run them through his hair, it looked good now, someone had fixed it, Ezra was looking at me like, lol, he'd seen a ghost.

"You should just fucking let her in," I heard Miggy say. Then Nozlee opened the door a little wider and my dead best friend who had told me himself that he wasn't able to obtain ghostly form, that he was only able to text me, he was there, sitting on the bed with Ezra.

"What!?" I shouted. "What!?" It wasn't shock that made me shout, it was a specific desire to cause a scene. It was a pleasurable feeling, actually, for all the anxiety I'd been feeling to quickly calcify into anger, to return me to the role that felt much more comfortable to inhabit, not the frantic nightmare friend who'd followed them into the desert, but the wronged party, vindicated in my choices. I'd been lied to, obviously, and every single fucking person in the entire Two Bunch Palms complex would know about it and be punished for proximity. I'd get Nozlee and Ezra kicked out of their nice hotel room; they could just *fuck off.* "You all can just *fuck off,*" I shouted.

Ezra sprang up, he grabbed my shoulder and pulled me inside, and slammed the door behind him, and I was in it with them now. I shrugged my shoulder as violently as I could and Ezra glared at me and aggressively flung himself back down on the couch, and part of his body passed through Miggy's body.

"Oh!" Noz said as Ezra's body went through Miggy's.

It didn't seem to bother Miggy a bit, he readjusted slightly so they were sitting like two people would normally sit next to each other if one wasn't a ghost.

"Oh shit, did I sit on him again?" Ezra said.

"Actually more like in me, but whatever," Miggy said.

"It's fine," Nozlee said to Ezra.

"It certainly isn't fucking fine," I said, picking my moment to remind them how I'd been lied to by Miggy and fucked over by Noz and ignored by Ezra.

"Oh, *you're* pissed?" Ezra said. "That's fucking ridiculous, Eve."

"He told me he didn't have a body!" I shouted.

"So fucking what, you were texting," Ezra shouted back. "You didn't tell me he was still around!"

"I wanted—" I stopped. What had I wanted? "That doesn't excuse ghosting me all weekend," I said.

"I'm mad at you," Ezra said. "That's what mad people do."

Noz slunk into a corner and sank down into an armchair. She put an indigo blue pillow on her lap for protection. I wanted very badly to find the door to the bedroom and to lie in the dark under the covers for a few hours, but if I did that maybe they wouldn't ever give me the full explanation of what was going on. I didn't want to sit on the couch with both Ezra and Miggy, who had betrayed me, so instead I sank to the ground and looked at the patterned tile. Miggy had the decency to look remorseful. The four of us were together again.

I looked up from the tile and through the glass of the suite's sliding glass door, and for a second I expected to see the blue flicker of water, like the swimming pool in that house in the Hollywood Hills. The room was dark, now, the sun was almost down. Noz turned on the lamp next to her chair and Ezra twisted to hit a switch on the wall, which turned the overhead light on. The furniture was cream colored, the accents were all blue, and we glowed in the lamplight.

"How long have you had non-corporal form?" I asked Miggy.

"Since the beginning pretty much, since I first texted you," he said.

"He's telling Eve stuff you already heard, about when she found his body," Noz said. She was translating for Ezra, who couldn't see or hear Miggy.

"Can we just talk for a second?" I asked Ezra and Noz.

Ezra scowled, his face had never expressed such brash displeasure with me. I understood suddenly the way some of his ex-girlfriends and ex-flings and ex-somethings carried still such vitriol for him, why some of our mutual acquaintances casually remarked that it was really bad to get in a fight with Ezra; he looked like someone who would fling a rock at your head and hang around after to watch you bleed out.

Nozlee stood up, "C'mon," she said to Ezra.

"Of course you'd do whatever she asked," Ezra snapped. I didn't understand, but I didn't dwell, because he was nevertheless standing up. He grabbed his cigarettes and Nozlee followed him out to that private back porch I'd imagined them fucking on.

"They don't seem like they're back together," I said.

"They're not," Miggy said.

I stood up and sat next to him on the couch. I wanted to hug him so badly.

"I want to hug you so badly," I said.

"Me too."

I held out my hand, palm up, and he held out his ghost hand, palm down, and rested it right on top of mine, and I could see that our hands were together but I couldn't feel him and he couldn't feel me. I moved away first. Miggy reached into his pocket and pulled out a ghost version of his cell phone, he typed something on it, then nudged me. I shifted onto my left hip and pulled my cell out of my right pocket; I had a bunch of new junk on my phone that I ignored, and a new message from Miggy.

Miggy

I loved all three of you so much

But it wasn't enough to keep me alive

Today 7:52 PM

It's good to see you.

"It's good to see you, too."

"I can't believe you wore Timbs to Two Bunch," he said.

"Oh god!" I reached down and yanked at the knots in the laces, I pulled them off as fast as I could, and stripped my sweaty socks off, and flung the whole mess into the corner near the door. I curled up on the couch so I was looking at him and he curled up to look at me. Between my toes: my own sweat, my own skin; the sweat in my armpits had dried up in the air conditioning into a salty film; I had such a living body next to his ghostly wisps.

"When I had a body again, I noticed I had a phone right away. At the time, I think I was just hands and a phone, actually. Which, like, some witch in their fifties should write some moral panic trend piece about how millennial ghosts are manifesting with phones. Anyway, I was drifting somewhere over Palm Springs, I could see the pool at the Ace Hotel, everybody partying there. If I could see that, does it mean I had eyes as well? Anyway, I texted you right away," Miggy said.

"Why didn't you tell me you had a body?"

"At first I was disoriented, like I was on some really strong edibles, and I was trying to figure everything out," Miggy said. "I tried to text everybody important, Ezra, you, my mom, and only you were answering. You and Nozlee. And I thought, of course. You two always said you could see ghosts."

"It's how we met," I reminded him. "We were witches together in New York."

"You were witches together in LA, too," Miggy said.

Sort of, yes, she'd moved and for a few days it seemed liked we'd shift into a version of our same closeness from New York, but then she'd met Ezra and started things up with him, and Miggy got pulled in, so instead of a twosome we'd become four. I didn't argue this history with Miggy, not now, when I was getting used to his body again. He wasn't bloody and hungry, he was as hot as he ever was, his muscular arms, his perfect face, the grace with which he held his limbs; he kept all his beauty in death.

"I found my footing," Miggy said. "I figured out how to touch down, how to walk around on the ground, and I was getting ready to tell you to come to Palm Springs and find me, I really was. It was strange, though, because I didn't regret killing myself, even though I felt this great sense of loss that I had given away my life. These contradictory feelings didn't feel at odds with each other, they both just were. Okay. I wanted to be dead, I wanted to keep on being a ghost and hanging out with you. How could that all be true at the same time? I felt lost.

"Around then, I texted Nozlee to ask how you were doing and she was very, very honest with me."

What could Nozlee have even said that would alarm him to such an extreme? "I had one bad weekend," I said, "which is pretty understandable when your best friend suddenly offs himself."

"You absolutely flipped your shit, you terrified everybody, and you definitely would've been 5150'd if Noz and Bea hadn't come pick you up."

"It absolutely was not bad."

"The manager of the motel had called the cops. It was going to have happened."

"That's a badly formed sentence."

"The sentence is not on trial here," Miggy said.

"Why didn't anybody tell me?" I asked.

"They thought it would make you flip again. Everyone gave you a lot of leeway to act out this year, Eve, and whenever there was a little bit of stress on you, you definitely acted out."

"I'm like one of those 1950s women whose husbands send them to 'institutions' to treat their 'hysteria,' and then the doctors will only tell the husbands what's wrong, keeping the probably totally sane-to-begin-with woman completely in the dark."

Miggy looked at me, droll. "You overreact."

"So what, conditions are dire."

"When you react more obsessively and dramatically than the people around you, it can come off—it *has* come off—like your suffering is worse than everyone else's," Miggy said.

This was alarmingly similar to something Georgie had said to me earlier that day; it felt like a million years ago, and it felt like the exact same moment, echoing.

"I don't think my suffering is worse than anyone else's," I said. "Anybody is welcome to be dramatic around me, I don't have to be the only one."

"It's not like it's 100 percent your fault," Miggy said, still my best friend despite his death. "There's no good way to react to a devastation, and you were all limping around, emotionally speaking."

He reached out to grab my wrist, like he used to when we'd had serious or difficult conversations. This time, though, his hand went through me, unworldly. I was used to the non-touch of ghosts, but I ached for Migs to be able to touch me again. I tried to put all my longing for his dead body into my face, and I looked at him. He shivered; I didn't know a ghost could shiver.

"You can't leave Palm Springs?" I asked, but I knew the answer. Ghosts get stuck in places.

"Well it's not as if I've tried," Miggy said, vibes of *it's not that I can't it's that I won't*, protesting too much, avoidant.

What was Miggy thirsty for, here, in the sand outside Los Angeles? Did he hover over the gay white parties in Palm Springs and drip his ghost saliva, unnoticed, over the glistening bodies of the hottest twinks and daddys alike? Did he sit unhappily at Tonga Hut and Melvyn's and the other historic Palm Springs bars, drinking in the depressive vibe of Old Hollywood and the desperate alcoholics it attracted? No, it had to be something that only existed in Desert Hot Springs. Was it rude to ask a ghost what kept them hanging around? I'd never before cared about being rude to them, or else they'd made their thirsts immediately clear.

What had Miggy wanted very badly when he was alive? He'd wanted his mental health issues to go away, the depression and the interlinked anxiety. When Miggy was alive he'd had panic attacks while he was driving, panic attacks at the

Glendale Galleria mall, panic attacks at the gay nightclub Akbar; his anxiety never seemed to abate, only expand, and he'd wanted very badly to feel calm and serene. We agreed that the desert skyline, palms and prickly Joshua trees and cacti blossoming against the beige sandy grounds and the rich blue skies—that was serenity. He was dead, he was in the desert, his panic was gone.

"Why did you tell Nozlee and not me?" I asked.

"I trusted her to know I was here and continue the work of getting over my death," Miggy said. "I worried you'd drop everything and move out to the desert and just, like, make that your life."

When ghosts encounter the thing they are thirsty for, they transform, like Babs had done in Verdugo bar when I gave her the gift of really good lesbian drama; I didn't want to see Miggy like that: ghoulish, animalistic. And perhaps, he didn't want me to see him like that. That would make sense if it were true, but if there was anything I'd learned over the past forty-eight hours, it was that I didn't have the first clue what anybody was ever thinking, especially when it came to what they were thinking about me.

"That's something I would do," I said.

"That's remarkable self-awareness, coming from you," Miggy said.

I guess it had been true that my lack of introspection had always been a joke among my closest friends. *Eve would rather look at a painting than think about a painting*, that kind of joking. I thought they'd just meant I had a keen eye. I guess everything means more than one thing at the same time.

"I've really grown up this weekend," I joked. Miggy laughed, I was grateful.

If he'd had a body he would've hugged me, or knocked his shoulder into mine like a playful older brother, "You still mad at me?"

I wanted to say no. "Honestly?"

"Honestly."

"I get what you did. And in my grief I've been selfish and too much to handle. You should be mad at me for snorting all that Cascarilla and being rude."

Miggy waved his hand as if warding off smoke, "We already had it out about that, it's fine."

"Yes, okay, I'm just saying, this might be me being selfish again, but I'm a little mad, and I'm mad because I'm hurt, but that doesn't mean I can help being angry."

Miggy nodded, "Okay, I get that."

I stuck my palm out again and he rested his ghost hand just above it. This would be our new way of hugging. We held our hands like that for as long a moment of a silence as either of us could stand, and I felt finally, for the first time since he'd died, like I was back in sync with Miggy, the way we'd been on all our good nights and days together when he was still alive. Together, simultaneously, our hands drifted away from each other and our faces turned towards the back glass door. Ezra and Noz were sitting in porch chairs next to each other. Ezra was leaning close to Nozlee, but not nicely, like he wanted to say something angrily directly into her space.

"So, they're definitely not getting back together."

"Definitely not," Miggy agreed.

"I've spent this whole weekend being pissed at Nozlee for breaking up with him."

"It's only Saturday," Miggy said.

"It's only Saturday! Holy shit."

Miggy left, dissolved into mist. Apparently he liked to float around a few feet above people and buildings.

Nozlee had been facilitating a conversation between him and Ezra all day long, and they'd all gotten a chance to talk things out with each other. I was jealous of the three of them, talking without me, even though Miggy assured me it had mostly been purging a lot of bad feelings. I wanted to be included, even when it was a negative experience. Too late, too bad. Miggy told me to tell Ezra he said goodbye, and I told Miggy that if Ezra ever forgave me, we could come to visit together next month. Making these plans made me feel really normal, like Miggy had moved to New York or something.

Noz and Ezra hadn't yet noticed that Miggy had left. Ezra wouldn't even see the change; they were still on the porch leaning forward in their chairs, arguing. I couldn't hear them, the glass was good and thick. Nozlee shook her head jerkily and her hair fell out of place, and she absently, furiously pushed it out of her eyes. I wished there was something I could do to stop them from fighting, some magic words to restore the peace. Seeing them together like this, their anger towards each other like a lightning storm, I lost my last shreds of stupid hope that we could go back to anything like the way we were, on the good nights when it was the four of together.

The night we took the Adderall, we were talking so much fun nonsense and I asked Nozlee, "What's a song you know all the words to?"

"'Strange Powers' by the Magnetic Fields," she'd said immediately.

"Sing it for me," I said.

She did, in a soft voice, not particularly melodic but beautiful all the same. The chorus went like this: *"And I can't sleep / Cause you got strange powers / You're in my dreams / Strange powers."* When she finished singing she said, "That song reminds me of you, actually."

Why hadn't I asked her what she meant? She had been close enough for me to touch. Why hadn't I thought of it since?

I walked up to the glass slowly but quietly, so I could get it open fast and hear a little of what they were saying.

I caught Nozlee hissing, "It's not as if I was lying to you," but they both stopped talking fast when I was suddenly there. Nozlee craned her neck to take a look in the living room behind me.

"He's gone," she said to Ezra. With me there, suddenly they were in cahoots again. I wasn't used to being anybody's common enemy, it was a bullshit feeling.

"He said bye, he said he'd see you before you left the desert, and I said I would text him for you whenever you wanted," I said.

"Well, he could've stayed to say bye to my face," Ezra said.

"It's not like you could've actually said bye back," I said, and the way Ezra's face got so mad and his eyes got so sharp at me, I knew I'd made it all worse.

"He's a ghost, okay?" Nozlee said. "You shouldn't take offense, he doesn't move in regular patterns."

"Don't take his side!" Ezra said, and simultaneously I said, "Ezra's allowed to be upset!" We were so much ourselves then, in that moment of overlap.

Nozlee shrugged in an exaggerated way, to express her incredulity. "Listen, okay," she said. "I'm devastatingly sober and today has not been the relaxing spa trip of my dreams, and I really want some wine. So I'm going to go find some."

"Yeah okay," Ezra said.

"That sounds good," I said.

Nozlee grabbed her purse and the front doorknob.

"Can you get me a nice dry white?" I asked. "I'll Venmo you."

"And can you get me some Budweiser bottles?" Ezra asked.

"Yes!" she said, exasperated. "You guys, I know what you like to drink!"

She let the door slam hard after her. And then it was just Ezra and me in that well-appointed hotel suite, everything was so clean around us.

"It's pretty dark in here," I said, and busied myself turning on every single light I could see, prolonging the moment before I would have to allow him to confront me, to express all his anger. The room blazed by the time I looked back at Ezra, who was sitting on the couch watching me move around. His skin was a little tan and his eyes glowed nicely in all the yellow lamplight. I couldn't tell if he looked older or younger with the shaved head but I knew that, from the back, we didn't look like each other anymore.

"You could've sent me a text, saying you were mad at me," I said. "And if you didn't want me here you could've texted me back saying I shouldn't drive in."

"Well today I was a little distracted by the revelation that I could communicate, indirectly but whatever, with my dead best friend, so I didn't look at my phone until after you got here."

"I guess, okay, that's fair," I said.

"Plus, I muted you," he said.

"Oh." I deflated; being muted made me feel so impotent.

"Sit down," he said. He gestured widely to the big sectional couch.

I sat. "Should I apologize for being here?"

He shrugged. Now that I was next to him, he couldn't look at me, which wasn't great. It's not like he'd been gone long but somehow I missed looking at his face. He was wearing this black-and-red-striped tank top he always grabbed when he was driving out to the desert, it suited him, it looked like him, it somehow matched the curve and flush of his lips (even scowling) and the way his face situated itself, now that his hair was gone.

"It's okay, it's fine, coming out to the desert is just a small thing, you know, comparatively."

"Compared to what?" I asked, even though I'd rather not have to talk through his answer.

"For a whole year, you and Nozlee were able to talk to Miggy, and you never told me. I thought that after you had your big breakdown, you were scared to express how sad you were. I assumed you were worried about going off the rails again," Ezra said.

I picked at a thread on the couch and looked at his hands, curved and still against the fabric of the cushions. I tried to tamp down all my knee-jerk rejections of his perspective, all my justifications of my actions. Ezra deserved for me to fully ingest all the ways I'd made him feel.

"But the truth was, you had stopped mourning in the same way I was," he said. "Not telling me separated our experience and I felt it but I didn't understand it, until this morning. I'm so mad at you. It was a big lie, Evelyn."

I laughed because I was hurt, and then I wanted to cry. Evelyn isn't my real full name, I'm Eve on birth certificate, passport, and credit cards; Ezra calling me Evelyn had been one of our little nonsense jokes. Did he call me that to show me that he still loved me or to remind me of the trust I'd betrayed? Ezra and I had quarreled tons and tons, but we'd never been in a real, serious fight.

"What can I do to fix it?" I asked.

"Talk it out with me, try to figure out what we need to do to get back on the same track," he said.

I said, "I don't want to be mean to you."

"So, don't be mean to me."

"I don't know how to be nice when I'm in a fight."

"So, let's not fight," Ezra said.

"You'll stop being mad at me?"

"Not unless we actually fight it out."

"You are the fucking worrrrrrrst," I said, and crumpled over my crossed legs. So, this was how Ezra fought; he said things that made a woman feel crazy, that made them do all the work of tying themselves into knots, while he came off as cool-headed and reasonable. I told him so.

"What the fuck do you want me to do then?" he asked.

"I want you to care that we're having a fight!"

"I fucking care!" Ezra leaned forward now, like I'd watched him do to Nozlee on those porch chairs. "You're my best friend and I love you so fucking much, you think I don't care? Like it's no big fucking deal that my girlfriend and my best friend were lying to me for a year?" Ezra picked up a plastic cup that was sitting on the coffee table and slammed it back down again; it sounded dramatic against the glass but nothing broke. Ezra had once mentioned that he talked to his therapist about "very typically male demonstrations of anger." I'd said, "Like what?" and he'd said something like, "You know what kind of stuff." But I hadn't known, and this must've been what he'd meant. You learn so much about a person when you finally fight. I'm not sure if I flinched when he slammed the glass or not, but he looked freaked out by himself.

"It's fine," I said, meaning the glass.

"It's not fucking fine," he said, meaning who knows what.

"I'm sorry," I said. "Okay, so, why I didn't tell you about Miggy. You didn't really know I see ghosts. You told me you thought the ghost thing was, what did you say, more metaphorical than real?"

"That is such a bullshit excuse. After Miggy died, that changed everything, you should've made me understand."

"And what would've happened then?" I asked. "Would you have made me text him every time you saw a meme that he'd laugh at?"

"Isn't that what you were doing? As my best friend, you should've given me at least what little contact you had with him. How would you have felt if I'd kept him away from you?"

I didn't have anything to say to that. If Ezra had done to me what I'd done to him, I'd have been mad enough to storm away from our friendship, maybe end it forever. I didn't want him to get that thought in his head, so I didn't mention it. "I'm sorry," I said instead, unqualified this time.

"You wanted to keep him for yourself," Ezra said. "You would've been fine if you'd been my best friend, and Nozlee's best friend, and Miggy's best friend, and we never developed connections independent of you. That's why I never got why you encouraged me to ask Nozlee out. It didn't make sense, especially when—no, let me finish—you got predictably shitty about it when Noz and I really started dating and suddenly we had a relationship you weren't invited to."

"That's not how I feel," I said. "I loved hanging out as a group. I didn't want to keep you from Miggy. It just seemed too hard to be the person to facilitate a connection between you two."

"Why? Don't we do hard shit for each other all the time?"

"Yes but—"

"But what?" he said.

"But I don't fucking know why, okay? If I fucking knew why I was like this I would tell you, but I don't know!" I was shouting now, even though my body wasn't moving. Fighting is so strange, so in your head and out of your body, so fast and rushed and hot-blooded. No space for pauses. Even as I was thinking, I was shouting. "I felt so bad every day and the only way I could not feel bad was to just not think about anything! It barely crossed my mind to connect you and Miggy! I was just trying not to have thoughts!"

"Well when you turn your whole self off it has consequences!"

"It's not on purpose!"

"It doesn't fucking matter if it's on purpose!" he shouted.

"What do you want me to do!?" I shouted back.

"Deal with yourself so you're less of a shitty friend!"

Ezra got up and went into the kitchen zone, to be a little bit away from me. I thought about maybe looking at something other than the couch but found I didn't have the emotional energy.

"Besides this one thing, I think I've been a good friend," I said.

"This was a big thing," Ezra said.

"All I've been thinking about for two days straight is you," I said.

"That's not good boundaries though. You were thinking about me in order to push this under the rug, but I can't do that anymore."

I finally tore my gaze away from the textured cream of the couch fabric. Ezra had his eyes on me unflinching and I bathed in the attention even though it wasn't warm or sweet. I would take him mad over silent.

"I will try to be better. I will seriously work on it," I said.

He came to sit with me again, as the energy in the room shifted from a boil to a simmer.

I leaned over to hug him and he hugged me back as tight as I liked it but said, "This doesn't mean I forgive you, I just want to be able to forgive you."

We unwrapped from each other and I wished badly for a drink that I could sip on to punctuate silences, to help transitions.

"You don't have to be perfect, you just have to try. And when you get freaked out you have to manage it, instead of running off or doing stupid shit like locking my phone," Ezra said.

"I was scared," I said.

"The point is, you have to be less scared."

"You should text Paris," I said. "I posted something on Instagram and she reached out to me. She's worried about you."

"Shit," Ezra said, fumbling for the phone in his pocket, sending off a quick text.

When he put his phone down, we gently told each other the stories of our weekends, all the little details we'd normally share with each other, but now we were tentative. All of the land mines we'd each been planting and stepping on as a surprise were suddenly dug up, so we were now obliged to walk around them carefully. I told Ezra about going into his house and reading the texts on Tommy's phone, and I kept saying *sorry sorry sorry*, knowing that with every rendition of the word, I was diminishing its effect.

Ezra filled in the blanks of his story with his usual writerly flare: Friday morning was strange and too-bright, dizzying cocaine hangovers and no sleep and the cold water in the pool at the house Paris was selling. Kissing her had made him miss Nozlee (and feel guilty for kissing her), so he cracked and texted her *Are you up, I still want you, where are you, can we talk?* Nozlee had eventually texted him back; she was still going to Two Bunch since she couldn't cancel the reservation and she still wanted to go to see the shaman here, and Ezra could come meet her later in the afternoon if he wanted, but he shouldn't get his hopes up, her mind was made up, they could talk but they were done.

Ezra didn't understand how set she was, Ezra didn't take her words at face value, he considered this invitation a loosening. He planned to text me when he got to the desert, a fait accompli, because he felt that what he was doing was emotionally reckless and somewhat masochistic, and he wanted to hurt himself without his friend stopping him. But then he got to the desert and Nozlee told him about Miggy. At first he didn't believe her and didn't know what kind of strange games she was playing, but then Nozlee said all these things that only Migg would/could know. He thought about all the times when I was drunk and had said things like, *The ghost at*

Little Cave won't talk to me because I'm a dyke or *The exorcism I did this morning was of a whole murdered family and it was really actually scary, they were all so mad.* All my ghost talk. And he started to believe her. Then he started to get mad.

"Why not confront me then, yell at me or whatever. Have this conversation? Why mute me and run away from me?" I asked.

Ezra rubbed the tiny hairs on his head. I wished I could touch them, they looked so soft.

He said, "This is what I'm like when I get mad. I ice out people. I've just never been mad at you."

Lydia had said as much, but I hadn't believed her.

"I have my own things to work on," he said.

"Let's thaw stuff out, then," I said. "Is there anything else you want to ask me?"

"I think I just need space right now, from both of you. You and Nozlee, I mean," he said. "I'm just really fucking hurt by both of you right now."

We were silent for a really long time; I felt a little bit like I'd been doing wind sprints.

"Were you out here to get back together with her?" I asked. "Because, I was the one who asked her not to tell you about Miguel's ghost. You shouldn't punish her for that."

"I came out here to talk to her, yeah," Ezra said. "But then, you know, we really talked and were totally honest with each other, maybe for the first time. We wanted to be that honest, that's how Miggy came up in the first place."

"Miguel's ghost," I insisted. "You have to think of it as the ghost of him, not him. That's what our witch-teacher taught us, to protect ourselves from getting too attached to a monstrous thing."

"Do you think of him like that, as a ghost of himself?" Ezra asked.

"No," I said.

Ezra drew in a breath loudly, "Look, there are other reasons Noz and I definitely aren't going to get back together, it's not just the Miguel thing."

"What are they?" I asked.

Ezra shook his head. "You can ask her," he said. "Maybe she'll tell you."

"Okay." I said. I brushed that away for now. "I need to say, ghosts are mostly the person they were when they were alive, but all ghosts are thirsty, and they become monstrous and awful sometimes. I'll admit, I was selfish and I kept Miguel for myself—and yes, okay, I *wanted* to keep Miguel for myself. But also, if you're not used to ghosts, I thought it might really hurt you to see an altered version of him, a scary thing, a monster. I'm used to ghosts and it wouldn't bother me to see him all freaked out, but it could've hurt you."

"I'm a fucking adult and you're not my mom," Ezra said.

"Yes, but, haven't you ever tried to protect someone you loved from something bad?" I asked.

Ezra put his forearms on his knees and dropped his head; his shoulder blades rose up from his back under that nice shirt. I reached out to scrub my fingerpads against his scalp, the way I always used to even when there was hair in the way. I was worried, but he didn't flinch or push me off; he leaned into my hand. I moved my hand across his scalp, I rubbed every inch of it, I know it felt good for him, it felt good for me to touch him. We stayed that way for a few minutes.

Ezra sat up, he grabbed my hand before I could pull it away and kissed my knuckles. He'd never been this tender, this semi-sexual, with me while mostly sober. All of our previous heated embraces had occurred on Molly, or at sunrise at the tail end of an all-night coke bender, or as spitty cheek and ear kisses while absolutely sloshed and sun-drunk at a daytime barbeque party.

"I've tried to think about what it would be like to have sex with you," Ezra said. "But I never got very far. I think I want to be you more than I want to fuck you."

"I want us to be the same person, sometimes, too," I said. "That's why I always took those pictures of our hair. Because we looked alike."

Ezra smiled brightly, for me, finally. He let go of my hand so he could touch his own head.

"It'll grow back," he said.

Saturday, 8:20 p.m.

Fifteen minutes later, Nozlee still wasn't back. Ezra was antsy, and I didn't want to tarnish our moments of deep understanding by lingering too long in each other's presence. He was still mad at me and would need to take time to get over how bad I'd betrayed him; I needed to learn how to be a good friend to him. To start, we needed to give each other space, we needed to create a jump cut like in a movie, so the scene didn't stretch out too long.

I went into the bathroom and sat on the toilet for a while after I'd finished peeing. I had so many notifications on my phone I didn't want to check. I opened Instagram, it reloaded, and Georgie's newest picture appeared on the top of my feed. It was from earlier, at The Grind. Most of the frame was full of sweating women mid-dance, but in the lower corner Bea was kissing Georgie's cheek and Georgie's eyes were closed and she looked happy.

Georgie

Today 1:09 AM

Where are you?

Today 8:25 PM

i have to mute you on Insta for a just little while

until im over it

im gonna get over it

and learn to be a good friend.

I went back to Instagram and muted Georgie. I unfollowed and blocked Bea. A new message popped up.

Georgie

im gonna get over it

and learn to be a good friend.

I understand

I'm glad you're working on your shit.

I could've said "thanks" or "thank you for helping me figure out I have a lot of work to do in order to be good to people," but Georgie didn't need to hear it and I didn't need to say it; I could just let our message chain ebb, I could let it fall to the bottom of the scroll until one day we were ready to forgive and ready to be better and she could jump to the top of my feed once again. I deleted my message chain with Bea; maybe she'd text me again, and I'd ignore it, but either way, I didn't need to keep the whole record of our back and forth anymore.

I left the bathroom and Ezra was leaning against a wall across the room, looking at his phone. He'd turned off some of the lights, so the hotel suite had less of an interrogation room feel and more of the dim glow of a romantic night in the desert. In the lower light, his face was illuminated by his phone's blue glow.

"The Saguaro has cheap rooms on HotelTonight," Ezra said.

The Saguaro in Palm Springs was where we were meeting up on Sunday, to have Miggy's vigil, because all our friends loved it there. Once, a huge swath of our group of friends had taken over about half the rooms at the hotel for a weekend and didn't leave once in forty-eight hours. We ate bags and bags of salt & vinegar potato chips and drank our way through a hundred beers. The few hours we slept, Ezra, Miggy, and I shared a bed; we woke up smelling like sunscreen and each other's underwear.

"You don't have to go," I said. "I can get a room."

"I think I need to be alone tonight," Ezra said. "I booked a room."

"Do you want to wait for Noz? To say bye?"

Ezra shook his head. He pocketed his phone, and walked

away, into the bedroom of the suite. I heard a bag unzip, I heard him shuffling around.

"I should get a room too!" I said. I pulled out my phone and tapped the HotelTonight app.

Ezra appeared in the doorway. "Wait before you book, okay? Can you do me a favor? Stay here until Noz gets back and update her and chat before you book a room and run off?"

"Yeah okay," I said. "Is she okay?"

"Not really," Ezra said.

Unsurprising; none of us were really okay, and it would be a while until we were.

With his bag slung over one shoulder, Ezra hugged me really hard and we stayed that way for a while, my chin over his shoulder and his chin over mine, my hand on his back and his hands in my hair.

"If you're ever mad at me again, please don't freeze me out." I whispered in his ear. "Yell at me, make me cry, just don't vanish. I was scared."

"I promise," he said, and kissed me on the ear, and let go of me, and left. I heard his car start and the tires crunch on that white rock road, and I was still just standing there in the middle of room. I didn't know what to do while I waited, I got antsy almost immediately.

I scrounged around a little and found the little binder all hotels have, with a guide to all the amenities. I checked the menu for their restaurant, annoyingly named "Essence," and ordered a totally ridiculous amount of mismatched food: gnocchi, a meze plate, grilled asparagus, crispy spiced cauliflower, seared scallops. Nozlee liked everything but it was hard to order for her because she ate based on her feelings on any given day rather than on a reliable list of preferences, and

I couldn't begin to guess what she was feeling and why it was taking her so long to go on an easy errand.

She came in a few minutes after I hung up the phone and explained, "I stopped at Tonga Hut just to be alone for a little while. I got a blue Hawaiian." She stuck out her tongue and it was stained, faintly, from the blue curaçao.

"I ordered a bunch of stuff from room service," I said.

"Oh thank god," Noz said. She collapsed on the couch, dropping her bags of booze on the floor. "I haven't eaten all day. Except crab rangoon with my blue Hawaiian."

I wrinkled my nose. Noz could eat anything and in huge amounts, but I couldn't really stomach all that fried bar food. I was better with liquids than solids. I found myself considering anew the familiar shape of her body, the way she always lounged in a sprawl instead of sitting like a normal person, the hugeness of her eyes, the way she didn't look at her phone when she was in the same room with you. I made myself useful gathering up the plastic bags of drinks and taking them to the kitchen area to sort them out.

"So he left?" Noz called from the couch.

"Maybe he's napping in the bedroom," I said, just to joke with her. I needed a little levity, I was starting to feel tired.

"His car's gone," Noz said.

"You're a good detective," I said. "He went to stay at the Saguaro, he needed space."

"So I bought that beer for nothing!" Noz said, but she didn't sound actually mad about it. She was talking just to talk, filling up the room, keeping me interested.

"Yeah," I said. Then, I caught her up on our convo, like Ezra had asked me to, while I put the beer in the mini-fridge and opened the white wine and poured us each a glass. I walked back into the living room, she was in a slump on the couch; I handed her a glass and she de-slumped so she could sip on it.

"That's the whole story?" she asked. "That's all you guys talked about."

"Yeah, that's pretty much everything," I said. "Why, wasn't it enough?"

She shrugged. I sat in the armchair. Someone knocked on the door. I stood up again and let in a man in a white, billowy uniform carrying a large tray, and Nozlee moved a few random objects—our wine glasses, decorative bowls—off the coffee table. The man put the tray down, lifted the cover, and said, "Enjoy." All the plates of food were steaming and Nozlee looked blissful. The couches and armchairs were too plush and elephantine to give us easy access to the plates so we both, automatically, slid to the ground, scooted close to the coffee table, grabbed our forks and started pecking.

I loved watching Nozlee eat. She opened her mouth very wide and put huge forkfuls of veggies or pasta in, she chewed silently but with exaggerated motions. She really enjoyed herself, no matter what it was that she was eating. She stuffed an entire scallop in her mouth and dedicated her entire body to eating it, while I slathered a triangle of toasted naan in unfortunately grainy hummus and took little bites of it, watching her.

Nozlee put a hand over her face and said with a full mouth, "What are you looking at?"

"I love watching you eat," I said.

She moved her hand away and opened her mouth, made an obnoxious *ahhhh* noise, I could see little white bits of the scallop on her tongue and between her teeth. She made the filthy elegant somehow. I giggled, a lot, and took down the last of my

wine. I scrambled up to grab more and she shouted after me,
"Bring the bottle over!" We were feasting. When had I eaten
last? Real food, not chips while driving to ward off a daytime
hangover? Enchiladas with Lydia, a million years ago? Would I
ever have enchiladas with Georgie again?

"Oh my god, can we talk about the ghosts around here?"
Noz asked, mouth full of fried cauliflower.

"It's like they're humming," I said. "They're so happy,
they're not even people anymore they're so happy."

I watched Nozlee dip her tender small pinkie finger into the
baba ganoush and suck the tip of her finger into her mouth and
pop it out again all bright and spitty.

"I had imagined this really calming, almost blissful weekend, connecting to myself, connecting to my magic, you know
what I mean." Noz gestured at me with her wine glass and I
lifted mine, and together we sipped.

Living in LA, I was constantly surrounded by communities and cultures leaning like a plant in light towards mindful
existences and an introspective understanding of one's self, but
never had I ever tried to look for myself. I was in my skin, what
more did I want? I was feeling my own feelings all the time,
what else did I have to know? But then, of course, Georgie and
Miggy—and Ezra, to a certain extent—had revealed that I
didn't know why I did what I did.

We were getting to the stage of our feast where we had
slowed down, but we wouldn't stop; I knew we'd keep picking
until there was nothing on the plates but a faint sheen of olive
oil and the dregs of the gnocchi's wild mushroom ragù.

"You really didn't talk about anything else?" Nozlee said,
switching topics as I opened the second bottle of wine and

poured us our third glasses. This would be her fourth total, but why would I count hers? We were going to run out of wine, so she had gotten the beer for something after all.

"What else would we have talked about?" I asked.

She said, without looking at me, "Me?"

"He said you're absolutely, definitely, not getting back together. Is it because of Miggy?"

"No," Nozlee said.

"Care to elaborate?"

She didn't answer; she stood up. She walked into the bedroom and came back a second later with her phone. She wasn't scrolling or checking anything; she walked it over to the vintage-looking speaker on the side table and plugged her phone into the AUX cable. She tapped and scrolled a bit. She was wearing these white baggy jeans I know she bought from Urban Outfitters online and a t-shirt with thin white and red stripes, tied at the waist, which made her looked very hourglassy. The knot in her shirt warped the stripes; I knew she'd picked up the shirt at the Highland Park location (the best location) of the vintage store The Bearded Beagle. I knew where she'd bought all of her clothes because I was there when she bought them; she'd asked me "How does this look?" and turned around so I could see it from the back before giving my opinion. Lana Del Rey started playing.

She sat back down next to me, her glass and eyebrow raised like props. "Do you always have to know every single little detail of my relationship with Ezra?" she asked.

That hurt so I said, "Ouch."

"Don't act idiotic," she said.

"I'm really not."

"It's not like we didn't invite you," Noz said. "But don't pretend you weren't always there."

"Are you mad at me too? I can't tell."

"I'm not mad, I'm pointing out that both Ezra and I were always inviting you to be this, like, *third*."

"Okay, so what?" I said. "Are you pissed at me for not being better than both of you and backing off?"

"That's not—"

I cut her off, "Because I think if this weekend proved anything, it's that I'm worse than all three of you, not better."

Nozlee shook her head, "That's not what I'm saying at all. I'm saying, did Ezra talk to you about that, like, *dynamic* between us?"

"We didn't discuss any *dynamic*," I said, sipping on wine. I hitched myself up into the armchair. "Ezra and I talked about how he and I were too close, how we sort of tried to be the same person sometimes. So maybe that created the *dynamic* you're talking about, and I'm sorry if that *dynamic* had some kind of negative effect on your relationship, but I'll remind you that you yourself admitted that you—not just Ezra, you!— invited me."

Nozlee looked up at me from her seat on the floor, and I was surprised to see her smiling big and wolfishly, like I'd just done something really wonderful.

"What?"

"You're really cute when you're ranting and defensive."

"I'm not cute," I said. It wasn't an adjective that Nozlee had ever, ever used for me before, I would've remembered; sometimes I hopped in her car in a good outfit and she said something like "You look hot" or "Those jeans are hot"; always

"You *look* hot," never "You *are* hot," and never, ever, "You're cute." "You're *really* cute."

Nozlee started laughing like an idiot at some joke I didn't get.

"What?" I said.

"I'm pathetic," she said, coughing and laughing into her hands while she tried to talk.

"What?" I asked again.

"You're an idiot," Noz said, and with her big eyes on me, she said. "I've been in love with you for, like, years. And that's why Ezra and I are absolutely, definitely broken up."

I shook my head, "That's absolutely not true, you're not even gay," I said.

Nozlee looked at me again and she wasn't amused anymore, "I told you over and over again that I'm bisexual! Over and over again Eve! It's like you weren't listening."

"Nobody's really bisexual," I said, reflexively, not even really believing myself all of a sudden.

"Yes they are," Noz said. She looked pissed still. "I basically moved to LA because you were here and the second I got here you were, like, 'You should fuck my friend Ezra,' and then, I don't know, I didn't want to be this pathetic person, pining for you all over the place."

I didn't know what to say; I stared at the perfect crest of her eyebrows and the glistening brown of her eyes and loved her face and wondered how long I'd loved her face, how long I'd watched her body, how long I'd ignored how hard I was looking.

"Oh god," she said, her face crumpled. "I guess I've fucked the rest of it up."

"It doesn't matter, our friendship is all fucked up already," I said without thinking.

"Oh god, I *am* pathetic," she said and she stood up and looked around like she was looking for somewhere to run away to, and I didn't want her to run away so I stood up too, a little frantically, and maybe I tripped a little.

"No, no, wait," I said. "I'm always talking without thinking, I just say the next thing! I just haven't thought about it enough!"

Nozlee stared at me, her face hard again. "Think about it, right now."

I didn't know how to think on command, I wasn't certain even what she wanted me to think about, but I could hear the hum of the ghosts and I liked knowing she could hear it too. How had Nozlee and I never been in sync? In New York I was intimidated by her and dismissive, and I hadn't understood why she always took the train to come to the one bar near my apartment in DUMBO instead of making me come to Williamsburg like everyone else I knew did. In Los Angeles, I'd mistaken our, whatever, *dynamic* for closeness, but we'd only ever been truly close once, on the night we swam and then stayed up together. Her platinum blonde hair had looked angelic spread over the soft white rich-person sheets, I had watched it fluff out while it dried, I'd smelled the chlorine on her when she'd put her hand close to my hand but hadn't touched.

Ezra and I had reached our uneasy stasis, and by doing something with what Nozlee was offering me, I was potentially delivering a killing blow to our friendship. Georgie had told me that my friendship was worth giving up for the potential of romantic happiness. I didn't feel that way about Ezra, but Nozlee's love felt powerful to me, like something that I needed to respect.

I stepped forward into Nozlee's space, I tried to take the

wine glass out of her hand. She moved her wine glass away from me, like she was suspicious of me, and her face looked concerned, but the swivel of her body just put her closer to me, more accessible. I reached as far as I could, I leaned forward; I took the wine glass at the stem while she gripped the curved body.

"Let go," I said. "I've got it."

She let it go. I took it, I put it down, and I put my hand on her face.

"Eve," she said, her eyes fluttered closed. "I'm really scared."

I tried to use every bit of the two inches I had on her to seem like someone she could fold into. I coaxed her with that hand on her face and another on her waist, I wrapped around her like bubble wrap, I put her face into the crook of my shoulder and my chin on her crisp blonde head.

"Do you remember when we went night swimming? You, Ezra, and Migs, and me?" I asked.

"When Miggy was housesitting in the Hollywood Hills?" she asked into the fabric of my shirt. I think she was sucking on it like a nervous child.

"Yes," I said. "I've been thinking about it all weekend, staying up all night with you. Did you give me that Adderall because you were in love with me?"

"Please don't make me embarrass myself," she said, and I felt bad for making her scared even though I hadn't meant to, and I kissed her.

Nozlee pressed her whole body into mine immediately and hummed performativity, like she was saying *I'm here, I'm here, I'm here. Where are you?* Her lips were very soft and I felt an instinctual understanding of where to put mine to fit in best with hers. I broke the kiss to suck at her warm neck and she panted. I pulled at the crew neck of her striped shirt to reveal the curved crest of her collarbone and I licked at it like it belonged to me.

Sharply, suddenly, Nozlee unwrapped her hands from around my torso and dropped her eyes and pushed at my shoulders; I thought she was trying to get me away from her, had the entire thing been a trick? Then she leaned into my space and pushed at me again and I landed on the couch and she crawled on top of me and I realized that the pushes had been to get me down so she could get on top of me. She kneeled on either side of my thighs and arched over me beautifully, and kissed me. I closed my eyes into it and discovered all the parts of her body I hadn't touched earlier: the hot skin of her lower back beneath her shirt, the sensitive place at the top of the back of her thighs, the abstract shapes of her shoulder blades. I was turning red and I could feel my cunt starting to pulse.

Nozlee released her grip on my face, finally, and scrambled at arm-holes in my shirt, trying to get a hand in there, while I was trying to kiss at her neck again and find the spot where her skin-smell was the strongest. My lips rubbed against her skin and my entire body jolted when she thumbed my nipple. *Bedroom* I thought. "Bedroom," I said.

In the bedroom, we scrambled and teetered; I pulled off my shirt in a ceremonious fuss, Nozlee unbuttoned her jeans while I fiddled with the light level until I figured out that the en suite bathroom light bathed everything in a soft blue glow. Nozlee stood still in her bra and underwear and asked, "Do you want me to take them off?" Though she'd asked it carelessly, it was the sexiest thing I'd ever heard.

"Take them off for me, Noz," I said.

She laughed as she reached around to her back to unhook her bra.

"What?" I said.

"Your voice gets all growly when you try to be sexy. Just let it happen naturally!"

"Most of the girls I have sex with don't give me so much shit when we're fucking," I said.

Nozlee looked right at me, her face suddenly tense with suffering; I might've ruined it. Then she blinked, and her smile was back, and all the pining and frustrated lust and loss was gone from her eyes.

"Forget I said anything," I said, "I've never had sex with anyone else."

Nozlee intertwined her legs with mine, completely naked now, and whispered in my ear, "Stop talking."

We made it, finally, to the bed. I laid myself out on top of her and mouthed at her nipples and breasts. She had tan lines, the skin on her breasts and around her neat but robust bush were paler brown than the skin on her stomach and arms. I stuck my tongue into her belly button and nibbled at her there. My fingers tugged lightly at her pubic hair curls and my fingers brushed downwards. "This okay?" I panted into the skin of her hip.

"Yes, keep going, please," she panted. I didn't know where her hands were, and then they were in my hair.

It felt like too much to go down on her right away, right then, so I pushed my head up against her hands and kissed her on that good-smelling spot on her neck while thumbing apart her pussy to find the gush of wetness and the nub of her clit. Her hips jerked up, looking for something. I was careful as I slipped two fingers inside of her at once; it was a pleasure to hear her gasp. I kissed her to keep my own heart rate up while concentrating on the mechanics of curling and thrusting the two fingers inside her while my thumb kept up a gentle strum on her clit. I lost myself in the smell of her pussy, in the feel of her lips, and though it was long minutes it felt like no time at all until she ripped her mouth away from mine to tell me she was close to coming.

I levered myself up, putting a little space between our bodies while my tired fingers continued to work. Her breath got sharp, she huffed out bursts; I kissed her and she came fast like she was blooming. I collapsed, sweaty, at her side, flexing my aching fingers. She pressed her face into my upper chest while I breathed hard and I could feel wetness on her fluttering eyelashes. She pressed her knee between my legs and could probably feel my wetness, too. She bit at my neck, she kept her knee there for me to grind against; she knew it was what I wanted because I had told her so, in so many conversations, so many nights ago. I take forever to come, and she let me build to it, and when the orgasm hit me, I felt so grateful for every inch of her skin she let me suck, for every chemical in her brain that made her who she was, and for the graceful arch of her knee that I'd fucked.

I felt like crying, too, but didn't. I wrapped my arms around Noz and tried not to think about how she would look at me in the morning and what would happen if Ezra came back unexpectedly.

Sunday, 2:35 a.m.

I came out of the mess of my sleep with a memory of a dream in which I'd gulped water voraciously and but couldn't slake my thirst. I can't ever slake my thirst. My mouth was dry and my breath was terrible, from all the wine. I dragged my body out of bed before I was really awake and tried to be light on my feet. I closed the door between the bedroom and bathroom before I turned on the bathroom light, and I rested my forearms on the basin of the sink. I ran the water, I drank directly from the stream. Unlike in my dreams, I was quenched. I was careful not to look at my face in the mirror, I was careful to turn off the bathroom light before opening the door.

Nozlee's body was balled up under the blanket; underneath she was naked. The bright light in the bathroom had made me too blind in the dark bedroom to see what was on her face. I was only just able to make out her shape.

I walked as lightly as possible to my side of the bed. I slid myself under the covers, tried to be as still as possible. I wasn't ready for her to wake up and either turn towards me or turn away from me. I didn't want to confront any signs or omens about what our morning would be like or what our relationship would be like from now on. I didn't think about the way

Ezra and Nozlee and I had systematically extricated our friend Andrew from our lives after Nozlee had slept with him.

Sleep was elusive; I grabbed my phone and burritoed myself using my half of the comforter, hopefully insulating Noz from my phone light. I turned the brightness down. The whole world of everyone I knew was in the palm of my hands and I could've gone anywhere, seen anyone, done anything, but I felt only the compulsion to go deeper. Noz's email, that I'd refused to read on Saturday, was lingering ghostly in my email's Trash folder, and I could see it, and read it still.

> Hi Eve,
> I'm writing to you from Desert Hot Springs, and it won't cool down even though it's the middle of the night. I'm typing this on my phone, I'm lying in the dark directly under an air conditioning vent. . . .

I stuck my head out of my burrito and saw, on the ceiling, that air conditioning vent.

> . . . Because you've obviously blocked my cell phone number, I'm going to tell you everything in this email where you can't avoid it, I won't let you avoid it like you avoid everything else you don't want to hear.
> I love you, I'm in love with you. I've been in love with you for years, maybe since New York. I wish I could say "I don't know how to tell you" but the truth is that I was too scared you wouldn't sit still for long enough to hear me out. At the same time, that was the excuse I used for being cowardly, and quiet, and not confronting my feelings for you head on. It was easier

to suffer from how much I felt for you than it was to risk you shutting me out of your life.

The thing is, I wasn't scared of you rejecting me, I was worried that you just wouldn't process what I was saying to you, and being left in a stasis, with no "yes" or "no," with just this being emotionally dismissed. I can handle being rejected, but I can't handle you pretending this isn't happening.

Tell me yes or tell me no, just tell me something.

Nozlee

Next to me, Noz shifted in her sleep, made noises. She loved me, she had loved me. I tried to stay with that feeling and I tried to understand what I was feeling in turn. Safety, maybe, and a little bit of joy that was corrupted by anxiety and regret.

I wished Noz and I had been able to begin with no history, no baggage, but that would've been impossible even if Ezra had never existed because we're all carrying our damaged pasts with us like snail shells; if it wasn't Ezra it would've been something else. This new dawn would break hot and ragged, and we'd slather on the fifty SPF sunscreen and sunbathe in the desert.

I was terrified that I would lay awake with racing thoughts, but everything inside me calmed, actually; I fell asleep fast under the same covers as Nozlee.

Sunday, 9:26 a.m.

Maybe if I didn't move, then nothing new would ever happen and time would stop and the world would forever be the time before Nozlee woke up and I had to look at her and think about what we'd done. I felt the place where she'd bit my lip when she came. I was completely still, aside from my tongue prodding at my lip, and Nozlee woke up anyway, and I felt her body start to move.

The night we swam, we hadn't slept at all, so there hadn't been a jarring moment where we woke up and in waking up, everything changed. Instead, we had slipped neatly from night into day; once we saw light in the cracks between the curtains, we had gone to the kitchen to make fizzy mimosas that were more orange juice than prosecco. While Nozlee peed, I'd crept into the boys' room and petted Ezra's hair while he slept. When he stirred, I fed him a bit of my mimosa.

"How was your girls' time?" he'd asked.

"Perfect," I'd said.

Miggy had slept through the whole exchange, he'd never had problems falling asleep or staying asleep.

Nozlee and I had passed out in the same bed plenty of other times, once or twice after a night out in New York when it was easier to get to her apartment in Williamsburg than my stupid rat-hole in DUMBO, and in Los Angeles, on Miggy's big couch bed that he'd inherited from a younger but richer boyfriend, or in hotel rooms in Koreatown and Palm Springs.

But never before had I been interested in the way her body moved as she woke up. I felt for the twitch and stretch of her arms, I wondered if she'd curl her body, but instead she stretched. I wanted, suddenly and very deeply, to know what her neck smelled like and to memorize the shape of her toes. Ezra knew both of those things; the knowledge rotted. I imagined I had a pit like a peach, but instead of a healthy core, my pit was toxic, it was burning me up, and getting all over everyone I loved, and everyone could smell it.

"Hi," Nozlee said, her voice croaky.

She couldn't have had any indication I was awake, I had been very, perfectly still.

Nozlee rolled, pressing the front of her body against the back of mine, she let her feather soft lips tickle the side of my ear. "Eve, I know when you're pretending to sleep."

"No."

She laughed, it was so loud.

"You better get up and face it," Nozlee said, stretching some more. "Today's going to be awful."

Yes, but she didn't have to just say it. I was afraid that being kind to her meant I would never get to be friends with Ezra again, and without alcohol making me live in the moment, I started to sour on the whole situation.

"You seem happy," I said, finally turning over so she could see my face and, with it, my little breasts and all of my naked stomach. "I guess getting what you've been craving for so long really burns away the guilt of fucking over Ezra."

Her face turned. I could see her get mad at me; I could see the dozens of angry things she wanted to say back to me. The question she—we were both—trying to answer was: Is Eve trying to ruin it because she doesn't want it or because she's scared and a bitch? I guess it's true that I'm like an animal, I bite when I'm afraid. I didn't want to lash out at her because I was scared of what I had done, but I had done it before I knew what I was doing, before I could help it.

Nozlee's anger settled into something much worse. "Don't do that to me right now," she said. "Today's going to be bad enough as it is."

I wanted to hug her and I gave in to the desire.

"You need to do some real thinking," Nozlee said into my ear during the hug. "You need to figure out what you want or at least what you *might* want. You need to figure it out pretty fast."

I didn't say anything but I initiated a de-hugging. Noz's eyes were a bit wet and so pretty.

"You should go soak in the tubs."

"What are you going to do?"

"I'm going to go to yoga," Noz said. She got off the bed and started pawing through her bag. "There's a class in the Celestial Dome."

"I can't soak. I don't have a bathing suit," I said, being obstinate.

She put on a pair of neon green stretchy athletic shorts. "Don't be shitty, you would never drive to the desert without a swimsuit."

"What if I was too overwhelmed to pack correctly?"

"You weren't." She had her sports bra on and a shirt that she would probably take off during the class when she got hot.

"You go soak and try to access your fucking emotions, okay? At least enough to stop being a bitch to me."

She left, but did the thing from the movies where she stopped in the doorway to say one last thing: "And you should look for the shaman."

On the way to the tubs, I passed a small, freestanding hut that Two Bunch used as its reception area. Taped to the door was a list of the daily programming for guests: Yoga and Pilates, and Meditation sessions with names like "Creating a New Book of Life" and "Shaman Blessing Honoring Your Dreams" and "Revealing Your Strengths."

"10:15 a.m., 'Balancing Your Chakras to Your Destiny:' Learn how your energy field plays a key role in your health and relationships and how to know if your energy is out of balance so you can rebalance and align with your destiny. Led by our resident shaman. Meet us in the Garden House."

"Where's the Garden House?" I shouted through the open doorway of the reception hut. The receptionist, and the guest who was checking in, both jumped; the receptionist glanced at the guest then at me, wanting to help but not wanting to shout. Would I help him by walking closer? I guess I would.

The receptionist gave me detailed instructions on which paths through the resort ground to take to the Garden House and, after following them, I found a room made of glass, built in the middle of Two Bunch's dense undergrowth. A collection of people were already waiting for the session to begin: a woman about my age wearing a thick blue robe who I maybe recognized from the failed Bravo reality show *Gallery Girls*; a shaved-head guy with a butterfly tattoo between his shoulder blades, shirt off, who looked like a queer punk type of which there was a semi-robust subculture back in LA; a couple in their early forties whose chairs were close together but whose hands weren't touching. Thankfully, the vibe was silent and internal, everybody on their own journey; they barely smiled at me and nobody wanted to talk. I was anxious about the noise my metal chair made against the concrete floor when I sat down. The vines were crawling up the glass, I tried to access my fucking emotions. My anger was a smoking volcano, so I closed my eyes and visualized the smoking volcano; I visualized it erupting and wondered when it would erupt. I visualized my friends covered in my lava. I didn't think this was what Nozlee wanted from me.

When I opened my eyes, the shaman was staring at me, and I remembered that the shaman was Colleen, I'd forgotten completely. Another person I owed an apology to. I felt exhausted by the prospect.

I interpreted her look as one of mild horror. I waited for her to unload on me, which was an idiotic thought, because she's a shaman and she doesn't *unload*; but based on my experience, she wasn't above being a petty bitch.

She jostled her head like she was clearing away a fog.

"Step outside with me," she said, her voice kind of scratchy and her tone authoritative.

"What, no 'please'?" I said, after not moving for an uncomfortable amount of time.

"Please," she said, surprisingly submissive.

I thought of Nozlee doing yoga in the Celestial Dome, an instructor telling her to lift her arms and take a slight backbend and Nozlee lifting her arms and backbending slightly. I remembered the two of us sitting around Witch Colleen's low table, shaking hands as we first met, shaking with excitement at meeting someone so new and yet so familiar. She'd set me up to go see Colleen because she thought there was something for me here. I realized that on the night we swam, if Nozlee had kissed me, I would've kissed back.

I stood up, almost tripping, and followed Colleen out of the Garden House. She led me a few feet down the slate rock path, until we were out of earshot of the others gathered.

"You owe me an apology for acting like a child and scaring my dear friend," she said, unconsciously turning her wrists so her palms were facing upwards, a gesture of asking. And maybe, dramatically, she channeled her power through her palms the way I did.

"I behaved badly," I said, the most I could muster.

"That's not an apology," she said sharply enough that I could see that vindictive streak rise up again in her, but this time she was able to squash it down. "I'll admit I created a negative atmosphere by coming at you so harshly. In my defense, I'd had an unusually terrible day and you must know how bad your energy was when you came into the meditation. I'd always thought of you as one of my best students, and you came to me ragged and broken."

"Well, what if I hadn't known that at the time?" I bit back, but a little less sharply than intended, in fact not sharply at all, but with a warble of barely repressed sadness. I hadn't known anything at the time. "In my defense, I'd also had a really bad day."

Colleen gestured to the greenery around us, the comforting setting, the safe space. "Justify your actions, then."

"One of my best friends had decided not to talk to me for no reason—what I thought was no reason—and it was simultaneously the anniversary of the day my other best friend killed himself," I said.

Colleen softened towards me, then, and I didn't understand. And then she said, "You're Miguel's friend?"

"Yes. You know him?"

"I've seen him around the grounds. Hold on for a minute. I'm going to see if someone else can cover the chakra workshop."

She pulled out her phone and bowed over it and texted. It was the first time I'd seen anybody on their phone on the grounds of Two Bunch.

I lingered awkwardly while she texted, feeling unmoored at even only ten seconds without a clear thing to do.

"Okay, good," she said finally, perhaps twenty seconds after she'd pulled out her phone. She tucked it back into the back pocket of her linen pants.

"Okay, good," I echoed. "I'm feeling a little unmoored here?"

"I'm going to cleanse you."

"What if I don't want to be cleansed?"

"I'm not going to give you a choice," she said.

"I'm not sure if I can afford a private session from a shaman here, actually," I said. "I've heard you're super expensive."

"This one's on me," she said, then gave me a mean little smile. "Sister to sister."

I shrugged again and let her lead me down the path. She went into a hut and made me wait outside. Through the window I saw the hut's walls were lined with wooden shelves, and the shelves were stuffed full of witchy supplies: colored candles, peacock and hawk feathers, chicken bones, logs of Palo Santo, baskets full of incense cones, jade beads, chunks of white and rose quartz and black tourmaline, abalone shells for smudging, lighters and matches and charcoal and plates to catch the incense ash.

"After this, you must promise me you won't take Cascarilla anymore," Colleen said.

I stood awkwardly while she pulled items from the shelf: A large ceremonial fan used for cleaning, a packet of dried herbs, a heavy-looking chunk of milky white quartz. Colleen made me turn around while she used the fan to scrub at my aura, chanting in Sanskrit and stomping on the ground to punctuate and evoke her incarnations. I felt a bit of my blackness fall away like I was a dusted shelf.

Eventually, she let me come inside the hut and told me to lie on a low cot in the corner and at her urging, shut my eyes and put my hands over my throat chakra. "You're completely blocked here," she said. "And I'm going to unstick you."

For an hour she chanted over me, moved the quartz around to various spots on my body to help channel energy into my throat, and gently massaged my neck and shoulders. Without meaning to, I relaxed into the drone of her voice, into the smell of her incense, into the fire-pricks at the top of her white candles. I felt my frantic thoughts soften away, and instead of finding the pain I was so scared to encounter there, I felt so deeply cared for. I felt love coming towards me so bright and huge that I couldn't keep myself from finally crying at the beautiful weight of it.

I reemerged from my meditative state as she was blowing out her candles.

"Am I fixed now?" I asked, rubbing my eyes hard with the back of my hand. They were burning; I'm sure they were red like I'd just taken a too-big hit off a never-washed bong in some smelly boy's dorm room.

The shaman took my hand and looked at me the way a nurse practitioner would before she told someone the chemotherapy wasn't working. "Your aura's pretty well patched up. You take to the cleansing and repairing really well, you don't fight it at all. I think that means you *want* to get better.

"But your aura didn't get full of tears by accident or by circumstance. Nobody hexed you, nobody degraded your aura with a toxic personality. You put the holes there yourself, and unless you change, you'll do it again."

"Okay," I said. "Okay."

She tilted her head. "It would be dangerous for you to be alone right now. Are you here with anyone?"

"Yeah," I said. "I'm here with my best friend."

Sunday, 11:42 a.m.

When I saw Nozlee again, on the back porch of the suite, she was covered in a fine layer of sweat; her ass looked fantastic in her green stretchy shorts.

"I've been healed!" I lifted my arms above my head and back bended in a performative, exaggerated way.

Nozlee laughed, and I laughed with her.

"But really," I said. "I was."

"Really?" She pulled out the second chair. The legs scraped loudly against the concrete. She sat. Unbothered by the noise, she scooted her chair closer to mine.

"Sort of," I said. "For now. I've been putting holes in my aura."

She raised an eyebrow skeptically, "Are you saying you've found a magic reason for all your bullshit?"

"No, actually, I'm saying there's a magic symptom based on my underlying problem."

"And what's your problem?" she asked.

"Boundary issues. Obviously. I mean, I don't have specific words for it yet, but you must have a sense of it. You've been here this whole time."

Nozlee twisted her neck like it was bothering her, but it wasn't bothering her, it was just something she did to fill time while she was thinking about what to say next. I remembered she had twisted herself like that whenever Witch Colleen asked her a difficult or obtuse question. Maybe she didn't even know she was doing it, but I could see it. There were probably things about me that she could see that I couldn't. We'd spent so much time looking at each other, and I was only realizing it now, I was catching up.

I grabbed her wrist and she gasped a little, I hoped in a good, sexy way.

"I love you, and I like you, and I think you're sexy," I said.

"Oh yeah?" she said, teasing. Her eyes were bright and the sun was making all of her so shiny. She let me lead her to the bedroom, and under milky sunlight, I got to spend time with her body. I watched a heavy droplet of sweat drip from the dent at the base of her neck down to the bone ridge between her breasts, and curved and moved my fingers until I found her g-spot and pushed on it.

After, we put on our bathing suits, my black one-piece that I absolutely of course had packed; hers was red-striped and purchased from a company that advertised on Instagram. We went down to the hot springs; we didn't hold hands as we walked but all of a sudden the idea of hand-holding loomed.

The deck chairs that surrounded the bigger pools were already mostly claimed; I looked around for a spot and saw first an empty wooden tub with empty chairs nearby, then saw that Miguel was there, sort of sitting on a chair, sort of floating. He was busy rolling a ghostly joint.

"Oh good," Miggy said, when he felt us approaching. "I've been saving this tub for you guys."

"You can fill it," Nozlee said, dropping her sunglasses on a nearby chair. "As hot or as cold as you like."

"Ooooh a private soak," I said, testing the faucets. The water ran out of old pipes fast and hot; it didn't smell but I could feel the magic radiating out of it, a psychic stink.

"I had to do a lot of work to keep this prime spot open for you," Miggy said. "It takes a lot of energy to repel people here, it's not easy to project bad vibes."

"I bet," I said. "The whole place is buzzing with positive energy."

Miggy glowed and hummed and I climbed inside my filling tub. The water was so hot it prickled me, and I could feel the magic of it soaking into the skin. I'd be glowing too if I soaked long enough. Nozlee climbed in next to me and this time I gave into the threat and slid my hand into hers. Miggy raised an eyebrow as he licked his joint closed.

"I know," Nozlee said, "I know. Ezra is going to be . . . I don't know."

"He's going to spiral," I said. "He's going to be very hurt."

"You can't worry about it," Miggy said.

"Shouldn't we though?" I asked. Noz fiddled with the faucet handles, making sure our tub didn't overflow. "My whole new thing is to try to be better to people, and what am I doing? Stealing his fucking girlfriend."

Nozlee made a gasped warble noise. "I think I've had a little more agency than, like, 'being stolen.'"

"Yes! Okay! Fuck! This is exactly what I mean," I said. "I'm bad."

Miggy toked his ghost joint, its end a haunting red spark.

Nozlee turned off the water and tipped onto her back; she floated, her arms splayed, her fingers brushing my thigh, a simultaneously accidental and deliberate touch. Like keeping a point of contact, like keeping a tether.

"The point, I think," Miggy said, exhaling smoke, "is to be thoughtfully good and thoughtfully bad. Random, accidental shittiness, based on anger or petty shit or ignorance of what is making your friends upset—that you have to cut out. But making a deliberate choice to be good to yourself even if it's hurting your friend, well that's a more complicated question. It could have a more complicated answer."

"But I'm at a deficit, now, I'm realizing," I said. I knelt on the bottom of the tub so I could get as much of my body under the water as possible. It lapped at my shoulders as comforting as a sweet puppy. "Maybe I need to make up for years of accidental shittiness by avoiding any deliberate shittiness for a while." I was doing this all backwards. I had just found Nozlee liked me, and already I wanted to hold onto her. And what was I supposed to do if being good to Ezra meant being bad to Noz? Who was I supposed to prioritize now?

"I don't think, like, repayment of a debt is a good way to think about it. You need to do the thing that's right, right now," Miggy said. "Sometimes that means wrecking things. Sometimes it's worth it."

I pondered this briefly. I tried to take the joint from Miggy, but my hands passed through the joint and Miggy's hand. Miggy laughed, he smoked.

"We're in a bad pattern too," I said to him, realizing it as I was saying it. "I've, like, been texting you as if you were alive, but you're not. I have to, like, process your death."

"Sounds like the healthy path," Miggy agreed.

"But what am I supposed to do?" I said. "Forget I can text you or come visit you here? Take Cascarilla all the time to shut you the fuck out? You hate that!"

Noz giggled.

"What!?" I said.

"It's as if the concept of balance has never occurred to you!" she said, still laughing. She grabbed my wrist and used it to tug on my whole body.

"What?" I said, again.

"Come float."

Miggy gestured: You better do what she says.

I shifted until my head was near Nozlee's; I let the water buoy me. The tub was wide enough for two, but narrow enough that we had to be close together as we floated side by side. Like those otters in that YouTube video, Nozlee again took my hand.

The water blocked my ears and I shut my eyes; I felt her near me and the rest of everything drop away. The water was gentle to me and I was calm and the world was happy to wait for me until I was done floating.

"It feels good," I said.

Nozlee murmured in agreement.

I was supposed to be there next to her, smelling my dead best friend's weed, feeling sun on my cheeks, realizing I should've put on sunscreen, realizing worrying about sunscreen was fine, that it would all be fine, that I didn't need to search all over the fucking state to find the solutions to my problems, just focus on floating.

Sunday, 2:00 p.m.

Around 2:00 p.m., our big group chat with all of our friends—
three years ago someone had named it "Who Wants To Go
Out?"—started blowing up. Everybody was piling into cars,
stopping at gas stations to get salt & vinegar chips, stopping at
In-N-Out to get a double double or animal fries extra crispy,
posting Instagrams of the iconic red-with-palm-trees In-N-Out
soda cup, Googling when the sun would go down and sending
it to the rest of the group so we knew when to look out for the
sunset, asking if the Saguaro had a hot tub.

WHO WANTS TO GO OUT?

Ezra:

Fuck yeah it does.

Then Ezra sent a selfie from the Saguaro's hot tub, his sunglasses low on his nose, the sun glistening off water droplets
on his face.

"Noz," I said, to get her attention.

She pulled her nose out of her book and stretched on her lounge chair. I sat up on mine.

"I think it might be time to head to Palm Springs," I said.

She sighed and stretched. "Vacation's over."

We'd already checked out and put our bags in my car and Nozlee had somehow gotten the hotel management to allow her to keep her car parked on the property for another night. Driving all the way back to Desert Hot Springs to get it on Monday would be annoying, but we both felt too uneasy to separate yet.

Miggy floated next to us while we walked to our cars, his body was present but wispy like a haunted breeze; I would've held his hand if I could. It hung unspoken that Nozlee and I were leaving Miggy's side to go to a gathering that would celebrate his life at the site where he took himself away from us. Should he be there, just out of reach, while we all lit candles for him? As little as three days ago, I probably would've begged him to come with. Instead, I held my hands out, palms up, and he held his hands out, palms down, like we were setting up to play the slap hands game: as close as we could get to touching.

"I miss you," I said. "I'm mad you're not here anymore. You left."

All ghosts are thirsty, all ghosts are beasts, even him. He told me he loved me, and I saw the blood between his teeth.

"I know you're going to take some space from me, and that's going to be good for you," the beast said, feeding on our growing emotional distance, because I realized the final way I'd been wrong. I'd thought Miggy's thirst was for conversation and connection, but his real thirst, his monstrous compulsion, was to leave people behind.

His face turned blue and his tongue got long and I saw so vividly the bruises around his neck from where he'd hanged himself last year.

"I'll love you for the rest of my life," I said, which was a more concrete promise than *I'll love you forever*, and also one I was prepared to keep. I'd take some time from him, I'd mourn his death and let him go, then text him back when I could determine the space between my friend and his ghost, and when I could create balance in my own life.

I lowered my hands, and Nozlee stepped in to say her goodbyes.

As we got settled in the front seats of my Fit, and Miggy hovered behind the car like a dad watching his kids drive off to college, Shaman Colleen walked by. She didn't see us in the car, but she saw Miggy, who was puffing on a new joint. I watched in the rearview mirror as Colleen approached Migs, and nudged Nozlee, so she was watching too when Miggy held out the joint to Colleen, who grabbed it and toked it. In all my twenty-nine years on this earth, I'd never seen anybody reach out and touch the spirit realm. I didn't think it was possible. I twisted my neck around so hard, trying to see it with my eyes instead of via a mirror; then Colleen exhaled ghost smoke, said something to Miggy as she handed him back the joint, and walked on.

"Holy fuck," Nozlee said.

"I want to learn how to do that," I said.

Miggy disappeared, I felt his energy lingering unbodied, and Colleen was walking away. The world was new, suddenly, the world was sparking, but there wasn't anything to do about it now. We had to get on the road.

The sky over the highway was so bright and big, I felt swallowed by it. As I drove, Noz played the music. She played me all her favorite guitar stuff, Colleen Green and Snail Mail and An Horse, and once or twice she slipped in a song about pining for someone, songs I already knew she loved, like that Shura song from a few years ago, "What's It Gonna Be?," and I realized that maybe all along she'd been thinking about me when she listened to them and that made me feel prickly with body heat, especially when she hummed along, *"I don't wanna give you up / I don't wanna let you love somebody else but me."*

When we passed a road sign that said "Palm Springs, twenty miles," I had an uneasy thought.

"Oh fuck," I said, "Where are we all going to sleep?"

Noz was supposed to be rooming with Ezra, and I was supposed to be rooming with Georgie.

"Don't worry about it," Noz said, watching the sky.

"Uh, I'm absolutely going to worry about it, there's no way I can sleep in the same bed as Georgie right now."

Noz smirked, "I promise not to be jealous."

"It's not that, she's fucking sleeping with Bea," I said.

"Oh shit! We'll absolutely talk about that later, but like, it's all worked out. You and I are going to stay in your and Georgie's room, Georgie's gonna go in with Bea and Lydia, and Ezra's going to stay alone in the one we were supposed to be in."

"When did all this switching happen?" I asked, flicking on my turn signal, sliding between lanes.

"We were texting," Noz said.

"I would like to be consulted about my own hotel room situation!" I said.

"Babe," Noz said, losing patience. "You're in the group texts, but you've been driving."

"Oh." I said. "I'm sorry."

"It's okay," she said.

"I've gotta work on that. Assuming the worst." There was a lot I had to work on, piles of nightmare habits to sort through and eradicate.

"It's a process," Noz said, rubbing my thigh.

Fifteen minutes later, I turned the Fit into the parking lot of the Saguaro; I pulled into a spot next to Ezra's red Volvo. I—we—were surrounded by cars we recognized, blue and silver, familiar dings and bumper stickers. In a minute we'd be surrounded by the people who traveled inside them. Through the lobby, checked in by a tired woman with her hair up, and then, together, Noz and I walking into the heart of the hotel.

The Saguaro is a big rectangular pool, surrounded on all four sides by two stories of hotel rooms with doors in bright colors like glasses of fruit juice. Everywhere, our friends were chatting. Almost a dozen of us who missed Miggy, in various stages of sunbathing; I waved at Chelsea and Lydia, who sat on lounge chairs, their hair still dripping from the pool, drinking from cans of rosé; in the deep end, Tommy floated alone, sunglasses low on their nose, on a pool float shaped like a cactus; nearby, Georgie and Bea sat partially submerged on the steps into the shallow end, Bea leaning onto Georgie's legs, her face turned towards the sun or maybe to look at Nozlee and me.

I saw them and I felt angry, and being angry and not saying anything about it or doing anything about it made the anger feel like there was a fire inside that was burning me up, but I finally felt strong enough not to let it burn anybody else down, and I knew that maybe, if I worked hard enough, it would stop burning me up too.

"You'll freckle," I said.

"I know how to put on sunscreen, Mom," Bea said with an eye roll.

And Ezra, on the second floor of the rooms, leaning over the wrought iron railing, his shoulders arched like birds' wings. He was wearing these short royal blue trunks and a neon green shirt and he shone, and he waved back at me. By unspoken agreement, everyone was squashing all their conflicts.

Noz and I quickly dropped our bags in our room and, swaddled by our friends, their familiar bathing suits and voices, we parted. Noz scuttled over to the deep end of the pool, shed her linen bathing suit cover-up, and pounced from the side of the pool onto Tommy's float. They yelped and flipped and Noz laughed manically and then dove to retrieve Tommy's dented old Ray Bans from the bottom of the pool before the chlorine could corrode the UV coating. I sprawled out on the empty lounge chair next to Lydia's and retrieved a can of rosé from the cooler for myself, and listened to her and Chelsea gab a bit before they folded me into their conversation. We talked until the sun dipped below the rim of the buildings, and then I hurried back to my room to get my supplies.

In the hotel room, Noz rustled through her bag. Over her bikini, she put on a white t-shirt with spray paint–style lettering that said "JAMES DEAN SPEED QUEEN," something one of the guys wore on the Netflix *Queer Eye*, which she and Migs had watched together. Then, she pulled out three hunks of raw crystal on chains, homemade necklaces. I recognized the stones: Ruby Zoisite facilitates releasing pain and sorrow— "This one's for Ezra to wear," Noz said; Apache Tear, a form of obsidian, which filters negative vibes into positive ones, was for Nozlee to wear. She put around my neck a chunk of Ruby Moonstone; it helps you forgive someone for leaving you. I kissed her, wet, and felt the little bumps on her tongue. When she stepped away from me, I grabbed my fat candles and we went back out to the pool area.

The sky was already dark blue and getting black, our friends were drinking from Solo cups and they spoke in hushed voices. Ezra was waiting for us by the steps into the pool. We were awkward with each other's bodies, as Nozlee almost put the crystal around his neck for him, but then handed it over for him to do himself instead. I held out the candles like I was passing a clean utensil to a stranger, careful not touch any part that they might touch.

"Black in the left hand, white in the right," I explained. Ezra switched his candles, and then I lit his, and Nozlee's, and mine, and threw the lighter into the grass, and the three of us walked into the pool, waist-deep. All of Miggy's friends sat down on the edges of the pool and hung their feet into the water.

"Black is the color of transition, ending a phase in your life, and it absorbs negativity," Noz told everyone. "White is the color of new beginnings and spiritual growth. It's also the color of Goddess energy, which I'm pretty sure Migs would've appreciated."

Everyone laughed a little bit, maybe remembering like me how Miggy could be a little fey whenever he felt a conversation had gotten too straight, slipping a warbling *yas queen* into a conversation about Dodgers baseball or bachelor parties in

Vegas. I cried then, enough burning tears to stream out of my eye and down my cheek, and with the burning candles in my hand I couldn't move my glasses to wipe them away.

Ezra said, "So, we Jews have a thing called Yahrzeit, which is the celebration of the first anniversary of a loved one's death. The actual day of Yahrzeit is based on the Hebrew calendar, actually, and the day changes if their death was before or after sunset. It's really complicated, and Eve and I couldn't figure it out. Considering that Miggy isn't even Jewish, we decided to do a Yahrzeit ritual on the goyim one-year anniversary, which is today. Obviously. For Yahrzeit, we light candles at sunset and leave the candle burning for twenty-four hours."

I sniffled in a gross, mucusy way and said, "We all shared our memories of Miggy at the wake, so instead of rehashing out loud and getting each other all riled up with deep sadness, we're going to just think about our favorite times with Miggy, and remind ourselves how lucky we were to have him in our lives for any amount of time." And maybe finally forgive him for leaving.

All weekend I'd been thinking about the housesit in the hills, thinking about being shut up in the room with Nozlee all night, and I'd barely given a single thought to the several hours Miggy and I had spent, just the two of us, in the kitchen, cooking lemony chicken and garlicky kale to feed each other and our friends. While the chicken had baked, we'd sat on the countertop and polished off a bottle of red wine. Our conversation had taken a turn for the serious, discussing something about dissatisfaction with our fathers, and I can't remember how I'd gotten there but I do remember saying to him, "Promise you'll never leave me," and, drunk, he kissed me on my shoulder and said, "I promise." I'd spent a year thinking about how he broke that promise, when I should've been thinking about how selfish it was, after he'd left, to make him stay.

Lydia held up her phone, taking pictures of us, and I knew that in the picture she would eventually post to Instagram, instead of some amalgamated mess of one personality and one desire spread over three bodies, I'd see separate people, missing their friend, standing next to each other.

Acknowledgments

Writing this book wouldn't have been possible without the support, encouragement, contribution, and attention of a murderer's row of my brilliant friends and some of the best publishing professionals in the business.

Thank you to Alyea Canada for understanding what I was trying to do with this story and helping me figure out how to stick my landing. Thank you to Dennis Johnson and Valerie Merians for believing in my work from the very beginning and not giving me grief about taking five years to write a second novel.

As a PR/marketing person myself, I deeply appreciate the often-thankless and always-exhausting work Amelia Stymacks and Selihah White put in to make sure this book made it into your hands. Marina Drukman designed the striking cover and I especially appreciate the work Betty Lew put into the interior, so that you could have the experience of holding Eve's phone and reading her texts. Thank you to everyone at Melville House who worked on this book.

I never would've made it to novel number two without the team behind my first novel. Thank you to Alex Shephard for your hard work, Liam O'Brien for your dedication and handselling, and Kirsten Reach for . . . everything (I can't narrow it down, Kirsten, you gave me everything I ever could've wanted).

I'm incredibly lucky to benefit from two groups of brilliant readers (one writing group called Shitty First Drafts, and one without a name): Maggie Murray, KK Wootton, Ana Reyes, Jon Doyle, Robin Tung, Darcy Vebber, Ann Holler, Paria Kooklan, Kristen Daniels, and Neela Banerjee. Without notes and encouragement from all of you, this book wouldn't be good, plain and simple.

A special thank you to Edan Lepucki, whose friendship, mentoring, and contributions to my books have added uncountable richness to my personal and professional life.

Anna Dorn gave me the courage to start writing this book when a different manuscript wasn't working. She sat next to me when I wrote the first words of this book, and made sure I didn't stop writing until it was done.

Thank you to my wonderful friends for their excitement and encouragement, especially Zan Romanoff, who helps me keep my head on straight when I'm spinning out. Thank you to Kelsey Ford and Aubrey Bellamy for always answering when I text you "Can I bounce a story idea off of you?" Our texting has made me a better storyteller.

Thank you to the Gorgeous Ladies of Strong Sports Gym (RIP), especially for help when I hit sticky career patches. Can't wait to get back in the ring with you guys.

Thank you to my parents, Nancy and Ted Disabato, for sending me to "poetry college" and otherwise encouraging me to follow my dreams.

Thank you to everyone who said it was a good idea to call my book *U Up?*.

About the Author

Catie Disabato's first novel, *The Ghost Network*, was deemed "a smart and thorny debut" that "reveals treasures" to readers, according to the *New York Times*. Disabato has written essays and criticism for outlets including the *LAist*, *BuzzFeed*, and *LA Weekly*. She lives in Los Angeles with her cats, Margot and Bambino.